The Sheikh Takes a Bride
by Caroline Cross

'Why? Because you have some ludicrous notion that if you hang around long enough I'll marry you?'

She regretted the words as soon as she said them. After all, she had no basis for the accusation other than her suspicions. And even if it were true, he'd hardly admit it.

Which was why it was such a shock when he calmly nodded his head and said, 'Yes. Precisely.'

She stared at him in stupefaction. 'You can't be serious! In case it's escaped your notice, this is the new millennium, the twenty-first century! I don't care who you are, you don't get to select a bride the way you would a piece of candy.'

'I assure you I put far more thought into this than I would choosing a bonbon,' he answered gravely.

'Oh! You're impossible!' She whirled away from him and, before he could make a move to stop her, swung herself lightly into the saddle. Instinctively adjusting her seat as the bay sidled nervously ben̲e̲a̲t̲h̲ ̲h̲e̲r̲ gathered the reins, fr̲ foot into place. 'In th message, the answer i you. No, I won't marr the last time, I want yo

The SEAL's Surrender
by Maureen Child

⊃ ⁊Ꙩ Ꙩ

He took a step closer.

He couldn't seem to help himself. Everything about her drew him in. She touched something inside him and though he knew he should be fighting it, he surrendered to the feeling instead.

Her scent drifted to him. Her eyes looked wide, troubled, and for some reason, Chance wanted to do something—*anything*—to help. As he came closer, she shook her head in warning.

'Chance,' she said, then corrected herself, 'Commander Barnett—Connelly—blast it.'

A flicker of a smile danced across his face and was gone again, but in that instant, Jennifer knew she was in trouble. This man was pure, undiluted, top-grade sex appeal.

The Sheikh Takes a Bride
CAROLINE CROSS

The SEAL's Surrender
MAUREEN CHILD

SILHOUETTE®
DESIRE™

*All the characters in this book have no existence outside the
imagination of the author, and have no relation whatsoever to anyone
bearing the same name or names. They are not even distantly inspired
by any individual known or unknown to the author, and all the
incidents are pure invention.*

*All Rights Reserved including the right of reproduction in whole or in
part in any form. This edition is published by arrangement with
Harlequin Enterprises II B.V. The text of this publication or any part
thereof may not be reproduced or transmitted in any form or by any
means, electronic or mechanical, including photocopying, recording,
storage in an information retrieval system, or otherwise, without
the written permission of the publisher.*

*This book is sold subject to the condition that it shall not, by way of
trade or otherwise, be lent, resold, hired out or otherwise circulated
without the prior consent of the publisher in any form of binding or cover
other than that in which it is published and without a similar condition
including this condition being imposed on the subsequent purchaser.*

*Silhouette, Silhouette Desire and Colophon
are registered trademarks of Harlequin Books S.A.,
used under licence.*

First published in Great Britain 2003_
Silhouette Books, Eton House, 18-24 Paradise Road,
Richmond, Surrey TW9 1SR

The publisher acknowledges the copyright holders of the
individual works as follows:

The Sheikh Takes a Bride © Harlequin Books S.A. 2002
The SEAL's Surrender © Harlequin Books S.A. 2002

*Special thanks and acknowledgement are given to
Caroline Cross and Maureen Child for their contributions
to the Dynasties: The Connellys series.*

ISBN 0 373 04861 0

51-0403

*Printed and bound in Spain
by Litografia Rosés S.A., Barcelona*

THE SHEIKH TAKES A BRIDE

by
Caroline Cross

SILHOUETTE®
DESIRE™

is proud to introduce

DYNASTIES:
THE CONNELLYS

Meet the royal Connellys—wealthy, powerful and rocked by scandal, betrayal...and passion!

TWELVE GLAMOROUS STORIES IN SIX 2-IN-1 VOLUMES:

CAROLINE CROSS

always loved to read, but it wasn't until she discovered romance that she felt compelled to write, fascinated by the chance to explore the positive power of love in people's lives. She grew up in Yakima, Washington, the 'Apple Capital of the World,' attended the University of Puget Sound and now lives outside Seattle, where she works (or tries to) at home despite the chaos created by two telephone-addicted teenage daughters and a husband with a fondness for home improvement projects. Pleased to have recently been No. 1 on a national bestseller list, she was thrilled to win the 1999 Romance Writers of America's RITA Award for Best Short Contemporary Novel and to have been called 'one of the best' writers of romance today by *Romantic Times*. Caroline believes in writing from the heart—and having a good brainstorming partner. She loves hearing from readers and can be reached at PO Box 47375, Seattle, Washington 98146, USA. Please include an SAE with return postage for a reply.

Special thanks to Ann Leslie Tuttle for suggesting me
for this story, Shannon Degen for patience above
and beyond the call of duty and Joan Marlow Golan
for believing in me. Silhouette Books is lucky to
have you, and so am I.

One

"**Y**ou're absolutely right, Kaj," Joffrey Dunstan, Earl of Alston, said in his usual thoughtful way. "She's even lovelier than I remembered."

Glancing away from the slim, auburn-haired young woman who was the subject of his observation, the earl retreated a step from the balcony railing overlooking the grand ballroom of Altaria Palace. Though more than two hundred members of Europe's elite milled down below in their most elegant evening wear, they might not have existed for all the attention he gave them.

Instead, with a bemused expression on his face, he turned to stare at his companion, who stood in a pocket of shadow, hidden from casual observance. "But marriage? You can't be serious."

Sheikh Kaj al bin Russard raised an ink-black eyebrow in question. "And why is that?"

"Because… That is…" Always the diplomat, Joffrey cleared his throat and tried again. "Surely you're aware that Princess Catherine has a certain… reputation. And Sheikh Tarik's will was quite specific—"

"That I marry a virgin of royal blood." Kaj grimaced. "Have a little faith, cousin. I haven't forgotten my father's unfortunate directive. I'd simply remind you that for all Catherine's reputedly wild ways, there's a reason she's known as the ice princess."

"I suppose you have a point. Still…"

Kaj took one last look at the woman he intended to marry, his hooded gray gaze admiring her auburn hair and slim white shoulders before he turned his full attention to his favorite relative.

He was quite aware that, despite the fact their mothers were sisters, there was no physical resemblance between himself and Joffrey. His cousin was five-ten, with a slim build, blue eyes, cropped blond hair and a fair, exceedingly English face. In contrast, he was a trio of inches over six feet, with a distinct copper cast to his skin and ink-black hair long enough to necessitate pulling it back for formal affairs like tonight's.

Yet for all their outward differences, he valued Joffrey's opinion above all others.

It had, after all, been his cousin's matter-of-fact friendship that had eased Kaj's crushing homesickness for his homeland of Walburaq when he'd been sent away at age eight to attend English boarding school. Just as it had been Joffrey's steadying presence and astute counsel that had allowed Kaj to get successfully through Ludgrove and Eton, where he'd stood out like a hawk among pigeons. In all the ways that mattered, Joffrey was the brother Kaj had never had.

The reminder softened the chiseled angles of his face. "If it will ease your mind, Joff, I've made certain inquiries. The princess may be a tease, but she's no trollop. On the contrary. I have it on excellent authority that her virtue is very much intact. Her pleasure seems to come from keeping her admirers at arm's length."

Joffrey's eyes widened in sudden comprehension. "You see her as a challenge!"

Kaj shrugged slightly, his broad shoulders lifting. "If I have to marry, I might at least enjoy the courtship, don't you think?"

"No, I most certainly do not," the other man retorted. "At least not to the exclusion of more important considerations."

Kaj crossed his arms. "And those would be what, exactly?"

"Compatibility. Mutual respect and understanding. Similar values. And…and love." A faint flush of embarrassed color tinted the earl's cheeks at that last, but his gaze was steady as he plowed stubbornly on. "This isn't a prize to be won, Kaj. This is your life, your future. Your happiness."

"Do you think I don't know that?" the sheikh inquired softly. "Trust me. I have no intention of making my parents' mistakes."

Joffrey looked instantly stricken, as well he should since he was one of the few people who understood the price Kaj had paid for Lady Helena Spenser's and Sheikh Tarik al bin Russard's disastrous marriage, bitter divorce and subsequent flurry of heated affairs. "Of course not. I didn't mean to imply you did. It's just that this hardly seems the answer."

"And what is?" Kaj's voice was studiously polite. "Given the need for my bride to be pristine, what are my choices? Should I marry one of those tremulous debutantes your mother keeps throwing into my path? Or should I make an offer for some Walburaqui chieftain's daughter, a sheltered innocent who'll build her whole life around me?" He sighed. "I don't want that, Joff. I want a woman who's pragmatic enough to see a union with me as a mutually beneficial partnership. Not some starry-eyed romantic who'll fall desperately in love with me and expect me to fulfill her every wish and need."

"Ah, yes, adoration can be so trying," Joffrey murmured.

Kaj felt a lick of annoyance, only to have it vanish as his gaze locked with his cousin's and he saw the affection and concern in the other man's eyes. His sense of humor abruptly resurfaced. "More than you'll ever know," he said dryly.

For an instant Joffrey looked surprised, and then his own expression turned wry. "Well, if it's any consolation, I doubt excess worship of you will be a problem with Princess Catherine," he said, matching Kaj's tone.

Kaj cocked his head in feigned interest. "Do tell."

The earl shrugged. "It's simply that the more I think about it, the more I understand your choice. Unlike every other female on the planet, the princess has never shown the slightest tendency to swoon when you walk into the room. And though she may indeed be a virgin—I bow to your superior sources—she doesn't strike me as the kind of woman who'll ever fall at your feet in girlish devotion. As a matter of fact—'' he glanced down at the ballroom spread out below them ''—you'll probably be lucky to get a date.''

Kaj followed his gaze. He quickly noted that Altaria's new king, Daniel Connelly, was about to kick off the dancing with his queen, Erin. Of more immediate interest to him, however, was the discovery that the group of young men vying for Princess Catherine's attention had grown even larger than before. He felt an unexpected pinch of irritation as one would-be swain said something that made her laugh. Vowing to put an end to such familiarity—and soon—he nevertheless refused to rise to his cousin's bait.

Catherine *would* be his. He'd given a great deal of thought to her selection, and one way or another he always got what he wanted. ''I appreciate your concern, Joffrey, but I assure you I'll do just fine.''

''Yes, of course.'' The other man's words were perfectly agreeable, but there was a note of skepticism in his voice that was distinctly annoying. ''I merely hope you're not counting on a quick courtship. Because from the look of things, it may take some time just to breach the crowd around her, much less win her heart.''

''Oh, I think not,'' Kaj said firmly. ''One month should do the trick.''

Joffrey turned to look at him, brows raised. ''You're having me on, right?''

"One month and I'll have Catherine of Altaria in my bed, my ring on her finger. Guaranteed."

Joffrey rocked back on his heels. "*Really.* Doesn't that first part rather violate your father's purity directive?"

Kaj rolled his eyes. "I think not. My intended is supposed to be chaste for me—not *with* me."

"I suppose you have a point."

"I suppose I do."

"In that case… Care to chance a small wager as regards to your success—or lack thereof—in this venture?"

"By all means. Simply name your terms."

"Well, I have always fancied Tezhari…"

Kaj nodded. His cousin had long coveted the exquisite Arabian brood mare. "Very well. As for me, I think the Renoir that graces your drawing room at Alston will make Catherine a lovely wedding present."

Joffrey winced but didn't back down. "It's a deal, then. And may I say good luck. Because in my opinion, you're going to need it."

For the first time all evening, Kaj smiled, regarding the other man with cool confidence. "That's very kind of you, Joff, but unnecessary. This hasn't a thing to do with luck. It's all about skill. Trust me."

At that his cousin laughed. "Why do I suddenly feel as if I should pen the princess a note of condolence?"

The sheikh nonchalantly flicked a nonexistent speck from his impeccably tailored Armani tux. "I can't imagine. But I do hope you'll excuse me." His gaze once more located Catherine down below, and he felt a distinct spark of anticipation. "I suddenly find I'm in the mood to dance."

"Oh, by all means." Joffrey stepped back, clearing the way with a flourish.

A twist of amusement curving his mouth, Kaj strolled away.

"Please, Highness." The handsome young Frenchman at Catherine's side gripped her hand and drew it toward his lips. "You are so very exquisite, with your Titian hair and your *yeux emerauds*. Take pity and say you'll dance with me."

Fighting an urge to roll her "emerald eyes," Catherine told herself to be patient. After all, the ball, for which she'd done the bulk of the planning, was going well. Overhead the thousand tiny lights in the mammoth chandeliers twinkled like iridescent butterflies. The lilting strains of the orchestra were neither too loud nor too soft, and the scent of blooming flowers drifting through the score of French doors thrown open to the mild March night was refreshing rather than overpowering.

Add the men in their sleek black tuxedos, the women draped in silk and satin and a glittering array of jewels, and it was perfect, a storybook scene. Most important to Catherine, the guests of honor—her cousin Daniel and his wife, Erin, Altaria's new king and queen—appeared to be enjoying themselves.

She watched for a moment as they danced, smiling at each other. There was such happiness in the looks they exchanged, such perfect understanding. Out of nowhere she felt an unexpected pang of envy.

What must it be like to share such closeness with

another person? Catherine couldn't imagine. She might be only twenty-four, but she'd long ago concluded that such intimacy wasn't for her.

Her conviction had its roots far in the past, when her nouveau-riche mother had happily surrendered Catherine to the royal family, making it clear in the years since that she regarded her illegitimate daughter as a stepping-stone to high society, nothing more.

It had been further shaped by Catherine's father, Prince Marc, who had always treated her like a unique trinket to be displayed when he wanted, then promptly forgotten once his need to impress others had passed.

Only her grandmother, Queen Lucinda, had ever truly cared for her. But that wonderful lady had passed away five years ago, and her loss had only underscored to Catherine how truly alone she was.

Oh, she had an abundance of suitors, but none of them had ever bothered to get to know the real her, the person beneath the public facade. They were too afraid of making a misstep and losing the chance to win her favor—and with it her money, her connections and, she supposed, her body.

Usually she didn't care. But every once in a while she caught a glimpse of what her life might have been if she'd been born plain Catherine Rosemere, instead of Her Highness Catherine Elizabeth Augusta. And she would suddenly feel unutterably weary of fawning admirers, frivolous soirees and always feeling alone no matter how big the crowd that surrounded her.

Oh, poor, pitiful princess, said a mocking voice in her head. *What a trial to be required to spend time in such a lovely setting, surrounded by the cream of high society. How unfair that you have to wear pretty clothes and listen to a few hours of lovely music and some meaningless chatter. What a tragedy that you're minus your very own Prince Charming.*

One hates to think how you'd stand up to a real problem, like being hungry or homeless. Or wait, how about this—you could be dead, like your father and grandfather, their lives snuffed out in an accident that now appears to have been no accident at all, but rather a deliberate act of murder.

Appalled at the direction her thoughts had taken her, Catherine cut them off. But she was too late to stop the anguish that shuddered through her. Or the guilt that came hard on its heels as she recalled the report by the Connelly family's investigator concluding that the speedboat involved in the disaster had been sabotaged. A speedboat meant to be manned by her, not her father.

"*S'il vous plaît, belle princesse.*" The Frenchman stepped closer, demanding her attention. She looked up to find him gazing limpidly at her, looking for all the world like an oversize, tuxedo-clad flounder. "Do say yes to just one dance. Then I can die a happy man." Practically quivering with anticipation, he pressed his wet mouth to the back of her hand.

The tight rein Catherine had on her emotions snapped. She snatched her hand away, just barely suppressing the urge to scrub it against the delicate chiffon of her midnight-blue dress. "I told you before, Michel, I'm not in the mood. What's more, I'd appreciate it immensely if you'd hold off expiring for at least the next forty-eight hours. Your absence would throw a decided wrench into the seating arrangement for Monday night's banquet.''

The young man blinked. Then, as her words sank in, his smile abruptly vanished. ''But, of course,'' he said, pouting in a way that made him look more fish-like than ever. ''A thousand pardons, Highness.'' Stiff-backed with affront, he turned on his heel and marched off.

Catherine felt a prick of remorse, but quickly dismissed it. After all, she'd been exceedingly polite to Michel the first three times she'd refused his requests to dance. She could hardly be held responsible that he refused to take no for an answer.

Sighing, she glanced at the miniature face of her diamond-encrusted watch. It was barely half past ten, which meant it would be at least another two hours before she could hope to make an unremarked-upon escape. She wondered a little desperately what she could do to make the time go faster.

She was saved from having to come up with an answer as a small murmur ran through the throng surrounding her. A second later everyone in front of her appeared to take a collective step back, clearing a path for the tall, ebony-haired man who strode toward her with a palpable air of leashed power.

Catherine tensed, the way she always did when she encountered Kaj al bin Russard. Although most of the women she knew found the enigmatic Walburaqui chieftain irresistible, she personally didn't care for him. Granted, his chiseled features, heavily lashed gray eyes and beautifully accented English had a certain exotic charm, but there was simply something about him—an innate reserve, the assured, almost arrogant way he carried himself, his indisputable masculinity—that she found off-putting.

She watched as he cut a swath through the crowd like some Regency rake from a bygone age, her edginess increasing as she realized his gaze was locked on her face.

He came to a halt and swept her a slight bow. "Your Highness."

She gathered her composure and inclined her head. "Sheikh."

"I don't believe I've had the chance to tell you in person how sorry I am for your loss."

"Thank you," she replied dutifully. "The flowers you sent were lovely."

He made a dismissive gesture. "It was nothing." He moved a fraction closer, making her intensely aware of how big he was. "Would you care to dance? The orchestra is about to play a waltz. Strauss's Opus No. 354, if I'm not mistaken."

Common sense urged her to simply say no and be done with it. But curiosity, always her curse, got the better of her. "How would you know that?"

"Because I requested it. I believe you once mentioned it was your favorite."

"I see." Ridiculously, she felt a stab of disappointment. In the past two months everything had changed: her father was gone; her position as court hostess was coming to an end; her entire future was uncertain. Now here was Kaj al bin Russard, apparently deciding to join her band of admirers. Though she hadn't liked him before, he'd at least been unique. "How resourceful of you," she said coolly. "Unfortunately, my favorite has changed."

"Then this will give you a chance to tell me what has supplanted it." Without warning he reached out and clasped her right wrist with his long fingers.

His touch gave her a jolt, and for a moment she felt anchored in place by the sheer unexpectedness of it. Then she instinctively tried to pull away, only to find that though he was careful not to hurt her, his grip was as unyielding as a steel manacle.

Her temper flared at the same time her stomach fluttered with unexpected excitement. "Let go of me," she ordered tersely, mindful of the interested stares suddenly directed their way.

"Oh, I think not." Matching her clipped tone, he stepped to her side, planted his hand in the small of her back and propelled her toward the dance floor. "It would be a shame to waste such enchanting music. Plus it just so happens—" he swung her around to face him, waited a beat as the orchestra launched into the waltz, then pulled her close and led off "—I'm curious to see how you'll feel in my arms."

Catherine couldn't believe it. Speechless, she stared up at him. She was shocked at having her wishes ignored, shocked by his statement—and more shocked still by the startling discovery that his hand felt deliciously warm against her cool, bare back.

She shivered as his fingers slid lower, unable to stanch her reaction. Only the sight of the faint smile that tugged at the corners of his mouth saved her from making a complete fool of herself by whimpering or doing something else equally mortifying. "How dare you!" she managed instead, finally finding her voice.

"How dare I not, princess." Never missing a beat, he guided her deeper into the phalanx of whirling dancers. "I could never forgive myself if I let the most beautiful woman in the room remain all alone during her former favorite waltz."

His outrageous flattery, coupled with the realization that he'd noticed her solitary state, brought her chin up. "Is there some reason you're toying with me?" she asked abruptly.

His gaze dropped to her mouth and lingered for an endless second. When he finally raised his eyes, they had a lazy, knowing quality that caused an unexpected clenching in the pit of her stomach. "You really must pay more attention. Toying is hardly my style."

"Just what do you hope to gain from this?" She managed to keep her voice steady, but just barely.

"Surely it's obvious. The pleasure of your company."

"And you believe *this* is the best way to attain it?"

One black eyebrow rose in question. "Isn't it?"

"No," she said flatly. "I don't like being commandeered."

"Ah." His expression lightened. "Does it happen often?"

"Of course not!"

He shrugged, and she felt the steely strength of his body beneath her fingertips. "How unfortunate. Perhaps you simply need to give yourself over to the experience. You might find you enjoy it."

Oh, what nerve! She opened her mouth to reply, then stubbornly shut it again. She would not let him provoke her into causing a scene. She would *not*. Besides, it was time he realized he didn't get to have everything his way. Pursing her lips, she deliberately

shifted her gaze to the weave of his impeccably tailored jacket and tried to pretend the rest of him didn't
exist.

To her surprise, rather than making another outrageous comment, he actually fell silent. At first she
was grateful...until it dawned on her that with the
cessation of conversation between them, she was
growing increasingly conscious of other things.

Like the hardness of the thigh brushing hers. And
the size of the hand now pressed firmly to the base
of her spine. Then there was his scent, all dark starry
nights and cool desert breezes. Not to mention the
warmth that radiated seductively from his powerful
body.

Suddenly, she felt...funny. Hot, cold, short of
breath and shivery. Alarmed, she tried to pull away,
but it was not to be. Instead of letting her go, the
sheikh gathered her even closer.

"Princess?"

She felt his heartbeat against her breast, and the
funny feeling grew worse. "What?"

"Relax. You're far too lovely to be so unyielding.
And far too intelligent not to accept that sometimes
the best things in life are those we initially resist."

It was too much. She jerked her head up to stare
at him. "I suppose you include yourself in the cate-
gory of 'best things'?"

He smiled. "Since you see fit to mention it, yes."

"Oh, my. And here I've always believed conceit
wasn't a virtue but a vice."

He made a tsking sound. "Such a sharp tongue,
little one. But then, the past weeks can't have been

easy. Tell me, does it bother you that much to be passed over as Altaria's ruler?''

Well, really! ''Of course not. I've known all my life that women are excluded from inheriting the throne. What's more, Daniel will be an excellent king. He has a very American sense of responsibility and a fresh way of thinking that should be good for the country.''

To her surprise, he actually appeared to consider her words. ''I agree.''

''You do?''

''Yes. I've had occasion to do business with the Connelly Corporation in the past, and found your cousin to be a very resourceful man. Still, it's not Daniel who concerns me, but you. It's never easy to lose a parent. Even a disappointing one.''

Wonderful. And just when she thought he might have some redeeming qualities after all. ''That's hardly any of your business.'' Particularly in light of the second part of the Connelly investigator's report, which had revealed that her father died owing considerable amounts of money due to extensive gambling. The now familiar shame pressed her, but she thrust it away. She had no intention of discussing her father's shortcomings with the sheikh, never mind her failures as a daughter.

He didn't seem to notice the chill in her voice, however. ''My own father passed away some seven months ago. I was never the son he wanted, just as he was never the father I needed. Yet it was still hard to lose him.''

''Oh.'' Suddenly confused, she set her own concerns aside, wondering again if she'd misjudged

him—and why he would say something so revealing.
"I'm sorry."

"Don't be. Typically, he's managed to complicate
my life even now."

"In what way?"

"It seems if I'm to inherit, I must marry."

She was so startled by the disclosure that for a moment she couldn't think what to say. "How...how
unpleasant for you."

"Not really. It's been a challenge, but I've finally
settled on a wife."

Her budding sympathy evaporated at the compla-
cency in his voice. "I'm certain she's thrilled," she
said tartly.

Incredibly, he laughed, a low, husky chuckle that
turned several female heads their way and had an odd
effect on the strength of her knees. "Perhaps not yet,
but she will be." He looked down at her, his eyes
gleaming with good humor...and something else.

It took her a moment to identify what she was seeing. And then it hit her.

Possessiveness.

Her breath lodged in her throat as she was struck
by a terrible suspicion. In the next instant she found
herself reviewing everything that had just passed between them—his sudden attention, his insistence they
dance, that surprising revelation about his father. And
for the first time she let herself wonder just what was
prompting his uncharacteristic behavior. It couldn't
possibly be because *she* was the future wife he'd
"settled" on. Could it?

Of course not. The very idea was ludicrous. Not
only didn't she care for him, she barely knew him,

any more than he knew her. And yet, why else would he be looking at her as if she were a prime piece of real estate he'd decided to acquire?

The waltz ended. Determined to make an escape, she looked around, relief flooding her as she spied her cousin, the king, standing alone a few feet away.

"Daniel!" Forcing a smile to her lips, she took a step back the instant Kaj loosened his grip and hastened to her cousin's side, linking her arm with his. "What luck to find you!"

Clearly startled, Daniel tore his attention from his wife, who was threading her way through the crowd, apparently headed for the powder room, and turned to look at her. "Catherine. Is everything all right?" Concern lit his jade-green eyes.

"Yes, yes, of course. It's simply that I was dancing, and then I saw you and realized I'd forgotten to tell you I talked to your mother earlier and she'd like me to visit Chicago soon since Alexandra has asked me to be one of her bridesmaids."

A frown knit her relation's sandy eyebrows. Catherine felt an embarrassed flush rise to her cheeks since she was fairly certain his distress was caused by her rapid-fire statement, rather than the reminder of his sister's recent engagement to Connelly Corporation executive Robert Marsh.

But all he said was, "I see." Before he could comment further, he caught sight of Kaj, his frown disappearing as a welcoming smile lit his face. "Al bin Russard. How nice to see you again."

"Your Majesty."

"I take it you're the one responsible for my cousin's rather breathless state?"

"I believe I am," Kaj said easily.

To Catherine's disbelief, the two exchanged one of those men-of-the-world looks she always found totally irritating. She drew herself up, gathering what was left of her dignity around her like a cloak. "I really do need to talk to you, Daniel."

"Right." With an apologetic smile for the other man, he said, "If you'll excuse us, then?"

Just as Catherine had hoped, Kaj had no choice but to take his leave. With impeccable manners, he tendered the pair of them a bow. "Of course, Your Highness." He shifted his gaze to Catherine. "Princess, thank you for the dance. I look forward to seeing you again."

Not if she could help it, Catherine vowed. With a flick of her head, she turned her back, dismissing him. Sheikh Kaj al bin Russard might not know it yet, but as of this moment she had every intention of excluding him from her life like the unwelcome intruder he was.

Two

"What are *you* doing here?" Catherine demanded from the doorway of the palace's family dining room.

For all its elegant spaciousness, the room suddenly seemed far smaller than normal, due to the presence of Kaj al bin Russard. The sheikh sat at the far side of the gleaming satinwood table, his suit coat discarded, the sleeves of his white dress shirt folded back, a newspaper in his powerful hands. At the sound of her voice, he looked up. "Princess. How nice to see you."

Catherine stared at him, clenching her teeth against a sudden urge to scream. Taken aback by her reaction, she struggled to rein in her emotions, assuring herself her extreme response to him was merely the result of surprise, frustration and a poor night's sleep. Add to that her worry about her favorite gelding who'd

turned up lame this morning, a meeting with her secretary that had run long so that she needed to hurry
to avoid being late for an engagement in town, and it
was no wonder the unexpected sight of the sheikh
made her feel a little crazy.

"That's a matter of opinion," she retorted, watching warily as he pushed back his chair and rose politely to his feet.

"I suppose it is," he said calmly.

She refused to acknowledge the way her pulse stuttered as he stood gilded by the sunlight that filled the
room or how she once again felt the force of his masculinity. She'd made her decision about him, and the
long hours she'd spent in bed last night tossing and
turning, bedeviled by an unfamiliar restlessness, had
only strengthened her conviction that he was best
avoided.

"I believe I asked you a question," Catherine said.
"What are you doing here?" Last night circumstances had compelled her to be on her best behavior,
but she saw no reason for false pleasantry today.

His gaze swept over her and a faint frown marred
his handsome features. "Are you always this tense?"

Oh! She struggled for self-control. "Sheikh al bin
Russard, this area of the palace is off-limits to everyone but family. I would suggest that you leave. Now.
Before I'm forced to call security."

A faint, chiding smile curved his sensual mouth but
otherwise he didn't move so much as an inch. "You
really must work on your temper, *chaton*. And not be
so quick to jump to conclusions. As it happens, I had
a meeting with the king this morning. When it concluded, he was kind enough to invite me to lunch.

Regretfully, something came up and he had to leave, but not before he assured me there was no reason for me to rush through my meal.''

An embarrassed flush rose in her cheeks. Stubbornly she ignored it. Daniel wasn't here now and she was. As for the sheikh, he might be fooling everyone else with his designer suits and civilized manner, but she hadn't forgotten the way he'd looked at her last night. Beneath that polished exterior she sensed something intense and formidable, and she wasn't about to lower her guard.

She glanced pointedly at the table, which was bare except for the paper and an empty cup and saucer. ''I see. Well, it appears you've finished, so don't let me keep you.''

''Actually, I was about to have some more coffee.'' He moseyed over to the sideboard and lifted the heavy silver coffeepot off the warming plate, then turned to her, his expression the picture of politeness. ''May I get you a cup?''

For half a second, she considered simply turning on her heel and walking away. Except that she was hungry, since she'd skipped last night's midnight buffet in order to avoid a certain interloper and she'd long since burned off the tea and croissant she'd had in her room at dawn.

She was also certain that if she left now, the sheikh would no doubt conclude it was because of him—and her pride wouldn't allow that. He was already too arrogant by half.

Squaring her shoulders, she strode around the table to the opposite end of the sideboard. ''No. Thank you.''

''As you wish.'' He poured a stream of steaming

brew into his cup and set down the pot. He turned, but instead of returning to the table, he stayed where he was.

She felt his gaze touch her like a warm breeze. And for a moment everything around her—the ivory silk brocade wallpaper, the richly patterned rug beneath her feet, the soothing gurgle of the garden fountain beyond the open windows—seemed to fade as her skin prickled and an unfamiliar warmth blossomed low in her stomach. Appalled, she gave herself a mental shake and tried to convince herself that her response was merely the result of extreme dislike.

It was a delusion that lasted no longer than it took her to snatch up a plate, fill it with cold cuts, fresh fruit and cheese from the buffet, carry her food to the table and set it down.

Because suddenly he was right behind her. "Allow me," he murmured, his bare forearm brushing her shoulder as he reached to pull out her chair before she could seat herself.

The heat from his body penetrated her every nerve ending; she might as well have been naked for all the protection provided by her cream linen slacks and sleeveless yellow silk sweater. Nor could she control the sudden weakness of her knees as his fingers closed around her upper arm and he guided her onto the chair. Or the way the warmth in her middle spread when his palm lingered far longer than was necessary.

Not until he stepped back and released her could she breathe again.

Shaken, she sat motionless on the chair, asking herself what on earth was the matter with her. She'd dealt with a variety of men's advances from the time she'd become a teenager, yet she'd never experienced this sort of acute, paralyzing awareness. It was unnerving.

Worse, it made her feel uncertain and out of control, and that made her angry. "Don't you have an oil deal or a camel auction or something that needs your attention?" she demanded as he picked up his cup, moved around the table and slid into the seat across from her.

"No." He cocked an eyebrow at her and took a sip of his coffee. "All of Walburaq's oil comes from offshore reserves, and its distribution is controlled by the royal family. As for camels, we don't have any since, like Altaria, we're an island nation."

Her annoyance shifted from his presence to his presumption that she was actually that ignorant. "Yes, I know. Just as I know Walburaq is located in the Arabian Sea, was a British protectorate until 1963, declined to join the United Arab Emirates and is currently ruled by your cousin, King Khalid." Doing her best to look bored, she picked up a small, perfect strawberry from the royal hothouse and popped it into her mouth.

"My, my princess, that's very good. I'm gratified that you've taken time to study my country."

She touched her heavy linen napkin to her mouth. "Don't be. It's nothing to do with you." Which was nothing but the truth. Not that she'd ever reveal that her knowledge sprang from a futile attempt when she was younger to impress her father by learning about Altaria's various trading partners. "I've always been good at history."

"Apparently." He took another swallow of coffee.

"It makes me wonder what other hidden talents you possess."

In the process of reaching for another berry, Catherine stilled, her gaze locking with his. She had an uneasy feeling that they'd just moved onto dangerous ground.

It was a sensation that increased as he added softly, "I look forward to finding out."

Alarm shot through her. She parted her lips to tell him in no uncertain terms that wasn't ever going to happen. But before she could say a word, Erin, Altaria's new queen, walked into the room.

Kaj came instantly to his feet. "Your Majesty."

Catherine, schooled in the strict protocol her late grandfather had insisted on, started to rise, too, only to sink back into her chair as her cousin-in-law sent her a remonstrative look. Although Daniel's wife possessed an air of reserve that sometimes made her seem rather distant, one of her first acts upon moving into the palace had been to insist that, among the family, royal etiquette was to be relaxed. It was a necessity, she'd wryly informed Catherine later, since there was little chance that Daniel's very American brothers and sisters would ever consent to bow down and call him Your Majesty.

"Catherine, Sheikh." Erin smiled. "Please, be seated." Letting the footman who'd suddenly appeared pull back her chair, she sat down herself and promptly reached out to touch her hand to Catherine's. "I'm so glad to see you. I haven't had the chance to tell you how much I enjoyed the ball last night. It was simply wonderful. Thank you for showing me how such an affair should be done."

"It was my pleasure," Catherine said sincerely.

The regal young queen gave her arm a squeeze and then turned her attention to Kaj. She sent him a warm and gracious smile. "My husband informs me you've agreed to be our guest."

"I beg your pardon?" Caught by surprise, Catherine couldn't keep the dismay out of her voice.

Kaj shot her a quick glance, and she could have sworn that his hooded gray eyes, so pale in contrast to his inky lashes and olive complexion, held a glint of triumph. Yet as he turned to Erin, his voice was nothing but polite. "It's very kind of you and the king to offer to put me up."

"I assure you, it's no problem. We have more than adequate room."

Catherine had heard quite enough. Setting her napkin next to her plate, she pushed back her chair. "I'm sorry, but I have an appointment in town. If you'll excuse me?" The last was directed toward Erin.

"Why, yes, of course."

She stood, but before she could take so much as a single step, the sheikh was on his feet as well. "Pardon me, ma'am." He bowed to the queen, then immediately turned his attention to Catherine. "Might I beg a favor, princess, and get a ride with you?" His smile—part apology, part entreaty—was charm itself. "I'm afraid I'm without a car today."

Catherine couldn't help herself. "Then how did you get here? Walk?" Erin shot her a startled look and she abruptly realized how she must sound to someone unaware that the sheikh had an agenda all his own. She swallowed. "It's only…I'm running late and I'd hate to cut short your conversation with Her

Majesty. I'm sure one of the servants can drive you later.''

''You mustn't concern yourself with me, Catherine,'' Erin interjected. ''It just so happens I have a meeting in a few minutes.''

''Yes, but I really need to go straight to my appointment—''

''I wouldn't dream of inconveniencing you,'' the sheikh said smoothly. ''I'd be honored to accompany you to your appointment. Afterward, if you wouldn't mind, we can go to my hotel and collect my things.''

''Good, that's settled, then,'' Erin said decisively, coming to her feet and heading for the door. ''I'll look forward to seeing both of you at dinner.''

Catherine simply stood, her face carefully composed so as not to show her horror.

Yet there was no getting around it. Her day had just gone from intense-but-survivable annoyance to major disaster.

Long legs angled sideways, Kaj sat in the passenger seat of the sleek silver Mercedes, watching Catherine put the powerful sports car through its paces.

Pointedly ignoring the ever present security detail following in their wake, she drove as she did everything else. With grace, confidence and—at least where he was concerned—a deliberate air of aloofness. The attitude might have succeeded in putting him off, if not for her breathless reaction to his touch at lunch or the way she'd trembled in his arms when they'd danced last night.

Try as she might to pretend otherwise, she clearly

wasn't indifferent to him. But it was also obvious she had no intention of giving in to her attraction to him.

That alone made her an irresistible challenge, he mused, since he couldn't remember a time when women hadn't thrown themselves at him. And though he'd be the first to concede that some of those women had been drawn by his power and money, he also knew that the majority had been attracted by *him*— his personality, his looks, his unapologetic masculinity.

But not Princess Catherine. To his fascination, she seemed intent on not merely keeping him at arm's length but on driving him away. Not that she had a chance of succeeding…

"Quit staring at me," she said abruptly, slicing into his thoughts.

He settled a little deeper into the dove-gray leather seat. "Now why would I want to do that?"

"Because I don't like it."

"But you're very nice to look at, *chaton.*"

Her grip on the steering wheel tightened. "Do *not* call me kitten," she snapped. "I have a name. And whatever your opinion of my appearance, I dislike being studied like some sort of museum exhibit."

"Very well. If it makes you uncomfortable… Catherine."

Her jaw tightened and he smothered a smile even as he dutifully turned his head and pretended to examine the view.

It was magnificent, he conceded. In between the small groves of palm trees that lined the narrow, serpentine road they were traveling on, aquamarine expanses of the Tyrrhenian Sea could be seen. Red-roofed, Mediterranean-style villas hugged the craggy-

coastline, while a dozen yachts were anchored in the main harbor, looking like elegant white swans amidst the smaller, more colorful Altarian fishing boats.

Yet as attractive as the surroundings were, they didn't interest him the way Catherine did, and it wasn't long before he found himself surreptitiously studying her once again.

He felt a stirring of desire at the contradiction of her, her air of cool containment so at odds with the banked fire of her hair and the baby smoothness of her skin, which practically begged to be touched. She wasn't a classic beauty by any means—her mouth was a little too full, her nose a little too short, and the way her dark-green eyes tilted up at the corners gave her a face a faintly exotic cast. Yet, looking at her pleased him. And made him hunger to do more.

The realization brought a faint frown to his face. Catherine, after all, was going to be his wife. He expected theirs to be a lifelong commitment, and if he'd learned anything from the debacle of his parents' marriage, it was that excessive emotions were not to be trusted. It was all right to find his future bride desirable. Just as long as he didn't want her too much.

Of course, given Catherine's current attitude toward him—and he'd known enemies of the state who'd been treated more warmly—being overcome by uncontrollable lust was probably the least of his worries.

With that in mind, he couldn't resist reaching out and resting his hand on the top of her seat as he turned to face her more fully. "Where, exactly, are we going?"

For a moment he wasn't sure she would answer. But then she sliced a quick glance at him. "If you must know, I like to drop in from time to time on the various charitable organizations supported by my family." She took advantage of a straight stretch of road to accelerate.

"Ah." He pictured her striding down a hospital corridor, doctors and administrators trailing like so much confetti in her wake as she looked in on patients. Or asking pertinent questions of the scientists at the Rosemere Institute, the cancer research facility founded by her grandfather.

Pleased by her sense of responsibility, he shifted a fraction more in her direction, just far enough to slide his fingers beneath the silken tumble of her hair.

A slight shiver went through her, and her lips tightened. "Today—" without warning she hit the brakes and made a sharp left turn, dislodging his hand "—I'm visiting an orphanage."

The explanation was unnecessary since by then they were sweeping past a high stone wall marked with a brass plaque that read "Hope House—where every child is wanted." Beneath that, in letters so small he almost missed them, were the words, "Founded 1999 by Her Highness, Princess Catherine of Altaria." He shot her a startled glance that she ignored.

Seconds later she slowed the car as they approached a rambling two-story house wrapped by a wide, covered veranda. Pulling into an adjacent parking area, she switched off the engine, opened her door and exited the car, all without another word to him.

With a slight shake of his head, Kaj reached for

the door handle. But before he could exit, an explosion of sound had him twisting around. He watched, bemused, as a small army of children burst out of Hope House's front doors, swarmed across the veranda and down the steps, all chattering at once as they ran toward the car.

"Princess, you came!"

"Amalie was ascared you forgot."

"I told her she shouldn't worry. I told her you'd be here soon!"

"Did you bring her a present?"

"Nicco said maybe the new king wouldn't let you visit. He said maybe the new king doesn't like kids like—"

"Children, stop!" To Kaj's surprise, Catherine laughed. It was a husky, musical sound that tickled his nerves like velvet against bare skin. "Of course King Daniel likes you." As she looked down at the dozen small people all vying for her attention, her remoteness melted away. "As a matter of fact, I've told him and Queen Erin all about you, and they've asked if they might come visit you themselves."

"They have?"

"Really?"

"Wait till Nicco hears that."

"Does that mean *you* won't come anymore?" This last was asked by the smallest of the children, a petite black-haired girl with big brown eyes in a too-serious face.

"No, of course not, Amalie," Catherine said gently. "We're friends, no matter what. Yes?"

The child nodded.

"What's more, today is your birthday. I couldn't possibly forget that."

A bashful smile crept across the little girl's face. She sidled closer and leaned against Catherine's hip, rewarded as the princess laid a reassuring hand on her thin shoulder.

Kaj felt a surge of approval. It was good to know the future mother of his children had a maternal side.

Yet even as he told himself he'd made the right choice, that Catherine of Altaria was going to make him a fine wife, he also felt the faintest flicker of uneasiness.

Because just for a second, as he'd watched Catherine's face soften and heard her affection for the children in her voice, he'd experienced an unfamiliar hunger, a desire to have her laugh at something *he* said, a need to have her reach out and touch *him.*

Which was ridiculous, given that he had every confidence that sooner, rather than later, he would be on the receiving end of her affection. All he had to do was stay close and he'd find a way to get past her reserve.

As for this nagging little itch of need she seemed to inspire… It was nothing he couldn't handle.

Three

Catherine sat on the padded chaise longue on her bedroom balcony. She stretched her tired muscles, then huddled a little deeper beneath the ice-green satin comforter she'd dragged from her bed. A golden glow pierced the gunmetal-gray horizon, announcing the sun's imminent arrival and the start of a new day.

For the second night in a row, she'd barely slept. And as much as it rankled to admit it, she knew exactly who was to blame for her second bout of insomnia.

The sheikh. Kaj al bin Russard. Or, as she was beginning to think of him: he-who-refused-to-go-away.

Perhaps she wouldn't be so disturbed if she could write him off as simply another pretty face. Or just a magnificent body. Or even an incredibly willful personality. But the truth was he was all of those things and more.

He was presumptuous, but also perceptive. He was arrogant, yet intuitive. And unlike most of the men she knew, his ego was disgustingly healthy; sarcasm, indifference, even outright hostility all rolled off him like rain off a rock.

Most disturbing of all, his lightest touch was all it took to ignite an unfamiliar fire inside her.

She shivered, not wanting to think about that last bit. Instead she did her best to concentrate on the chorus of birds tuning up to welcome the sunrise—only to make the unfortunate mistake of closing her eyes. The scene at Hope House when Kaj had climbed out of the car yesterday promptly popped into her mind.

Without exception, all the children's eyes had widened at the sight of him. "Who's he?" Christian had asked.

Marko had sucked in a breath. "Is that the king?"

Catherine had been tempted to make a sharp reply—until Kaj had come to stand at her side. The same faint breeze that tugged at his gleaming black hair had carried his clean, masculine scent to her, and suddenly he'd seemed much too close. To her disgust, she'd found she had to swallow hard in order to locate her voice.

"Children, I'd like to introduce Sheikh al bin Russard." Not wanting anyone to get the wrong idea, she'd added, "The sheikh is a friend of my family's."

There were several nods and an "Oh."

And then Christian burst out, "Is he a real sheikh?

Does he live in a tent? How come he doesn't have one of those sheet things on his head?''

Catherine had hesitated a mere instant, and Kaj had stepped into the breach. ''Those sheet things are called ghotras,'' he'd said easily. ''I wear one when I'm in my country, as is the custom. But when I'm here, I try to follow your fashions. And much like you, I live in a home made of mortar and stone. Though I do own several tents. For the times—'' he displayed a quick flash of white teeth ''—when I feel a need to escape and sleep under the stars.''

Whether it was the sentiment or the brief, impish grin that accompanied it, the children all nodded in understanding and several of the boys murmured, ''Yeah!''

Isabelle, one of the older girls, looked earnestly up at him. ''Do you have a camel?''

He shook his head. ''I'm sorry to say, no.'' Although his expression was suitably apologetic, his eyes gleamed with humor as he glanced briefly at Catherine. ''That seems to be a common misconception. What I do have is horses. Beautiful Arabian horses. Oh, and I'm also the keeper of a truly magnificent tiger.''

''You have a tiger?'' Christian, Isabelle and Marko all exclaimed at once. ''A real, live tiger?''

''Mmm-hmm. His name is Sahbak and he was a gift to my father. He's quite a wonderful fellow. Do you know, if you scratch him behind the ears, he purrs?''

''Wow,'' Marko murmured.

That seemed to be the general sentiment. Eyes rounded, the children had stared up at him with a combination of awe and admiration. And though un-impressed by his status as a big-cat owner, Catherine had found that, as the afternoon went along, she couldn't fault his manner. He was wonderful with the children, relaxed, down-to-earth, friendly without seeming too eager. Even little Amalie, who was usu-ally standoffish with strangers, had eventually low-ered her guard.

Catherine wanted in the worst way to blame the latter on the exquisite gold coin Kaj had given the child as a birthday present. But honesty forced her to admit it probably had more to do with the coin's pre-sentation. Who would have suspected a Walburaqui chieftain could, with a flick of his long, elegant hands and a widening of his eyes, make a coin vanish once, twice, thrice? Or that, with a subsequent snap of his fingers, he could make it reappear—much to the delight of a giggling little girl—from its hiding place behind one of her shell-like ears?

Certainly not Catherine.

She pulled the comforter up a little higher and sighed. Perhaps it was the earliness of the hour, but for the first time she admitted that keeping the sheikh out of her life was turning out to be more difficult than she'd imagined. And not just because he'd man-aged to finagle an invitation to stay at the palace, either. But because no matter how hard she pretended otherwise, when she was with him his presence took center stage. A part of her seemed always to be hold-ing its breath, waiting to see what he would do or say next.

Which was annoying but not totally surprising, given the dominant force of his personality.

Far harder to accept was his ability to invade her thoughts. To her horror, every time she let down her guard even the slightest bit he seemed to be there, making her wonder all manner of things.

Like why was he pursuing her when he already had money, power and connections of his own? And what would happen if, in a moment of temporary insanity, she allowed him to get close? How would it feel if she let him kiss her? Or if she let him draw her into the strength of his embrace and touch her? And what would it be like to touch him back, to let her hands roam over his smooth, bronze skin…?

She scrambled off the chaise. Enough, she chastised herself, doing her best to ignore the way her heart was pounding. Clearly two nights of inadequate sleep were addling her brain. A condition that lying around brooding wasn't doing a thing to help.

Her time would be far better spent if she got moving, got some exercise, found a focus for her untrustworthy mind. And the time to start was now.

Impatiently she tossed back the tangled skein of her hair and marched into her room. Fifteen minutes later she was washed and dressed in a white shirt, slim beige twill pants and her favorite knee-high riding boots. She gathered her hair into a high ponytail, snatched up a thin navy vest to guard against the morning chill and slipped out her door.

Kristos, one of her bodyguards, sprang to attention. "Your Highness. Good morning."

She motioned for him to relax. "I'm going for a ride. I promise I'll keep to the palace grounds, so why don't you take a break."

He was clearly not thrilled, but after a moment he

nodded. "I'll let the stable detail know you're on your way."

"If you must." Swallowing a sigh, she started down the corridor, knowing the heightened security was necessary in light of what had happened to her father and grandfather, yet still disliking the increased loss of privacy.

Thanks to the thick, intricately patterned runner that covered the stone floor, the sound of her footsteps was muffled as she began the long, familiar walk toward the west stairway, which was closest to the stables. She reached the intersecting hall that led to the king and queen's apartments, nodded to the pair of guards standing sentinel there, and continued on, moving briskly until she reached a solitary door set midway down the remaining stretch of corridor.

And there she faltered.

She wasn't sure why. After all, she'd passed the entrance to her father's quarters numerous times since his death. And though she'd experienced any number of emotions—disbelief, grief, guilt—not once had she been tempted to step inside.

Until now.

Yet suddenly she wanted to know if Prince Marc had read the note she'd sent him the last day of his life. The note thanking him for going boating in her place with King Thomas and apologizing for disrupting his schedule. The note asking if they might meet later that day so she might explain the real reason she'd begged off at the last minute.

Whether her need sprang from simple curiosity, a belated need to reconnect with her father or some sort of subconscious attempt to occupy her mind with a subject other than the sheikh, she didn't care. She simply had to know. She opened the black-wreathed door and stepped inside.

The elegant sitting room looked the way it always had, as if it was waiting for the prince's imminent return. The carved mahogany furniture was freshly polished, the plush gold, maroon and navy carpet recently vacuumed. Her father's favorite smoking jacket lay folded over the arm of the Queen Anne chair next to the fireplace, and the cut crystal decanter on the wet bar in the corner was three-quarters full.

A lump rose in her throat, but she swallowed it. This was no time for self-indulgence; she'd already given in to enough rampant emotion this morning. Clinging to her composure, she dragged her gaze from her surroundings, crossed the room and let herself into her father's study. She walked to the desk that held his computer and switched the machine on.

Waiting as it hummed to life, she reflected on the contradictions of her father's personality. In so many ways—his belief in the superiority of nobility, his attitude toward women, his resistance to societal change—he'd been a nineteenth-century man. Yet he'd also been fascinated by new technology and had fully embraced the instant access of e-mail. Most likely, Catherine suspected, because without a paper trail he could ignore whomever he chose. In any event, during the past year it had become the best way to communicate with him.

She brought up his on-line server and clicked on the mail-waiting-to-be-read icon. Two entries appeared, and her heart sank as she saw that one of them was indeed hers.

Regret, sadness and a familiar sense of inadequacy washed over her. Well, really. What had she been thinking to harbor even the slightest hope that the prince would have considered anything she had to say of interest? She'd always known she was low on her father's list of priorities.

The only thing that was unexpected was that for once she didn't appear to be alone. Like hers, the other e-mail was timed and dated hours before the prince had left for the marina. Unlike hers, however, the subject line read "urgent."

She frowned, wondering what that could be about even as she clicked the read button and the entire message popped into view.

Your Highness,
The powers that be have agreed to your request, and everything is now in order. As long as the operation continues smoothly, your loan will be reduced as previously discussed.
Your servant,
The Duke

What on earth? Perplexed, she started to read the e-mail again when a faint sound behind her and a sudden prickle at the back of her neck warned she was no longer alone. Unwilling to explain what she was doing—not entirely certain herself—she instinctively clicked off the program before swiveling around.

Gregor Paulus, her father's aide and most trusted servant, stood in the doorway, his usual polite mask firmly in place. "Your Highness. What are you doing in here?"

Although his manner was perfectly civil, there was something in his tone that made Catherine feel like the hapless child she'd been, the one whom Gregor had excelled at discovering at her worst possible moments. Like the time she'd beheaded all her grandfather's prize hothouse orchids to make a bouquet for her nanny. Or the night she'd hidden in her father's closet to surprise him with a good-night kiss only to be trapped when he brought Lady Merton home with him.

She didn't think she'd ever forget the fury in her father's eyes—or the disdain in Gregor's—when the servant had hauled her out of her hiding place the next morning. It most certainly hadn't been one of her more shining hours.

But she wasn't six anymore. She had every right to be here. And even if Gregor didn't agree, it was hardly his place to question her. She drew herself up and stared haughtily at him. "I felt like it. What about you? Isn't it early for you to be on duty?"

He assumed an expression of wounded dignity. "I beg your pardon, but Prince Marc liked having me here first thing in the morning. Carrying on, doing my best to get his affairs in order, is the least I can do to honor his memory." He sounded so sincere that Catherine felt a prick of remorse—until he added piously, "Someone must."

The verbal slap hit its mark. Try as she might to tell herself that Gregor wasn't worth it, that with her father's death he'd lost his power to harm her, his words hurt. Only her pride kept her chin up. The one thing worse than how she felt would be for him to know he'd succeeded in getting to her. "And who better to honor Father than you, Gregor?" To her relief, her voice sounded steady. "No one. So I'll leave you to it."

She could have sworn she saw a flicker of triumph in his pale blue eyes. Yet it vanished as she took a step toward the door and his gaze flicked to the workstation behind her. He stiffened. "Why is the computer on?" he asked sharply.

She shrugged. "I haven't the slightest idea. It was running when I came into the room." She doubted he believed her, but she didn't care. It suddenly felt as if the palace were pressing in on her and all she wanted was to escape. "If you'll excuse me, I'm due elsewhere." She brushed past him, not waiting to hear his response.

Just as she'd intended earlier, she'd go to the stables. By now a groom would have a horse saddled and warmed up for her. Except for the usual exchange with the stable master, she wouldn't have to talk to anyone, much less answer questions or explain herself. She would be able to simply climb into the saddle, take up the reins and head out. She could clear her mind, try one more time to put her feelings about her father into some kind of perspective and drive a stake through any lingering, inappropriate thoughts about the sheikh.

For a little while she'd be free.

Catherine swept into the short end of the L-shaped stable block, her boot heels clattering on the well-swept cobblestones. Blinking as her eyes adjusted from the sunlight to the shadowed corridor, she felt some of the tension drain out of her at the familiar scene.

A dozen roomy box stalls, six to a side, lined each wall, and were occupied by a dozen horses of varying sizes and colors. Some of the animals were still enjoying their morning meals, some were dozing, some stood alertly with their heads thrust out the upper halves of their stall doors. Although there was no sign of another human being, she knew that could be deceiving. "Chalmers?" she called.

There was a sudden movement in the stall to her left and a groom appeared, tipping his head shyly when he saw it was her. "Mr. Chalmers is in the long block, ma'am."

"Thank you, Carlo."

He nodded and she headed briskly down the passageway, swept around the corner—and plowed straight into what felt like a warm steel wall.

Her body knew instantly who it was. Her skin flushed, her nipples puckered, her heart thumped as a pair of strong hands reached out to steady her.

A second later her mind caught up with the rest of her, and she jerked her head up. Just as she feared, she found herself confronted by a pair of bold gray eyes in a familiar face. Her stomach flip-flopped. "You!"

Kaj looked down at her with a wry smile, a faint pair of grooves scoring his lean cheeks. "Good morning, princess."

She parted her lips to ask what he was doing here, then abruptly clamped her mouth shut. She'd asked that question far too often lately, and there was no way she was going to ask it again. Besides, a quick glance at his attire pretty much told the story. Like her he was dressed in a white shirt, breeches and a gleaming pair of tall boots. All he needed to complete his ensemble was a horse.

The discovery was as alarming as his presence. Or would be, she amended, if she gave a whit about how he spent his time. Which she didn't, as long as it wasn't with her.

She pulled free of his hold. "Pardon me," she said sharply, stepping around him. "Chalmers!" She lasered a gaze at the stable master, who stood no more than ten feet away, holding the reins of a compact blood bay as well as a rangy gray. "I assume Cashell is ready?" Not waiting for an affirmative—why else would he be standing there?—she strode forward and snatched the bay's reins from his hands. She glanced at the gray, automatically sliding a reassuring palm down her mount's neck when he pranced sideways. "Why is Keystone saddled?"

Chalmers looked uneasily from her to the sheikh and back again. "Mr. al bin Russard requested him, Your Highness."

Kaj moved to her side. "I thought we might go for a ride."

"Oh, did you?" Once again she moved away from him. Even so, he was still so close that with a sideways glance she could see the faint shadow of beard beneath his bronze skin and a faint scar that bisected his left eyebrow. Out of nowhere, an urge to reach out and touch him—to lay her palm against his cheek, run her fingertips over that inky eyebrow—swept her. Appalled, she wrenched her gaze away and slid the

nearest stirrup iron down the saddle leather. "I don't
think so."

There was a moment's silence, and then he inquired softly, "Are you all right, Catherine?"

She heard the concern in his voice and looked
down to see her hands were shaking. Mortified, she
bunched them into fists and rounded on him. "No!
Yes! That is, I would be if you'd just leave me
alone!"

"Ah." He nodded, his expression almost sympathetic. "I'm sorry, *chaton,* but that's not going to happen."

"Why? Because you have some ludicrous notion
that if you hang around long enough I'll marry you?"
She regretted the words as soon as she said them.
After all, she had no basis for the accusation other
than her suspicions. And even if it were true, he'd
hardly admit it.

Which was why it was such a shock when he
calmly nodded his head and said, "Yes. Precisely."

She stared at him in stupefaction. "You can't be
serious! In case it's escaped your notice, this is the
new millennium, the twenty-first century! I don't care
who you are, you don't get to select a bride the way
you would a piece of candy."

"I assure you I put far more thought into this than
I would choosing a bonbon," he answered gravely.

"Oh! You're impossible!" She whirled away from
him and, before he could make a move to stop her,
swung herself lightly into the saddle. Instinctively adjusting her seat as the bay sidled nervously beneath
her, she gathered the reins, freed the far stirrup and
slid her foot into place. "In the event you still haven't

gotten the message, the answer is no. No, I won't go riding with you. No, I won't marry you. Not now. Not ever. For the last time, I want you to leave me alone!'' She urged Cashell forward, not caring as the bay responded with an eager lunge that forced the sheikh to jump out of the way or be run over.

Somehow she found the control to keep the bay at a trot until they were clear of the stable and courtyard. But the minute they reached the path that led to the cliffs above Lucinda Bay, she gave the high-strung gelding his head. With a toss of his silky black mane, the animal leaped into a ground-eating canter that became a flat-out gallop as they turned onto the wide track that skimmed the edge of the headland.

The reckless flight perfectly matched her mood. She'd had enough of reining herself in, of behaving like some witless pushover. She was done allowing Kaj to alternately outrage and sweet-talk her. She was done with him, period. Marriage? What incredible nerve! She didn't even know the man—or him, her.

As for the inexplicable ribbon of loss curling through her, it had nothing to do with the sheikh. Yes, he was charming. Yes, he was attractive, in a purely physical, hormonal sort of way. And yes, she supposed that deep down a tiny, juvenile part of her may have been somewhat flattered by his attention. But that was all it had been; she didn't *care* about him. She didn't.

Cashell stumbled, startling her. He quickly regained his footing, but his misstep was enough to bring her back to the moment. Realizing the bay was tiring, she reined him in, bringing him first to a canter and then to a walk.

That was when she finally heard the sound of hoof-beats, coming on strong. She twisted around in the saddle, incredulous as she saw the sheikh atop Keystone bearing down on her. So what if the Walburaqui chieftain rode divinely, so flawlessly balanced in the saddle that he and the big gray might have been one body? How dare he follow her? How dare he disregard her direct order that he leave her alone?

Catherine couldn't remember the last time she'd completely given in to her temper. But now anger, hot and unfamiliar, bubbled through her. She reined in and waited, and when Kaj caught up with her moments later, bringing the gray to a sliding halt, she let go. "This is the outside of enough, sheikh! I want you to leave this instant—"

He cut her off, saying something in Arabic that sounded as fierce as it did profane. Then he vaulted to the ground, closed the space between them in two big strides, reached up and clamped his hands around her waist.

Catherine stared at him in shock, a funny feeling blossoming in the pit of her stomach. At some point during his ride his rich black hair had come loose and now brushed his open white collar. The bronzed vee of his chest rose and fell with his every agitated breath, while his gray eyes glittered like shards of silver. He looked achingly beautiful, more than a little uncivilized—and every bit as furious as she was.

She told herself that was his problem and vowed not to let him intimidate her, regardless of how formidable he might appear. "How dare you! Let go of me this instant or I swear I'll have you deported!"

"*Bes.*" Enough. He yanked her out of the saddle,

her feet barely touching ground before he gave her a hard shake. "What do you think you're doing, riding so recklessly?" he demanded through his teeth. "You could have broken your neck!"

She blinked. She'd expected him to berate her for her treatment of him, not care about her welfare. Not that it mattered. "Well, I didn't! And even if I had, what I do is none of your business!"

"The devil it's not." He pressed forward, looming over her. "Everything about you concerns me."

"Oh!" She shoved at his broad shoulders, but she might as well have tried to move the promontory they stood on. "Either you're profoundly hard of hearing or simply the most conceited man to ever walk the earth! Whichever it is, I don't give a damn. Just go away!"

"No. And don't swear."

"Or what?" she said scathingly. "You'll say something else I'll choose to ignore?"

She knew she'd made a mistake even before his jaw tightened. Still she wasn't prepared when he abruptly pulled her so close she could feel his heart thudding against her breasts. She parted her lips to protest, but that too proved unwise. With a savage murmur he lowered his head and sealed her mouth with his own.

Her mind reeled. She couldn't believe his sheer audacity. Or that rather than struggling to escape, she was standing statue still, allowing him to take such a liberty. But then, nothing in her life had prepared her for the pleasure suddenly pouring through her in a scalding tide.

The world around her vanished. There was only

Kaj, his heat enveloping her, his scent filling her head, his big, hard angular body the perfect fit for her smaller, softer one.

Far away, she heard someone start to moan. Vaguely she recognized her own voice, but it didn't seem to matter. What was important was the firm, knowledgeable mouth fixed to hers, the tongue breaching her lips, the heat spinning downward to pool in the tips of her breasts and the juncture of her thighs.

She couldn't seem to get enough. Not of the drugging warmth of his kiss, the hands clamped possessively to her hips, the tantalizing friction as their bodies pressed against each other.

He tugged her shirt out of her breeches and slid his hand over her bare abdomen. His thumb swept the lower curve of her breast. She sucked in her breath at the foreign sensation and willed his hand to move higher. When it did, she squeezed her eyes shut, unable to contain a whimper when his fingers closed around her distended nipple.

Her whole body flushed. She arched her back, pressing closer until she felt him, thick and hot against her. Startled and uncertain, damning her lack of experience, she hesitated, not sure what to do next.

Kaj had no such reservation. Reaching down, he slid one powerful arm under the curve of her bottom and lifted her up, bringing her to rest against the bulge of his erection. He pressed her against him, and all the hot, liquid sensation thrumming through her seemed to converge in one aching, sensitive spot.

It was way too much and not nearly enough. Guided purely by instinct, she wrapped her legs

around his waist and rocked her hips, rewarded as a
groan escaped his lips. He tore his mouth from hers
and she started to protest, but the words caught in her
throat as he shifted her upper body away from his and
his lips found the underside of her jaw. He began to
string a chain of kisses downward, into the open vee
of her shirt. When he ran out of bare skin, he lifted
his head. In the next second his mouth settled greedily
over the swollen tip of her cotton-covered breast.

Hot. Wet. Urgent bliss. Sensations flooded her.
Who would have thought that being with a man could
be like this? That she—justifiably referred to as the
ice princess by a legion of spurned suitors—could feel
dizzy with desire? Not her.

The idea that she'd finally found a place where she
belonged whispered through her mind.

And then it vanished, forgotten as a throbbing, unfamiliar need began to build in her, growing and
growing until she couldn't think, couldn't breathe,
couldn't stand it a second longer. "Kaj." She pressed
her face into the silk of his hair. "Please. Make love
to me."

For a moment he didn't seem to hear her. Then
he went very still. A violent shudder racked him
and the delicious pressure of his mouth at her breast
ceased, replaced by the ragged wash of his breath.
He slowly raised his head. "Catherine. *Min fadlak
fehempt—*"

She might not know the exact meaning of his
words but she recognized *no* when she heard it. Even
so, for the space of several heartbeats she still didn't
understand. And then it struck her. He didn't want
her.

An icy fist seemed to close around her heart. As if emerging from a dream, she realized she was clinging to him like a starfish plastered to a rock at high tide. And that despite his obvious arousal, he was still very much in control of himself.

Her desire drained away, replaced by stinging humiliation. For the first time in her life she'd actually wanted a man to make love to her—and he'd said no. Her face burned and it was hard to breathe over the mixture of shame and embarrassment suddenly clogging her throat.

"Catherine?"

She pushed hard against him, and this time he let her go, which she took as a further sign of his rejection. "I…I beg your pardon." Unable to meet his gaze, she addressed the vicinity of his right ear. "This was clearly a mistake."

"No," he said roughly. "You don't understand—"

"Oh, yes, I do." She lifted her chin and forced herself to speak clearly, although she still couldn't bring herself to look directly at him. "I don't know what game you're playing, sheikh, but this never should have happened. Stay away from me. Just… stay away."

To her horror tears suddenly filled her eyes. Not about to break down in front of him, she swiveled on her heel, located Cashell and crossed to him. Her body felt leaden, but somehow she still managed to climb into the saddle where, without so much as a backward glance, she put her heels to the bay's barrel and urged him away.

Back ramrod straight, she pretended not to notice the tears running down her face. After all, there was no reason for them: it was her pride Kaj had bruised, not her heart.

She paid no attention to the small, inner voice that called her a liar.

Four

"**A**h, there you are."

At the sound of his cousin's voice, Kaj looked up to see Joffrey step through the wide glass doors that opened onto the palace's west balcony. Backlit by the warm light that spilled from the first-floor drawing room, the Englishman looked dapper as always, his evening clothes impeccably tailored, his pale hair gleaming as he strolled across the exquisitely patterned tiles that comprised the floor.

Reaching a spot just short of where Kaj stood, his back to the balustrade, Joffrey came to a halt. "Getting some air?" he inquired.

Kaj inclined his head. "Yes."

"I must say, it is a lovely night out. Not too warm, not too cold. Full moon, beautiful sky. And while I'm a little disappointed in you, I suppose your aversion to being inside with the rest of us is perfectly understandable under the circumstances.''

''I beg your pardon?''

''I'm referring to Princess Catherine's choice of company this evening, of course. One can hardly blame you for conceding the field. Although personally I've always found that Italian bloke to be a tad cheeky. Then again, if the princess looked at me that way, I'd no doubt feel a bit brazen myself.''

Unable to help himself, Kaj glanced toward the drawing room. Catherine, exquisite in a black lace gown, stood inside next to the grand piano. She was listening intently to something Ricco Andriotti, the internationally known race car driver, was saying to her.

The two had had their heads together all through dinner. By the time the company had quit the table to stretch their legs and mingle, the brash young playboy had even grown bold enough to occasionally touch her. Which he did now, first gesturing ebulliently as he spoke, then reaching out to run a finger down her cheek to underscore his point.

Kaj forced himself to look away, afraid if he watched one second longer he might do something he'd regret. Of course, he wouldn't regret it nearly as much as Andriotti.

''She really does have incredible eyes, doesn't she?'' Joffrey mused. ''And those lashes. They're as thick as the imported paintbrushes Great-Aunt Marietta was so fond of. Add in all that lovely alabaster skin and one can hardly blame Signor Andriotti for wanting to leave his handprints all over—''

''*Shut up, Joff.*''

There was a brief silence. Then Joffrey delicately cleared his throat. "No need to inquire how the courtship's going, I see. So do be a dear boy and remind me to call home tomorrow. It appears I need to instruct my people to hurry putting the finishing touches on the stall I'm having readied for Tezhari."

Kaj sliced him a look as sharp as a razor blade. "Tell me, cousin, are you simply feeling reckless tonight, or are you deliberately courting a death wish?"

Joffrey had the brass to chuckle. "Oh, dear. As bad as all that, is it? Would it help if you told me all about it?"

Kaj smiled humorlessly. "I think I'll pass."

"Now, don't be hasty. You know what they say— confession is good for the soul."

"Yes, and silence is golden." Too bad he was the only one who seemed to know it, Kaj thought as he glanced back at the drawing room in time to see Catherine smile at something Andriotti was whispering in her ear. To his disgust, the race car driver's hand seemed to have taken up permanent residence on her forearm. He had a brief fantasy of snapping the man's fingers one by one.

Unfortunately, it didn't help that Catherine seemed to be hanging on the Italian's every word. She'd never looked at *him* that way. But then, he might as well be invisible for all the attention she'd paid him tonight. Hell, for the past two days she'd barricaded herself in her room, refusing to take his phone calls or accept either the notes or flowers he'd sent her. And the one and only time their gazes had met this evening she'd looked right through him.

Not that he didn't deserve her scorn. It was bad

enough that he'd lost his temper the last time they'd been together. But to also lose command of the situation, to first lay hands on her and then give in to the temptation to kiss her...

But that wasn't the worst. Oh, no. That designation was solely reserved for how close he'd come to mindlessly stripping Catherine of her breeches and taking her right then and there, out in the open, on the hard ground with nothing but gorse for a bed, where anyone could have seen them.

With no thought for her pleasure, but only his own.

A nerve jumped to life in his jaw. Never, ever, had he experienced such a monumental failure of control, not even when he'd been a raw, inexperienced youth and his father had arranged for a courtesan to instruct him in the art of love.

A part of him still couldn't believe what he'd almost done. And he certainly couldn't excuse it. Any more than he could excuse the clumsy way he'd handled things when he'd belatedly come to his senses. Thanks to his self-absorption, his shock at his behavior, he'd unwittingly hurt Catherine's feelings.

Not that she seemed to be suffering unduly, he noted grimly, his gaze never leaving her.

Nevertheless... For one of the few times in his life, he wasn't sure what to do. He was a man accustomed to taking command; sitting on his hands was no more his style than being on the outside looking in. But what could he possibly say to her? That she made him a little crazy? But not so much that he'd been willing to do what she'd asked and make love to her? He swallowed a sigh. Perhaps, if he gave it enough time, she'd come around all by herself...

"You know," Joffrey said suddenly, "I must say I'm surprised. It's not like you to so readily concede defeat. You still have three weeks remaining, after all."

"I haven't conceded anything."

"Really? You could have fooled me. Hiding out here in the dark, brooding and licking your wounds—"

Kaj frowned, beginning to feel irritated. "I am not brooding."

His cousin regarded him with raised eyebrows. "Then you're doing a bang-up imitation. And may I add, it doesn't suit you."

"What would you have me do? Go in there, grab the princess and cart her off to my room?"

"If that's what it would take to get that pathetic look off your face, yes."

"*Pathetic?*" Kaj repeated in a dangerously low voice. He drew himself up to his full height. "I'm never pathetic—" He broke off as he saw Andriotti sidle even closer to Catherine. Something primitive took hold of him, and his displeasure with his cousin shifted solidly to the Italian.

Joffrey was right, he decided abruptly. Standing around waiting for the perfect moment to approach Catherine wasn't accomplishing anything. It was time to take action. "Excuse me," he ground out, shoving away from the railing and heading for the drawing room.

"Does this mean I should hold off on phoning home?" Joffrey called after him.

Kaj ignored him and stepped inside. Whether it was his grim expression or the purposeful set of his shoulders, the other guests took one look at him and scurried out of his way, clearing a path as he strode toward Catherine.

She and the Italian seemed to be the only two people in the room oblivious to his presence. Though that made him feel grimmer still, he made a conscious effort to unclench his teeth when he reached them. "Catherine. Andriotti." He zeroed in on the smaller man, whom he topped by more than a head, and managed the facsimile of a smile. "Would you be so kind as to excuse us? There's something I need to discuss with the princess."

"Don't be ridiculous," Catherine contradicted immediately, laying a hand on the Italian's arm. "The sheikh is mistaken, Ricco. He and I have nothing to talk about. Nothing at all."

Kaj's gaze flicked from her hand to Andriotti's face. "I would suggest that you go, Ricco. *Now.*"

Whatever the Italian saw in his expression, it was enough to make the other man take a hurried step back. "Yes, of course," he said hastily, sending Catherine an apologetic look. "*Arrivederci, bella principessa.* For now." With that, he went.

Catherine shifted her attention to Kaj, her exotic green eyes glittering with anger. "You simply don't know when to quit, do you?"

"Let's take a stroll through the gardens," he countered, reaching out to clasp her elbow.

She jerked her arm away. "No. I'm not going anywhere with you." Her voice was frigid enough to cause frostbite.

"Yes," he said, "you are. Your only choice is

whether you prefer to do so under your own power or over my shoulder.''

She stared at him. "You wouldn't dare."

He didn't deign to answer but simply raised an eyebrow.

Furious color touched her cheeks. She glared at him for the space of several heartbeats, then with a little "hmph" averted her gaze and flounced toward the French doors. He fell in behind her, doing his best not to stare at the lissome line of her exposed back or the enticing sway of her hips.

She crossed the terrace, marched down the wide, shallow steps that led to the gardens, then turned to face him, her slender arms crossed over her breasts. "Now," she said. "What is it you want?"

Such an interesting choice of words. For an instant he actually considered telling her the truth. *You. I want you. Under me, on top of me, around me. Hot, wet, willing. For however long it takes to sate this exceptionally bothersome hunger you induce in me.*

Yet even without the protectiveness of her posture or the wariness in her eyes, it didn't take a genius to guess how that declaration would be received. Like it or not—and he didn't like it one bit—he was going to have to take a different, far more humbling, tack. "I'd like to apologize."

"For what?"

"For what happened between us on the bluff."

Although he wouldn't have thought it possible, her expression grew even more remote. "There's absolutely no need for that. You made your regret crystal clear at the time. So now if you'll excuse me—" She started to step around him, intent on gaining the stairs.

"Catherine, don't." He moved into her path and reached for her.

She jerked back. "Don't you touch me!"

He raised his hands. "Very well. As long as you stand still and listen."

Once again she crossed her arms. "I'll give you exactly one minute. Then I'm calling the palace guard."

He took a calming breath and marshaled his thoughts. "As I said, I'm sorry about what happened. There's no excuse for my behavior, but if you only had more experience—"

"Oh! If you think I'm going to stand here and let you insult me on top of everything else, you're sadly mistaken. Get out of my way. Now!"

"*No*. Not until you hear me out. What I'm trying to say is that you deserve better—"

"Finally something we agree on!"

"—than for the first time we make love to be some quick, mindless encounter. My only defense is that I lost my head. I've known a number of exceptional women, but I've never desired anyone the way I do you. Which, I can assure you, you'd know if you had more experience."

For what felt like an eternity she said nothing. And then he heard her utter a faint, "Oh."

"Make no mistake, Catherine," he said, picking his words with care. "I want you. And I intend to have you. But not until the time is right. Not until you trust me and know that I want you for who you are, not just for the physical pleasure you make me feel."

"But...why bother?" The chilly note had left her

voice, replaced by defensiveness—and a faint note of uncertainty. "Why not just take what you can when it's offered? After all, you've already decided we should marry."

"Because you deserve better. You have a right to expect candlelight and tenderness, to have a man take his time with you. You deserve a lover who makes you feel cherished, not just drunk with desire. You shouldn't have to settle for a quick toss in the grass with someone you don't trust."

Again she was silent. Then, after what felt like a very long time, a sigh escaped her lips. "I don't understand you, Kaj," she said softly. "I don't understand you at all."

"All I want is a chance, *chaton.* A chance for us to get to know each other, to spend some time together. Perhaps we'll find we don't suit. But then again, perhaps we'll find we do. What can it hurt to find out?"

The question seemed to hang in the moonlit air between them. "I'm not sure," Catherine answered finally. "But you may not feel that way when you learn that I decided a long time ago that I'd never marry. You or anyone else."

"So perhaps I'll have to settle for our being friends."

"Do you mean that?"

"I always mean what I say." It wasn't a lie. He did want to be her friend, just as he wanted to be her lover. That he still intended to marry her despite her naive and unrealistic, if rather touching, intention to remain unwed, was a mere detail. One he had every confidence she'd come to view the way he did, as a practical necessity, once they spent more time together.

After all, she had no place here in Altaria now that Prince Marc was dead, while as the wife of Sheikh al bin Russard she'd have a position in society, unlimited wealth and the personal freedom to do whatever she liked. She was an intelligent woman; given a little time and the proper attention, she was certain to see the advantages of a union between them.

"All right," she said a trifle breathlessly. "As long as you understand how I feel."

"I believe I do. Now, what do you say to the proposition that we get away from the palace tomorrow?"

"To do what?"

He smiled. "I can't tell you that, Catherine. It would ruin the surprise. Simply say you'll meet me at the south portico at noon." By then he'd have figured it out himself, he thought wryly.

"All right. I'll be there."

"Good. Then there's just one more thing." Eliminating the space between them, he cupped her face in his hand. Her cheek felt baby smooth against his fingers, her jawbone light and delicate.

Apprehension flared in her eyes. "Kaj... I don't think—"

"Hush." He pressed his thumb to her lips; he knew he was taking a chance, but the need to erase every trace of Andriotti's touch on her was riding him hard. "Trust me." He slid his thumb to the base of her chin and lowered his head, ignoring the heady rush of need that deluged him as he settled his lips against hers.

Damn, she was sweet. Her scent, her taste, the texture of her skin...all of it pleased him. For a few seconds he let his hunger off its leash, sliding his arm around her, finding the bare valley of her spine with his hand, allowing himself the sheer sensual luxury of exploring that warm satin hollow with his fingertips.

Yet he had no intention of jeopardizing their newfound understanding. Just as quickly as he'd let himself go, he reined himself in, shifting his hand to the lace-covered indentation of her waist and easing his mouth away from hers.

"Ah, you're such a temptation," he murmured, pressing a kiss first to one corner of her lips, then her cheek and finally her temple. He rested his forehead against hers, allowed himself a moment to catch his breath, then eased back. He looked down at her with a rueful smile. "But I swear to you that the next time we kiss—if there is a next time—it will be only at your invitation. Now, we'd best go in, before you succeed in unmanning me completely."

Even in the moonlight he could see the look of satisfaction that crossed her face, and he congratulated himself. Admitting to a temporary weakness couldn't be all bad if it succeeded in restoring her self-esteem.

"Come." He held out his hand and after the briefest hesitation, she took it. Try as he might, he couldn't entirely contain a sense of triumph. Or quiet the deadly serious little voice that whispered, "Mine," as, side by side, they headed inside.

Five

"Amazing," Catherine murmured, still trying to take in the sight before her: the glistening blue-white ice filling the temporary skating arena, the bubble dome enclosing it, the stereo speakers issuing pop music.

It would have been a surprise even without the presence of the children from the orphanage. But they were very much in attendance, dotting the ice like sprinkles atop an ice-cream cone. Some clung to the tubular rail that encircled the rink, some stood wind-milling their arms in desperate bids for balance, some were actually gliding around the mirrorlike surface. All together they were as noisy as a convocation of crows, expressing their delight in their surroundings with a mixture of shrieks and laughter.

Catherine turned to look at Kaj, unable to keep the

wonder out of her voice. "Whatever made you think of this?"

He shrugged. "Your cousin Daniel deserves some credit. He and I were enjoying a game of chess the other night when he mentioned you'd visited his family one winter in Chicago, learned to skate and had seemed quite taken with it."

"But that was a decade ago, at least. I can't believe—" She broke off as she realized she was about to say, You went to so much trouble to please me. Taken aback, since she certainly didn't consider herself as needy as such a declaration implied, she deliberately lightened her voice. "That is, however did you manage this? Skating rinks don't grow on trees, and there's certainly never been one in Altaria."

"I have an acquaintance in the amusement business in Trieste. I made a phone call. He took care of the rest."

He was obviously downplaying his role. Even if his friend had all the equipment to put together an ice arena in less than twenty-four hours, Kaj still would've had to secure the site, get a permit, arrange for power and water hookups and take care of a dozen other things she was no doubt overlooking.

"The most challenging part was having it ready by this afternoon," he confided. "It seems this much water takes a certain amount of time to freeze."

"Surely you realize I could have waited a day."

He shook his head. "I promised you a surprise. As I believe I've mentioned before, I always mean what I say."

To her dismay, his declaration made her suddenly remember something he'd said last night. *Make no mistake, Catherine. I want you. And I intend to have you.*

And just like that her mouth went dry and her nipples tightened. Hastily she crossed her arms, reminding herself sharply that that had been before. Before she'd made it clear that marriage wasn't for her. Before he'd conceded the most they might ever be was friends. Before he'd demonstrated his good faith by bestowing a kiss on her that had been a model of respect and restraint.

As for the tiny but willful part of her that persisted in hungering for more—it was her cross to bear. While Kaj's explanation for putting a halt to their encounter out on the bluff had eased the worst of her hurt and embarrassment, it wasn't an experience she had any intention of repeating. And surely, given time and familiarity, the shivery feeling she got when she was around him, as well as the zing of pleasure she experienced at even his most innocent touch, would dim. It had to, since the alternative was simply unthinkable.

"What about the children?" she asked. "What made you think to invite them?"

"Self-preservation." At her startled look, the skin around his eyes crinkled. "Given recent events, and your effect on me, princess, I thought it would be best for us to be chaperoned."

Some of her anxiety eased. "I'm glad you did. Otherwise, I suppose I'd have to skate alone, since I don't imagine they do much ice-skating in Walburaq."

"You forget I went to school in England."

"You skate?" She tried to picture it and couldn't.

He was simply too big, too intent, too seriously masculine for something so lighthearted.

A rueful smile curved his mouth. "In a manner of speaking. My mother's family has an extensive holding in Northumberland, and my cousin Joffrey and I spent our winter holidays there. He made certain I learned the local pastime. Initially, I've no doubt, because he enjoyed seeing me fall."

She considered his wry expression. "You're not serious."

"Ah, but I am."

"But I've met your cousin. Blond, rather serious, lovely manners?" He nodded his confirmation, and she couldn't contain a protest. "He seemed so civilized."

"A facade, I assure you," he responded dryly. "A devil in tweed would more accurately describe him."

As if a veil had been torn away, she suddenly heard the affection underlying his tone. "The two of you are close?" As fond as she was of her own cousins, she'd never spent much time with them. The idea that Kaj had a warm relationship with a member of his family, particularly one who seemed so different from him, was oddly endearing.

"Very. Despite his limitations as a skating teacher. Not to worry, however. Today I thought I'd limit myself to just being an observer."

She forgot all about their respective families. "No. You can't!"

One elegant black eyebrow rose. "I can't?"

"No." The mere idea of being watched by him made her skin tingle; she didn't want to think how her body would react to the real thing. "You can't go to all this trouble and then just sit on the sidelines like some kind of all-powerful pasha expecting to be entertained.''

"But I *am* a pasha, dearest Catherine, albeit an Arabian one.''

"Not today,'' she said firmly. "Today you're a participant.''

Their gazes met. He studied her a moment, and then his face softened and he inclined his head. "Very well. If that's what you wish.''

Her stomach did an unexpected flip-flop, and once more she tried to tell herself the cause was nothing more than sexual chemistry. Only, this time she didn't totally believe it.

She liked him. Or at least she could, she quickly amended, if this was the real him and not some carefully constructed act. Which she didn't think it was.

Not that *that* was necessarily good. She could handle being physically attracted to him, though it wouldn't be easy. But to actually become friends, to have someone in her life who was genuinely interested in her, who wanted to know her in more than just the Biblical sense...

She drew in a shaky breath. Giving him a second chance had seemed like the right thing to do last night. But now she wasn't so sure. Could she trust her instincts? Could she trust *him?* Or *was* she really so needy, so starved for attention, she'd lost all perspective? Even worse, what if she was just looking for an excuse to go after what she'd already decided she shouldn't have?

"Catherine.''

She jumped as he touched his palm to the small of her back. "What?"

"Quit thinking so hard." He urged her toward a bench near the curving, puffy plastic wall. "Today is about having fun. Relax." He motioned to a young man standing next to a large chest.

"I am relaxed." It wasn't a total lie, not really. As soon as she put some space between them—and got away from the delicious weight of his hand resting against her—she hadn't a doubt she'd feel much, much calmer.

She took a jerky step and abruptly sat down on the end of the bench, feigning interest in the youth approaching with a pair of large, square boxes. He set them down, retrieved two pairs of skates, and in no time at all she and Kaj were booted and laced.

"You're certain I have to do this?" Underlying Kaj's inquiry as they headed for the ice was a distinct note of reluctance.

"Yes."

He uttered a faint sigh, and to her surprise, she found she wanted to smile. Although it was hardly to her credit, there was a part of her that was looking forward to seeing him be less than his usually competent self.

But first she had a more immediate concern. The instant she stepped onto the ice, children approached from every direction, drawn to her like filings to a magnet. "We've been waiting and waiting for you," Marko exclaimed.

"Watch me, Princess Cat!" Christian demanded, doing an awkward pirouette.

"Look at my skates!" Isabelle pointed at her feet. "Aren't they pretty?"

"Will you skate with me?" Elizabeth asked.

"Me, too?" Nicco chimed in.

Just for a moment Catherine wondered what it would feel like to be free of obligation. The thought quickly faded, however, as she looked around at the faces turned hopefully up at her. If there was one thing she understood, it was a child's need for adult recognition. She summoned a smile. "Of course I will—"

"But later," Kaj said firmly. "First Her Highness needs to practice." He ignored the chorus of dejected oh's that greeted this pronouncement and leaned close to Catherine, his warm breath tickling her ear. "Quit looking so surprised. You deserve some time just for you." Straightening, he addressed the children. "I, however, would be delighted to skate with you. Or perhaps some of you might prefer to have a ride on my shoulders?"

There was an instant uproar. "I want a turn!"

"Me first, me first!"

"No, me!"

He raised a hand to silence the jangle of young voices, looking around until his gaze settled on Amalie, who was hanging back as usual. "What about you, little one? Would you like to go skating with me?"

She considered, then shyly nodded.

"Very well." As easily as that, he leaned down, turned her around and gently lifted her up, settling her squarely on his broad shoulders. "Don't worry," he murmured as the child took a death grip on his hair. "I won't drop you."

"Promise?" came her tremulous voice.

"On my honor."

Amalie thought about it, then relaxed enough to give him a tentative pat on the head. "'Kay."

He took in the other children's disappointed expressions. "Everyone who wants one will get a turn," he said, and the youngsters' faces immediately brightened. He turned to Catherine. "If you'll excuse us?"

Hopelessly if reluctantly charmed, she nodded. "Of course."

He nodded back, then turned and skated away, skimming over the ice so effortlessly he might have been born with blades on his feet.

So much for incompetence! She'd been conned, and though she told herself she ought to be mad, it was impossible. Still, she couldn't allow him to escape completely unscathed. "Has anyone ever told you you're a scoundrel, Sheikh al bin Russard?" she called after him.

He executed a graceful half turn so he was gliding backward. His teeth flashed whitely. "As a matter of fact, yes. I believe they have."

Oh! The man had more nerve than anyone she'd ever known. Which was precisely what made him so entertaining.

Deliberately she turned her back on him, doing her best to ignore the amusement dancing through her like sunlight on water. Still, she couldn't seem to stop smiling even as she took a few tentative steps of her own. To her delight, so quickly did she find her footing, it might have been days instead of years since her last outing. In no time at all she was lost in the sheer exhilaration of flying over the ice, and the next hour flew by. By the time she finally conceded to a break to catch her breath, she felt as giddy as a teenager.

And every bit as mischievous. Gliding out of the far corner, she eyed Kaj, who stood down the rail, standing to one side of a half circle of attentive children. Carefully judging velocity and distance, she sped up, then slid to a showy stop—a move that just happened to spray a certain Walburaqui chieftain with a shower of ice.

The children gasped. Then the gasps turned to smothered giggles at the sight of the frosty coating clinging to the sheikh's face. "Uh-oh," Marko murmured as said sheikh turned to consider Catherine.

Kaj deliberately wiped the clinging crystalline droplets from his face before raising one black eyebrow. "Having fun?"

She smiled sweetly at him. "Yes. I am. Thank you for asking. And you?"

His gaze flicked to her upturned mouth. Just for an instant something hot and dangerous seemed to flare in his eyes. Then he smiled and his whole face changed, leaving her to wonder if she'd just imagined that torrid look. "Yes, I believe I am. Despite a certain person's warped sense of humor."

"We're all having fun," Christian chimed in brightly. "But it would be even better if you'd skate with us, Princess Cat."

Wrenching her gaze away from the sheikh, she glanced around to find the children all staring expectantly at her. Grateful for the distraction, she nodded. "I'd be delighted."

"Good!"

"I want to be first," Isabelle declared.

"No, me!" Marko chimed in.

Christian pursed his lips. "How about if we all hold hands? Then everyone can skate together!"

There was a moment's silence as his suggestion was considered, then a sea of small heads bobbed up and down.

"Is that all right with you, Mr. Kaj?" Elizabeth asked, staring up at him with a worshipful expression.

"Certainly." He glanced at Catherine. "What do you say? Want to give it a try?" He held out his hand.

Once again she looked into his handsome face, her heart giving a familiar little stutter as their fingers brushed. "Yes," she said impulsively, "that would be—"

"Perfect!" Christian thrust between them, bristling with importance. "You can be on the inside, sheikh, because you're the biggest. And Princess Cat can be at the other end—" he took Catherine's hand and tugged her toward the rail "—because she's the fastest. And everybody else can be in between." He gestured at the other children to fall in.

Catherine glanced over her shoulder at Kaj, expecting him to protest. When instead he gave a philosophical shrug, she felt a prickle of disappointment.

She looked away, telling herself not to be foolish. The last thing she needed was to hold hands with the sheikh like some sort of vapid schoolgirl. Yet she couldn't deny the pang she felt when she glanced back and was just in time to see him reach down to clasp little Isabelle's skinny fingers with his much bigger ones.

In that instant she knew she'd been deluding herself.

Despite all her protestations to the contrary, what she wanted from Kaj al bin Russard was not a platonic friendship. So what, exactly, did she want?

Kaj strode along the headland path, moonlight lighting his way. Like a lover's playful fingers, the ocean breeze skimmed over his face, plucked at his white silk shirt, tugged at his pulled-back hair. He barely noticed. He was far too intent on identifying the cause of the uncharacteristic restlessness powering his steps.

He tried to tell himself it was merely the result of his longing for home. As had often happened during his school years in England, he was fed up with well-ordered gardens, constricting clothes, too many people and too many rules.

He wanted—no, he needed—to strike out with a few trusted kinsmen, to lose himself in the vast silence of the desert where he could travel for days seeing nothing more than a sun-drenched horizon or the endless black dome of a star-spangled sky. He needed to shake off civilization, speak his native tongue, drink in the hot, dry desert air and not this softly misted imitation fluttering in off the Tyrrhenian.

And it certainly wouldn't hurt if somewhere in there he could take Catherine to bed.

The last thought brought a sudden, reluctant smile to the tense line of his lips.

Very well. So perhaps there was more to his present mood than mere homesickness. Something resembling an ocean-size pool of lust that rose with each passing day, threatening to breach the dam of his restraint.

Ah. And I suppose that explains why finding a way to coax a smile from Catherine has become such a priority. Or why she's constantly on your mind. Yes, and let's not forget the growing need you have to protect her from any and every hurt.

He stubbornly gave a mental shrug. The truth of the matter was he'd always had a penchant for defending those weaker or less fortunate than himself. How could he not? Both his parents had been so self-absorbed while he'd been growing up that someone had had to look out for the hundreds of people who looked to the Russards for guidance, protection, support. He'd had no choice but to step in and do what had to be done.

As for Catherine, she understood duty and obligation, was exceedingly nice to look at, had breeding as well as style—just as he'd foreseen when he'd chosen her to be his wife. Of course he wanted to protect her. She now belonged to him, whether she wanted to or not.

That he found her interesting was simply an added bonus. As was her underlying kindness and the vulnerability she did her best to hide with her tart tongue and that raised, elegant chin. He was beginning to understand her well enough to know she'd deny she needed, much less wanted, a champion. But he hadn't missed her extreme surprise and genuine delight today at the skating rink—and he was glad for the chance to make her happy. If nothing else, having her depend on him could only benefit the long-term success of their marriage.

Yes, of course. But how does that square with your growing possessiveness?

Kaj hunched his shoulders and lengthened his stride. There was no way he could outpace his own misgivings, however, and after a moment he had to concede that that development was a trifle unsettling. Although he'd always viewed women as fascinating and complex, he'd also seen them as fairly interchangeable. If an association with one didn't work out, there was always another charming creature waiting to step into the breach.

Yet for some reason he didn't feel nearly so cavalier about Catherine. She was *his,* and while it made perfect sense that the idea of her being with anyone else was absolutely unacceptable, at some point during their little skating party today he'd realized she was the only woman he wanted. At least for the present—and even that was unprecedented.

Not to mention crazy. If he didn't get a firm hold on such fanciful thinking and soon, the next thing he knew he'd be wondering if perhaps he was on the verge of falling in love.

He abruptly stopped walking, which was just as well, since he'd reached the farthest point of the promontory. Thrusting his hands in his pockets, he blanked his mind, disgusted that he would entertain such a ridiculous idea even in passing.

With an iron will he forced himself to concentrate on the waves down below, watching as they dashed themselves against the projecting jumble of rocks, retreated, then came rushing in again.

He wasn't sure how much time passed before he realized he found the age-old action decidedly suggestive.

The discovery startled a laugh out of him, and like a puzzle piece snapping into place, he suddenly realized he'd been correct at the start of his walk. His uncharacteristic mood really *was* just frustrated desire. Catherine was the first woman to hold herself aloof from him, and as Joffrey would put it, he was in a "bad way." The fact that such a thing had never happened to him before explained why he'd allowed himself to get caught up in all these other unacceptable thoughts and uncertainties.

But now he knew. He wanted Catherine, pure and simple—and not just to fulfill the dictates of his father's will. Oh, no. He was way past the point of making her his solely out of duty. When he finally claimed her, he wanted her hot, slick, wet, whimpering with need, straining against him, her legs locked around his back, begging him to sheath every thick, aching inch of himself in the tight glove of her womanhood.

Even as his body throbbed at the images tumbling through his mind, he breathed a sigh of relief. Looking back on the day from this new perspective, he thought it safe to say he'd made definite strides toward achieving his goal. The skating idea had been nothing short of inspired, and Catherine had clearly been pleased. Add in his gentlemanly behavior, and he'd made definite progress in winning her over.

The next step would be more of the same. After

that, he'd find a way to get her off by herself, away from the palace, away from her friendly group of orphans, away from all other distractions.

Once he got her truly alone, she'd have no choice but to focus solely on him. And once she did, it shouldn't take much to get her into his bed. Then finally all these disturbing and uncharacteristic doubts would be vanquished for good.

As for the fantastical notion that he could be falling in love—it was absurd. Truly, absolutely, unequivocally absurd. Hadn't he seen what ''love'' had done to his parents and everyone around them? Hadn't he vowed never to get caught in a similar trap?

Absolutely. And he had no intention of changing his mind, now or ever.

No matter the temptation.

Six

_____

"**Y**ou, my dear *chaton*," Kaj said, "are a menace."

Accepting his steadying hand as she climbed out of the gleaming-hulled cigar boat, Catherine turned to look up at him the instant her feet touched the palace dock. "I beg your pardon?"

"You heard me." He jumped lightly down beside her. Wrapping his long fingers around her upper arm, he gently urged her toward shore as the dock attendants moved in to secure the mooring ropes. "Was there some purpose in cutting in front of that ocean liner? Other than giving me a heart attack? Or attempting to make my hair turn white?"

She glanced at the hair in question. Black as a winter night, as shiny as a raven's wing, several of the thick, straight strands had come loose from the leather thong anchoring them at his nape and now framed the strong angles of his sun-kissed face. Her fingers suddenly itched to touch him.

She looked away, filled with the by-now-familiar confusion she'd been immersed in since they'd gone skating.

The past handful of days had been amazing. She and Kaj had spent most of their waking hours together, engaged in activities from horseback riding to dancing the tango at Altaria's hottest nightclub. They'd gone on a picnic, spent an afternoon hang gliding, flown to Rome for a day of shopping, stayed up an entire night playing a cutthroat game of baccarat, which Kaj had waited until after he'd won to cheerfully inform her was Walburaq's most popular pastime.

Such were his persuasive abilities, he'd even convinced her to show him Altaria from the water—no mean feat since she hadn't gone near a boat since losing her grandfather and father.

Most amazing to Catherine, through all the things that they'd done, was how they'd talked. Perhaps not about their most private feelings—she still couldn't bear to discuss her father or the circumstances surrounding his death—but about more than fashion or the weather. To her surprise she'd shared happy memories of her grandmother, admitted how as a child she'd longed to go to a real school rather than be tutored, had even talked about her Connelly cousins and how she'd always envied them their bonds with each other.

For his part, Kaj had regaled her with tales of his schooldays in England, disclosed some of the difficulties he'd had growing up caught between two cultures, revealed an unexpectedly sentimental side when he'd described the ancient fortress built around an oasis that was his home.

And though none of their conversations had seemed particularly serious at the time, at some point Catherine had realized she knew that Kaj's parents' marriage had been an unhappy one, that he had no intention of repeating that particular bit of family history, and that for all his easygoing charm, he took his responsibilities seriously.

She'd also learned firsthand that he really was a man of his word. Just as promised, except for legitimate reasons like holding her when they danced, shielding her from the occasional paparazzi or helping her in and out of various vehicles, he'd kept his hands to himself. He'd been gallant and gracious, thoughtful and polite, concerned at all times with her comfort and pleasure—the perfect gentleman.

And it was starting to make her a little crazy. When they were apart, she wondered where he was, what he was doing and with whom. When she was with him, she wondered what he was thinking. And all the while her senses seemed to be operating on overdrive. A part of her was constantly tracking everything about him—the tone of his voice, the warmth that emanated from his skin, his scent, his relative proximity, his facial expression.

She was starting not to recognize herself. She'd tried to convince herself that her unusual behavior was the result of prolonged sleep deprivation, since she hadn't slept through an entire night since their first meeting at the ball—but she didn't really believe it. Something else was happening, and she was very much afraid she knew what it was.

He was getting under her skin, sweeping her off her feet, making a place for himself in her heart.

She had no intention of letting him know that, though. What she felt was too new, too unexpected, too fragile and ultimately uncertain to share. She was having a hard enough time explaining it to herself.

Suddenly aware that he was still waiting for a response to his accusation that she'd tried to scare him, she did her best to match his light manner. "Don't be such a baby. Everyone knows that big ships are notoriously slow. Plus we had scads of clearance time, and I was only at three-quarters throttle. Although I have to admit, I did love hearing the warning horn blare out. It sounded wonderfully dramatic, don't you think?"

His response would have been deemed a snort had it been made by anyone half so sophisticated.

She felt the corners of her mouth start to curve up, but quickly controlled herself. "In any event," she said, trying to sound austere, "I'd watch whom I criticize, sheikh. Let's not forget just who it was who attempted to take that wave sideways and very nearly flipped the boat. In the future you might want to consider sticking to those things you know."

"Very well. If you insist." He ceased his unhurried walk and pulled her around to face him. Then, his movements deliberate, he moved his hand slowly up her arm, slid it under her hair and cupped the back of her neck. "I'm just not sure where around here—" he lowered his head so she felt his warm breath

against her lips, and her eyelids suddenly felt heavy
"—I'd be likely to find a camel. Do you?"

It took a second for his words to sink in. When
they did, her lashes snapped up and she found he was
mere inches away.

He raised an eyebrow at the same time that a slow,
devilish smile transformed the perfection of his lips.
"What? You were expecting me to ravish you?"

She laughed. The sound burbled softly up, the result of an odd combination of exhilaration and embarrassment. "The thought did cross my mind," she
admitted recklessly.

He shook his head and a loose strand of his hair
tickled her cheek. "Not until I receive an invitation."

"Yes. So I understand." And finally she did. With
a sense of wonder, she realized she trusted him.
Enough to take a chance.

Her gaze locked with his, she brought her hand up
and brushed his hair behind his ear. The errant lock
was silkier than she'd expected, as was the arch of
his ear. Intrigued, she traced the curve of his jaw with
her fingertips. His bones felt larger, denser than her
own, but his skin was surprisingly smooth despite the
faint prickle of beard that lurked just beneath the surface.

"Catherine—"

"Shh." Then she breathed in, filling her head with
the essence of him, a heady combination of spicy af-
tershave, soap, saltwater and sun, and suddenly such
limited contact wasn't nearly enough. Sliding her
hands around his neck, she pushed his collar out of
her way, took a half step forward and buried her face
in the warm hollow where his neck met his shoulder.

As it had that day on the cliffs, pleasure enveloped her. Only this time there was none of the frantic urgency, the uncertainty of being completely out of control, to distract from the experience of being close.

She closed her eyes, soaking up sensations like a sponge. She felt the steady thud of his heart against his chest, the hardness of his thighs through the finely spun material of his slacks. His chest was broad, solid, warm, a welcome refuge protecting her from the breeze blowing in off the water.

It was the smooth, taut, velvety texture of his skin beneath her cheek that made her head spin, however. With a sigh of pleasure, she snuggled closer, more than a little intoxicated by the pleasure of being in his arms.

She wasn't sure how long they stood there, bodies pressed together. Finally Kaj made a sound that was midway between a chuckle and a groan. "I was right," he murmured, his lips brushing her temple. "You *are* a menace." The words might have stung if hadn't added, "A beautiful, much too desirable one." His movements firm but gentle, he reached up, disengaged her arms from around his neck and set her away from him. "Now come." Linking his fingers with hers, he resumed his unhurried walk. "Let's see if we can't find some refreshment. I find I'm feeling a little overheated."

Any embarrassment she might have felt was banished by his admission. "I believe I could use something cold to drink myself," she conceded, breathless but happy as she strolled beside him. "And something to eat. All of a sudden I'm famished."

In companionable silence they reached the end of

the dock, crossed a swath of emerald lawn edged with bright splashes of blooming flowers, and proceeded up the wide stone staircase that led to the palace's main back terrace.

They hadn't taken more than a step or two across the tile floor of the gallery when a movement in the shadows of an archway to her right caught Catherine's eye. Her attention arrested, she came to a halt, tensing as Gregor Paulus emerged from the darkness.

He inclined his head. "Your Highness. Sheikh al bin Russard."

Something in the way his gaze flicked from her to Kaj and back again made her suspect he'd been watching them for some time, an idea she found extremely distasteful. "What is it, Gregor?" she demanded.

"Might I have a moment of your time?"

"Is it really necessary?"

"Yes, Your Highness. As much as it pains me to interrupt your…tête-à-tête, I believe it is."

She bit back a sharp reply. Sinking to his level would accomplish nothing. "Very well." She glanced at Kaj. "Would you excuse me? This shouldn't take more than a second."

Flicking a speculative look at the servant, he nodded. "Of course. I'll wait here for you."

She smiled, then turned away. As she approached Gregor, he stepped back into the gloom of the shadowed archway, beckoning her to follow with a crook of his long skinny fingers.

She barely had time for her eyes to adjust to the change in light when he came straight to the point. "I found this among His Highness's private papers this morning. I thought you'd like to have it." He held out a palm-size envelope, that she instantly recognized as bearing the crest and distinctive gold-edged design of the stationery used exclusively by her father.

A knot coiled in her stomach, part hope, part dread. Yet years of practice helped her retain an outward calm. "Thank you," she said, taking the missive from him. She waited, willing him to leave. When he didn't budge, she managed a cool smile. "Don't let me keep you. I'm sure you have other, more pressing duties to see to."

"How gracious of you to be concerned." Despite his words, he made no move to depart. "But before I take my leave, may I say how glad I am to see that the prince's death hasn't had an adverse effect on your enjoyment of the water?" His unblinking gaze didn't leave her face.

Catherine recoiled. Although the words were perfectly benign, the sentiment behind them was anything but, as was obvious from the chilly dislike in his eyes.

Then and there, she made a vow to speak to Daniel about the man's insufferable attitude. In the meantime, she lifted her chin and said with all the hauteur she could muster, "Leave me. Now."

For the briefest instant he looked surprised, and then he inclined his head. "As you wish." He made a cursory bow, turned and walked away.

She waited until he was out of sight, then slipped her finger under the envelope flap. She slid out the heavyweight piece of card stock. Her hands trembled slightly as she looked down and her father's distinctive handwriting jumped out at her.

Daughter,
I see no need for further discussion between us. Sadly, your decision to indulge your own desires rather than do your family duty doesn't surprise me. I will see to it your grandfather receives your regrets.

It was signed with Prince Marc's trademark looping *M*.

For a moment she couldn't seem to breathe. She'd been distraught when she believed her father had never received her e-mail message; now it appeared he had, but not only hadn't he cared, he'd continued to believe the worst of her, and oh, how it hurt.

It also served to revive her guilt: *she* should have been on the boat that day with King Thomas. If she had, perhaps she would have noticed something or somehow prevented the tragedy.

She suddenly could no longer contain her pain. She sagged back against a marble pillar and squeezed her eyes shut, fighting for control.

I will not cry. I will not. After all, this really isn't any great surprise. Father was angry; he hated having to dance attendance on Grandfather and clearly he wrote this before he had a chance to cool off and get over his pique. He didn't mean it, not really…

"Catherine? Has something happened?"

It took a moment for Kaj's concerned voice to penetrate her misery. Realizing how ridiculous she must appear, she straightened her spine and opened her eyes, doing her best to pull herself together. She dredged up a determined smile. "No, of course not."

"Then what's the matter?"

"It's nothing. I'm sorry I kept you waiting—"

"Don't," he said sharply. "Don't lie to me. Tell me. Now."

There was no mistaking his absolute determination to hear the truth. Still, she continued to resist, not entirely comfortable with sharing either her feelings or her problems. "Truly, Kaj, there's no need for you to be concerned."

His jaw hardened just for a second, and then his face abruptly softened. "Please." He reached out and lightly laid his palm against her cheek. "I'm not going away, nor do I intend to take no for an answer, so you may as well tell me what's upset you and be done with it."

His kindness nearly undid her. She swallowed, forcing down the tears suddenly clogging her throat as she conceded defeat. For all his gentle manner, it was clear he meant what he said. And she was in even less of a mood to argue with him than she had been with Gregor. Reluctantly she handed him the card.

He read through it in a handful of seconds, then looked at her questioningly.

She drew in a shaky breath and tried to put her thoughts in some sort of coherent order. "The day my father and grandfather died, I was supposed to be on the boat," she began. "Grandfather's eyesight was failing and I knew he didn't feel safe piloting the boat by himself anymore, but he was such a proud man. He absolutely refused to acknowledge that he needed help, so for several months I'd been going with him on one pretext or another.''

She couldn't contain a shaky sigh. ''But that day—that day I wasn't feeling well—I was suffering from some sort of nasty food poisoning—so I called Father and asked him to go in my place. He said he would, but it was obvious he wasn't happy about it, and before I could explain that I was ill, he accused me of being selfish, always thinking of myself, just like my mother. God forgive me, but I lost my temper. I told him he was absolutely right, that I was begging off because I had an absolutely essential appointment for a facial and manicure, and he—he hung up on me. The instant I heard the phone go dead, I realized how childishly I was behaving. I called him back but he wouldn't come to the phone, and as I was too indisposed to leave my room, I sent him an e-mail, asking if we might talk when he got back.

''This—'' she tapped the note card still in his hand ''—was his answer. His man Gregor, who's in charge of putting his affairs in order, apparently just found it.''

The line of Kaj's mouth had turned grim. Not at all certain what he was thinking, she turned to look blindly out at the last of the sunshine sparkling on the water. She cleared her throat. ''I should have been the one on the boat that day,'' she said, finally saying aloud what she'd been thinking for months. ''No matter how ill I felt, I was a better driver than Father. If only I'd been there—''

''That's nonsense,'' he interrupted harshly. ''For all you know, you would have been killed, too. You have to accept that accidents happen.''

"I'd like nothing better," she said fervently. "But it wasn't an accident."

"What? What do you mean?"

She felt his gaze sharpen but continued to stare out at the horizon. "At first we just assumed it was some terrible, unforeseen mishap. Then there was an attempt on Daniel's life in Chicago, and he and his family began to wonder. They hired an investigator, who's since found evidence the boat was sabotaged." Gathering her courage, she turned to face him. "Don't you see? If I'd been there, I might have seen something, or sensed that something was wrong—"

Looking into her anguished face, Kaj felt something fierce stir to life deep inside him. "And what if you hadn't?" he demanded, catching her by the arms and pulling her into the shelter of his body. "It would be you who was gone—and *that* is totally unacceptable to *me*."

In point of truth, while logically he could see that any ongoing threat most likely centered around Daniel and the succession, he felt a stab of anger that nobody had seen fit to even consider that Catherine might also be in danger, much less provide her with added protection.

Until now. Resolve hardened his voice. "What happened was not your fault," he said flatly. "It was a terrible thing, one we will talk about in greater detail in the future, but for now there's something else we need to discuss."

Clearly confused by his manner, not to mention the sudden change of subject, Catherine tipped her head back to directly meet his gaze, still looking pale and fragile from too much emotion. "And what is that?"

Her hair slid like silk against his hands; he ignored the instant stirring in his groin. "I have to leave for a few days. There are some things that demand my attention at home."

For the merest second her lips trembled, and then she got herself under control. "Oh."

He hesitated, but only for a moment. Cupping her chin in his hand, he stroked his thumb over her lips. "I don't want to go without you, Catherine. Come with me."

Seven

"**Y**ou're very quiet, *chaton.*"

Taken aback by Kaj's observation, Catherine considered a moment, then realized it was true. She gestured at the view beyond the tinted glass limousine window as their driver negotiated the busy downtown streets of Akjeni, Walburaq's main city. "There's so much to take in."

That was a decided understatement. Everywhere she looked there was an eclectic mix of East and West, old and new. Shiny new high-rises pierced the azure sky several blocks away, while directly around her sprawled the low stone buildings of what Kaj called the Old City. Booths from a variety of small markets or *soukhs* crowded the side streets. As the limo slowed to negotiate around a donkey-powered cart, she glimpsed swatches of jewel-colored silks, the glitter of gold jewelry, vast stacks of baskets and piles of colorful rugs all in a single narrow alley.

And the crowds! Clustered on the narrow sidewalks, men in traditional white headdresses and the long white robes that Kaj called *dishdashas,* rubbed shoulders with men in European-style suits. Similarly, women wearing the newest New York and Paris fashions looked like bright butterflies as they flitted among their more conservatively attired, black *abaya-*wearing sisters with their modestly covered heads.

It was all very exotic, and for an instant she almost convinced herself what she'd told Kaj was the truth—that her silence stemmed from a preoccupation with her surroundings. Augmented, perhaps, by continuing distress about yesterday's encounter with Gregor Paulus.

Except, Catherine the princess had traveled the world and had seen far more startling sights than this prosperous and beautiful city. And Catherine the daughter had long known better than to allow her father's manservant to upset her.

More to the point, much as she might like to pretend otherwise, Catherine the woman knew that the true cause of her reticence was sitting right beside her.

She still found it hard to believe she'd actually confided in him the way she had yesterday afternoon. For as long as she could remember, even when her grandmother had been alive, she'd kept her own counsel. No matter what the provocation, the public Catherine always raised her chin and put on a show of regal indifference. Tears and fears, hurts and disappointments, even hopes and dreams, were handled alone, in private.

Until Kaj. From the moment he'd thrust himself into her path at Daniel and Erin's ball, he'd managed to get beneath her practiced reserve. And though she'd long recognized the power of his personality—it had been her primary reason initially for wanting to avoid him—in the past twenty-four hours she'd come to see that she'd underestimated his sheer charisma and commanding presence.

That had never been more evident than earlier today when they'd stepped aboard his private jet and set course for Walburaq. A subtle transformation had come over him. Although he'd been as polite and attentive to her as ever, there'd been a tone in his voice when he'd dealt with subordinates, a decisiveness about his every move, an ease of manner that had made her more aware than ever that he was accustomed to being in charge and enjoying instant obedience.

And though that was hardly a surprise, her reaction to the palpable power he exuded was. Not only was she even more hyperaware of him than usual, but for the first time in her life she also felt a desire to cede control, to lean into his big, hard body and simply let go.

It scared her to death. And excited her no end.

"Shall I turn down the air-conditioning?"

Kaj's concerned inquiry penetrated her musing. She turned to look at him. "What?"

"You're shivering. Are you cold?"

"Oh. No, I'm fine."

Despite her assurance, his concerned gaze swept over her like a lick of fire and her nipples promptly puckered. She felt them pressing against the lace of her bra and a splash of heat burned her cheeks since she knew very well her reaction had nothing to do with the temperature and everything to do with him.

In the next moment he seemed to realize it, too. Realized it, but still—thankfully—misunderstood.

He reached across the plush leather seat, captured her hand and brought it to rest against his muscled thigh. "It's all right, you know. Even here in Walburaq our agreement still stands. Nothing will happen between us without your express permission. However much—" his voice dropped ever so slightly, at odds with the twist of amusement that lurked at the corners of his mouth "—I might like to lock you in the seraglio and keep you solely for my pleasure."

"Seraglio?" Her lips parted in surprise. "You have a harem?"

He gave a theatrical sigh. "Yes—and no. I have the structure to house one, but not the requisite concubines. Fortunately—or unfortunately, depending on one's viewpoint—my great-grandmother put a stop to that."

"Really?" Grateful for any diversion to keep her mind off his proximity, she cocked her head. "How on earth did she manage that?"

His silvery eyes, so startling, framed by his inky lashes and bronze skin, warmed. "Her name was Anjouli, and the story goes that she was very young and very, very beautiful. She was also exceedingly clever and wise, and it is said that it took Khahil, my great-grandfather, a very long time to coax her into his bed. Once he finally did, he was entranced. So much so that when she eventually gave birth to his first son— until then he'd been blessed only with daughters—he impulsively told her he would give her anything her heart desired. I can't help but believe he thought she'd request her own palace or a trunkload of jewels, but instead she asked that he be hers exclusively. He agreed, and that—'' his teeth flashed in a rueful smile ''—set a precedent for future Russard sheikhs.''

His smile was irresistible and she answered it with one of her own. ''Oh, dear. Is that regret I hear?''

He shrugged, careless, elegant, infinitely masculine. ''I think not. Even without a harem, I've managed to acquire a more than adequate amount of carnal knowledge. Enough to know what—and whom—I want.'' Once more, his gaze played over her, then settled on her face, riveting her in place.

Another shiver went down her spine, and this time she didn't even attempt to deny that he was the cause. Yet some proud and obstinate part of her still wasn't quite ready to reveal the depth of her growing desire for him.

Not here, not now, not yet. Not when she still wasn't sure if she intended to act on what she felt or keep him to his word and make this trip a purely platonic one.

Doing her best to look thoughtful and nothing more, she nodded. ''I see.''

Outside, the city fell away and the road opened up. Fine white sand stretched in every direction, framed in the west by the aquamarine glimmer of sky meeting sea and to the east by the jagged upthrust of the Kaljar Hills.

After a score of miles, their driver turned onto a side road that climbed through a series of rising sand dunes. Eventually the road leveled out and in the near distance Catherine could see the brilliant green foliage of a large oasis, ringed by a cluster of buildings whose rooftops could be seen over a mammoth, crenellated wall. Behind them, soaring upward, was a storybook palace built of glistening white stone, with gilded domes and exquisitely shaped towers that looked as if it had been plucked from the pages of *1001 Arabian Nights.* "Oh, my," she murmured.

"Home," Kaj informed her, pride and affection unmistakable in his voice. "It's called Alf Ahkbar—which roughly means a thousand shades of green."

"I can see why."

Minutes later the limo swept through the compound's main gates, then slowed as it advanced down a narrow stone road set between a double row of chenar trees. Off to one side was a plaza where a spring bubbled up to fill a large, rectangular reflecting pool. Several dozen people, mostly women and children, looked up from various tasks, smiling and waving as the car went past.

The vehicle approached another set of gates, these fashioned of elaborate ironwork. Their driver spoke into the car phone, and the gate opened, then slid shut behind them. Five hundred feet later the limo pulled into a circular courtyard and came to a stop before the massive front doors of the palace itself.

Catherine drew in a deep breath as the full magnitude of her agreeing to come here sank in.

For the first time in her life she was alone with a man on his home ground. And she still didn't know what she wanted to do. Marriage, of course, remained out of the question. But did she really want to spend the rest of her life as a virgin?

* * *

A faint knock jarred Catherine awake. Blinking the sleep from her eyes, she shifted on the azure velvet divan, taking a moment to get her bearings.

The tiled ceiling overhead was ornate, decorated with an intricate pattern of vines and flowers in shades of turquoise, indigo and celadon green. Thick blue-and-cream rugs covered the stone floor, and diaphanous silk panels lavishly embroidered with silver thread draped the arched doorway that opened onto the balcony. Matching silk panels encased the bed, which boasted a delicately carved headboard inlaid with lapis lazuli and a peacock-blue bedcovering scattered with tasseled pillows in shades of green and blue, amber, orchid and rose.

Unlike the more sedate furnishings of her rooms in Altaria, the chamber was lush, playful and exotic, a feast for the senses, and Catherine felt a return of the delight she'd experienced when she'd first laid eyes on it.

Which had been two hours ago, she realized with a jolt as she glanced at her wristwatch. Appalled, she sat up and swung her feet to the floor, doing her best to quell her fascination with her surroundings and force herself to think.

She remembered climbing out of the limousine, and her surprise at the sweet scents of roses and jasmine that had laced the crisp desert air. She recalled crossing the courtyard and passing through a tall, arched doorway. Once inside, she'd given a sigh of pleasure at the lovely detail of the tile and latticework walls, the tall ceilings and the cool serenity of the interior that had greeted her. There had been a wide staircase with shallow steps that climbed unhurriedly up to a long gallery, a formal-looking reception area furnished with exquisite Georgian furniture to the left and a mirrored hallway dappled with shadows and sunlight to the right.

But it had been the view directly ahead of her that had most enchanted her. A series of carved arches had opened onto a shaded inner courtyard. Stands of bamboo had whispered beneath a nearly imperceptible breeze, while plants in enormous pots provided brilliant flowers in shades of magenta, scarlet, and lavender. Small, colorful birds darted among the foliage, and a peacock strutted along a paved path past a three-tiered fountain that was the courtyard's centerpiece.

It had been hushed, soothing and beautiful and Catherine had loved it on sight. She'd been nearly as entranced by the rest of the palace when Kaj had given her a quick tour. If she'd also felt relieved when he'd escorted her to her own quarters, tacitly revealing that he didn't expect her to share his room, well, that wasn't surprising given the current turbulence of her feelings. But it certainly did not excuse her lying down to rest for a few minutes and promptly sleeping away the afternoon—

Another knock at the door interrupted her musing. Positive it must be Kaj wondering what had become of her, Catherine shook off her languor, scrambled to her feet and raked her fingers through her hair. "Come in," she called, stepping forward as the door opened. "I'm so sorry—"

She broke off in confusion. In place of the tall, powerful figure she expected, there was a slim, pretty girl of perhaps fourteen. *"Masa'a alkhayr,"* the teen said, making a quick curtsy. "I am Sarab."

Catherine shifted gears, trying to remember some of the Arabic words she'd been studying. *"Marhaba,* Sarab." Hello.

The girl's dark, liquid eyes sparkled with interest. "You speak Arabic?" she asked.

Catherine shook her head. "No. Only a very little. I'm sorry."

"That is very much all right, Highness," the girl assured her. "Most fortunately, as you can surely tell, I speak the English very, very well. That is why my *jaddah* sent me to assist you."

"Jaddah?"

"My grandmother. She is the sheikh's...how do you say?...keeper."

Although she knew the choice of word certainly had to be a mistake, Catherine couldn't contain a smile. "Keeper?"

The girl nodded earnestly. "Yes. For many years now she has had the charge of the entire palace."

The pieces fell into place. "Ah. You mean housekeeper."

"Housekeeper, yes." Sarab nodded enthusiastically, then flashed Catherine another melting smile. "Please, I may come in?"

"Yes, of course." Stepping back out of the way, Catherine gestured for the girl to enter.

Sarab crossed the threshold, looked around and headed straight toward Catherine's suitcase, which lay open on a stand next to an enormous satinwood wardrobe inlaid with mother-of-pearl. She glanced politely at Catherine. "It is approved by you that I unpack your things?'' Catherine nodded, and the girl began the task, her slender fingers deft as she started to transfer clothes to the wardrobe's padded hangers.

Catherine watched, feeling strangely ill at ease. Although she'd lived her entire life surrounded by servants, she'd never known one so young, and it bothered her. "Have you worked for the sheikh long?" she asked after a moment.

"Oh, no, Highness!" The quick shake of the girl's head was accompanied by a small, amused giggle. "I'm just visiting while my parents attend a conference. They are doctors." Her pride was unmistakable. "My mother grew up here at Alf Ahkbar and has always been exceedingly clever, so Sheikh Kaj sent her to medical school as was her dream. He never forgets his people. He's a very great man, you know."

This last was said with such reverence that Catherine was tempted to roll her eyes. Except that at the same time she felt a swell of something akin to pride.

Where on earth had that come from? she wondered, a little unnerved.

Sarab removed a stack of lacy lingerie from the suitcase. Holding the items as if they were made of cobwebs, she opened one of the wardrobe's drawers and laid them carefully inside. Worrying her lower lip, she appeared to ponder something, then turned to Catherine. "A thousand pardons, Highness, but… might I ask you a question?"

Even temporary help in Altaria knew better than to be so forward. Catherine parted her lips to say no, then hesitated. "Yes, I suppose," she said, her curiosity getting the better of her. Besides, it was better than trying to sort out the confusing mix of her feelings for Kaj.

"Are you going to marry the sheikh?"

So much for a diversion. "Why would you ask that?" she demanded.

Hot color tinged the girl's smooth cheeks. "Just…everyone is wondering. Sheikh Kaj has never brought a woman here, you see. He has a house in Akjeni where he…entertains. Not that I'm supposed to know that," she added hastily. "But you're so very beautiful and you seem so very nice, and Jaddah and my mother—all the village really—think it's time for him to settle down, even if one didn't have to consider Sheikh Tarik's most unfortunate will—" She broke off, her face growing even more flushed as she seemed to decide she'd now completely overstepped her bounds. "You do know about that, yes?"

There was nothing like having everyone know your business. Catherine felt a sudden sense of kinship with her host, as well as a perplexing protectiveness. "I believe the sheikh has mentioned it," she allowed.

Sarab continued to stare at her expectantly.

She lifted her chin. "As for the other, I haven't decided."

"But—" The girl swallowed whatever she'd been about to say, Catherine's cool tone apparently registering. She looked thoughtfully down at the open suitcase, then reached in and extracted two of the four negligees Catherine had impulsively brought with her, and placed them in the wardrobe. She delicately cleared her throat. "Sheikh Kaj is very handsome, is he not?"

"He is."

"And he would give you many pretty babies, yes?"

"Yes, I suppose."

"And he is generous and kind, brave and smart, tall and vigorous and very strong. He has much wealth and many beautiful homes and— Oh!" The girl's eyes rounded and her hand flew to her mouth. "Oh, no!"

Catherine jerked her thoughts away from the idea of having Kaj's baby, which she found absurdly appealing. "What on earth is the matter?"

"I forgot!" the girl wailed. "Jaddah said I was to tell you the sheikh would be most pleased if you'd honor him with your presence in the Peacock Garden. And I forgot!"

"Oh." Her initial alarm faded. "Is that all?"

"All? You cannot keep him waiting. He is the sheikh!" The teenager made a vague, shooing motion. "You must hurry!"

Catherine started to protest, then reconsidered as she took in the girl's very real distress. Her expression softened. She agreed, "I suppose I shouldn't keep him waiting."

Yet even as she allowed Sarab to lay out fresh clothes and help her with her hair, Catherine couldn't quell a prickle of amusement as the girl's words about making Kaj wait kept playing through her mind.

Poor Sarab, she thought wryly, if only she knew. Compared to what else I've been keeping Kaj waiting for, this is nothing.

But perhaps—just perhaps, since she still hadn't made up her mind—that was about to change.

* * *

Kaj stretched his legs, pleased to feel the familiar comfort of the fine white cotton of traditional Arab dress against his skin.

It was good to be home. Settling a little deeper into one of the oversize garden chairs in the inner court-yard, he soaked up the familiar sound of the soft splash of water from the fountain. He could hear the usual evening breeze blowing beyond the sheltered walls of the courtyard, but within the compound the flower-scented air was still. The only movement came from the scores of candle-filled lanterns illuminating the garden, their flickering light painting gilded shadows on walls and foliage.

The only thing more beautiful, he reflected, as he lifted his iced coffee and took an appreciative sip, was his company.

He regarded Catherine across the intimate width of their wrought-iron table-for-two. With her elegant bones, creamy skin and gleaming, shot-with-fire hair, he'd always considered her lovely. But tonight there was something different, something special about her. And after painstaking consideration, he'd finally figured out what.

"So." He took another sip of coffee. "Are you going to tell me what has you so amused?"

Her eyes widened slightly—but not before a telltale gleam of comprehension sparked in their emerald depths. "Pardon me?"

He unhurriedly set down his tall, narrow glass. "Ever since you joined me there's been the ghost of a smile lurking at the edges of your mouth. It was there all during dinner and dessert, it's continued to tantalize me as the sun has set and the moon has risen, it's teased at my senses during our every conversation I'd simply like to know if you're ever going to share its source with me."

Her eyes gleamed mischievously. "I don't know. I'm not sure that I should."

Like a silken vise his desire for her tightened its hold on him.

He ignored it. Instinct told him that here, in what was indisputably his territory, it was more important than ever that *she* come to *him*. If keeping his hunger for her in check had also become a point of honor, an exercise in willpower that had his intellect pitted against his libido, so what? Eventually he *would* emerge the winner. "And why is that?"

Her lips curved a fraction more. "Perhaps because I think your ego is already more than healthy."

He raised an eyebrow. "You don't say."

"I do. Although you've proven to be such a gracious host I suppose I might make an exception."

"How generous of you."

"Yes, isn't it?"

Their gazes locked. Again his body stirred, and again he disregarded it. He took another sip of coffee. "Well?"

"Oh, all right." She gave an amused little sigh and made a production of crossing one leg over another. "It appears you have a fan club."

He told himself sternly not to notice the way the thin fabric of her dress clung to her rounded breasts and slim thighs. "I do?"

"Mmm-hmm. Your housekeeper's granddaughter couldn't refrain from singing your praises."

"Ah, Sarab. A lovely child. And exceedingly intelligent, too."

"You don't say?" She made no effort to hide the irony in her voice as she repeated his earlier words to him.

"But I do. What's more, I think it's extremely unkind of you to keep me in such suspense. What did she say?"

"I'm afraid I don't remember exactly." Her voice was airy. "Something about you being tall. And healthy, for someone your age. And I believe the word *handsome* may also have been used. But then, she *is* just a child."

The tartness of her humor pleased him. Too much. Suddenly restless, he came to his feet. "One with excellent taste," he said, stepping around the table and holding out his hand. "Come."

She was clearly puzzled by the abrupt change in his manner. "Where?"

"The moon is up. Let's take a walk."

To his gratification, she asked no further questions but pushed back her chair, took his hand and came to her feet, following his lead as he made his way to the far side of the garden and up a narrow set of stairs. He unlocked the gate at the top, and they stepped out onto the wall walk.

"Oh, Kaj," she murmured in an awestruck voice.

Bathed in pearlescent light, the desert seemed to stretch endlessly before them, still and silent except for the invisible play of the wind, while to the east a full moon lay low in an immense cobalt-blue sky. Not to be outdone, stars shimmered overhead, some spilled in swaths like vast rivers of sequins, some solitary and immense like the finest of diamonds.

It was breathtaking. But not half so much as Catherine's upturned face as she turned toward him, her eyes shining with reflected starlight. "It's beautiful. Absolutely beautiful."

There was something in her expression.... He tensed with anticipation, expecting her to come closer, to reach out and touch a hand to his arm or face or shoulder, to finally tell him she wanted him.

Instead, as their eyes met, her expression changed, transforming from warm delight to something he couldn't identify. Puzzled, he tried to put a name to what he was seeing—doubt, longing, chagrin? Before he could reach a conclusion, a trace of brilliant light streaked across the sky and Catherine hastily turned away to watch it. "A shooting star!" she exclaimed. "How perfect."

He considered her averted face and stiff spine. Whatever she felt, her body language spoke for itself. She may as well have donned a sign that said Don't Touch Me.

Frustration and what felt alarmingly like need roared through him. "I suppose it is," he managed.

She fixed her gaze on a distant spot, gingerly ran the tip of her tongue over her lower lip, then quietly ventured his name. "Kaj?"

"What?"

"Thank you for asking me here. For being—" she paused, as if searching for just the right words "—such a good friend."

Friend? She couldn't mean it. What about *lover?* He clenched his jaw, excruciatingly aware the cotton pants that had been loose earlier in the evening now felt damnably confining—a ridiculous state of affairs for a man of his age and experience.

"A ridiculous state of affairs, period," he could just imagine his cousin Joffrey drawling in his usual amused way.

The thought of what else his relative would have to say about the current situation made him grimace. Yet it also served to remind him of what was at stake. He wanted Catherine to be his wife, not just a one-night stand.

And not because he had designs on Joff's painting, he thought impatiently. But because he was now more convinced than ever that she was the perfect choice for him. She was smart, interesting and beautiful, generous of heart but nobody's pushover. He had every confidence she'd be a caring mother to his children, a thoughtful and responsible guardian of his people, a gracious hostess, an asset to his varied business dealings. She was clearly not inclined toward promiscuity, but still spirited enough that he doubted he'd ever suffer from boredom.

And hadn't he learned by watching his parents the incalculable value of making a well-thought-out match, of never letting his body or emotions overrule his common sense?

Of course he had.

He slowly let out his breath. "I'm honored to be your friend, *chaton*. Thank you." Bracing himself against the increased desire that touching her, no matter how innocently, always brought him, he reached out and clasped her small, elegant hand. "Come. I'll take you to your room. It's been a long day and you must be tired.''

She parted her lips as if to protest, then appeared to think better of it. "I suppose you're right," she said in a subdued voice.

By way of an answer he walked over and opened the gate, indicating with a flourish of his hand that she should precede him down the stairs. Avoiding his gaze, she did as asked. Congratulating himself on his self-control, he closed the gate and started after her.

And that was when he discovered his mistake. All it took was one look at the firm, rounded cheeks of her derriere flexing beneath her thin dress to send his testosterone level soaring again.

Scowling, he flicked a baleful glance at the heavens, knowing he was doomed to spend yet another restless night alone.

Eight

Coward.

Catherine paced her bedroom, her self-condemnation gaining ground as she replayed her exchange with Kaj over and over.

Despite what some of the men in her past had assumed, her virginity didn't make her either naive or unworldly. And while she was currently of the opinion that that didn't always qualify as an advantage, she still couldn't escape the truth: the moment she'd stepped into the courtyard tonight and seen Kaj sitting there, something inside her had shifted and she'd known he was the one she wanted to be her "first."

The reasons then—as now—seemed obvious. She admired how comfortable he was in his own skin, the way he could be commanding without being a bully, the fact that he could make her laugh. She liked his strength and tenacity, his willingness to stand up to her, his wry sense of humor. She cherished his unexpected kindnesses and respected his honesty.

Young Sarab had gotten it right when she'd said he was a good man.

That he was also heartbreakingly handsome and wonderfully exotic Catherine had always known. But seeing him this evening, dressed as befitted the Arab half of his heritage, so clearly at ease with himself and so assured of his masculinity, she'd also realized how tired she was of fighting her attraction to him.

So she'd let down her guard just as she had after her encounter with Gregor. Only this time instead of telling Kaj her troubles, she'd given herself permission to reveal her softer, more playful side. She'd done her best to make sure he knew she was enjoying herself. And that she enjoyed being with him.

And everything had gone well—until the time to speak up had come and she'd faced the prospect of admitting she'd changed her mind, that she wanted him in every way the word *want* could be defined. Looking up at him, her fingers tingling with the urge to touch him, to brush back a stray strand of his glossy black hair, to trace the line of his eyebrow, to explore the muscular contours of his chest, she'd panicked. Not only hadn't she confessed she wanted to make love with him, she'd actually thanked him for being her friend.

Just thinking about it made her wince.

In stark contrast to her sorry performance, Kaj had been an absolute gentleman, not pressing her to deliver what they'd both known she'd been promising.

Which might not have been so bad if she hadn't clearly seen both the desire, the surprise and the disappointment in his eyes in the moment she'd lost her nerve and turned away.

But she had. And she couldn't get his expression out of her mind. Making matters worse, no matter how many times she went over it, she didn't understand why she'd behaved as she had. After all, her decision to have sex with Kaj hadn't been a sudden whim. Over the years she'd known plenty of attractive men but had never felt the slightest urge to share her body with any of them. Yet, where Kaj was concerned, one way or another she'd been thinking of nothing else ever since they met.

So why, why, *why,* having finally made a decision, had she acted the way she had?

Restless, uneasy, agitated, she reached the far end of the room. She started to turn to retrace her path, only to freeze as she caught sight of her shadowy reflection in the mirrored wall of the bathroom a dozen feet away.

Her long, nearly transparent silk robe of peach, pale-green and cream clung to her bare shoulders. The flimsy garment did nothing to hide the way her ice-green satin nightgown molded to her high breasts or rounded hips or the long line of her thighs. Her hair was tumbled around her shoulders, her cheeks were flushed, her lower lip plump and swollen from being gnawed on.

She looked like a woman who'd just rolled out of her lover's bed. Or a woman in a fever to climb in....

She whirled away, unable to bear her own image, much less the ideas it provoked. Pacing back the way she'd come, she felt as if she couldn't breathe. Her heart began to pound; her skin felt tight; the walls seemed to close in, making the same space that earlier had been such a source of pleasure now feel like a gilded cage.

Unable to stand it a moment longer, she fled toward the balcony, threw open the French doors, took a half dozen steps outside—and just as suddenly jerked to a halt, sucking in what little breath she had left.

Twenty-five feet to her right stood Kaj, his head bowed, his back to her, his hands braced against the parapet. He was barefoot and naked from the waist up, and, despite the distance between them, thanks to the moonlight she could see the muscles in his wide shoulders and lean waist bunch with every slight shift of his weight.

Her stomach hollowed. Her throat went dry and she felt a sudden throbbing at the apex of her thighs. Most alarming of all, however, was the way her heart squeezed at the tension of his posture.

In a burst of clarity, she understood what she'd refused to face only minutes earlier.

She cared about him. More than she'd ever cared about another person. Enough that earlier tonight some self-protective part of her had made one last desperate attempt to keep him at arm's length and keep her heart safe. Enough that the only word powerful and exclusive enough to describe what she felt was…*love*.

She remained stock-still as the idea washed through her, half expecting her sanity to return and tell her to stop being ridiculous. She didn't love Kaj. She couldn't. Hadn't she long ago decided that love wasn't for her?

Yet as the seconds ticked by, as the sensual play of the wind cooled her cheeks, tugged at her hair and ruffled her gown, her inner voice remained silent. With a growing sense of wonder, she realized that loving Kaj al bin Russard simply felt…right. That this time there were no doubts.

She wasn't sure how long she stood watching him, her heart hammering in her chest, her throat tight, her eyes stinging with her newly realized feelings.

But eventually, watching him wasn't nearly enough, while the need to touch him became overwhelming.

She began to walk, drawn to him like a compass to true north. Desire beckoned, tempting her to keep going until she was pressed against his gleaming bronzed back. Only her sense of fair play held her back, insisting he deserved something more.

Something better.

She stopped when a mere arm's length separated them. "Kaj."

His head jerked up. Although only an instant passed before he swiveled around on the balls of his feet, she was so attuned to him she saw the slight shudder that went through him before he turned. Nevertheless, he didn't look happy to see her. "What are you doing out here?"

Raising her chin, she stood her ground. "I need to tell you something."

He was shaking his head even before she finished. "Whatever it is, I'm sure it can wait until morning."

She might have been discouraged if not for the

sheen of perspiration suddenly sleeking his skin, the tautness rippling his abdomen, the effort he had to make to control his breathing as his gaze flicked over her. Despite his attempt to convince her otherwise, he was anything but indifferent to her. "No," she said softly. "I don't think so."

Impatience flashed across his face. "Catherine—"

She stepped close enough to reach up and press her fingers to his mouth. "I want you, Kaj. Make love to me."

He went still as a statue. His eyes locked on hers, not wavering even as she allowed herself the luxury of stroking the strong line of his jaw.

He cleared his throat. "What did you say?"

"Make love to me. Teach me how to make love to you."

For another second he remained anchored in place. Then he slowly let out his breath, looped his hands around her waist and tugged her close. "Damn. I was beginning to think you'd never ask." Bending his head, he covered her mouth with his own.

Magic. Madness. Bliss. Her body seemed to melt like a candle overrun by a forest fire. She molded herself against him, exulting in the satin-over-bronze texture of his skin, the flat planes and rounded curves of muscle in his chest and arms, the sleek power of his legs as he pulled her into the cradle of his thighs.

He became her universe. His breath fed her lungs, his strength held her up, the beat of his heart dictated the rhythm of her own. A rhythm that began to race as he slid his hands lower and gently squeezed the sensitive curve of her bottom.

She whimpered and pressed even closer.

His mouth still fused to hers, he swept her off her feet and into his arms. She vaguely registered that he was carrying her somewhere, but it didn't matter. What did was the delicious heat of his tongue tangled with hers, the sweet sensation of having one of his hands press the side of her breast while the other cupped her hip. Then there was the way the swelling ridge of his erection pushed against her with his every step.

Angling sideways, they passed through a doorway. Surprised by the faint smell of sandlewood and cloves, she broke the seal of their mouths, lifted her head and looked around.

She knew immediately she was in Kaj's bedroom. It was larger than her room and more lavishly decorated, the walls embedded with bands of gold and silver tiles in a diamond pattern. An opulent rug covered most of a pale marble floor. She had an impression of dark gleaming furniture, dimly realized the soft, exotic music she heard was spilling from hidden speakers and that the scents that had first caught her attention were coming from a dozen glowing candles grouped together in a wall niche.

But it was the oversize bed that quickly became her focus. Backed by a massive headboard of gold and silver latticework, it was framed by gold cloth drapes that swept to the floor. The matching satin comforter lay folded across the bed's foot, exposing rich black sheets. The effect was uncompromisingly masculine and breathtakingly handsome.

Which perfectly described the master of Alf Ahkbar, she thought, her gaze swinging back to Kaj as he set her on feet. Cupping her face in his palm, he brushed his lips over her cheeks, jaw and brow. "You're sure?"

Tenderness flooded her. For all that his voice sounded calm, she felt the slight tremor in his hand. "Yes."

"Very well." He took a half step back, unwound the band of fabric at his waist and stepped out of his pants. Her breath lodged in her throat as his erection sprang free and she had her first unobstructed view of what a real man looked like.

Massive. Impressive. Impossible. The thoughts tumbled through her mind a little hysterically before her reason reasserted itself. After all, men and women had been procreating for untold centuries, she reminded herself, and everyone seemed to survive. At least everyone she'd ever known.

Then Kaj slid her robe off her shoulders and her gown over her head, and her thoughts fragmented yet again as she glanced up to find *him* looking at *her*. Too aroused to be self-conscious, she watched, flattered and fascinated as the skin across his nose and cheekbones drew tight at the same time a muscle ticked to life in his jaw.

"Ah, princess... Do you know how beautiful you are? How perfect?" He brushed the pad of his thumb across the straining tip of her left nipple. "How much I hunger to make you mine?"

His thumb strafed her tender flesh again and her knees nearly buckled. Instinctively she stepped forward to clutch his broad shoulders for support, only to shiver as she felt his thick masculine length press firmly against her stomach. "As a matter of fact—" she did her best to ignore the heat she felt rising into her cheeks "—I believe I do." She pressed a kiss to the shallow valley between his pectoral muscles.

His response was midway between a groan and a chuckle. Gently weaving his hands into her hair, he tipped her face up to his. "Why do I suddenly have the feeling you're going to make me as crazy in bed as you do out of it?"

"I can't imagine. Perhaps because you're beginning to know me?"

Although her words were lightly spoken, as he looked down at her his amusement drained away. "Yes," he said, slowly running his thumbs over the curve of her cheekbones to frame her mouth. "I think perhaps I am." With that he leaned down and once more began to kiss her.

The play of his lips was even more drugging than before. A fever of need seemed to spread through her, and instinctively she locked her arms around his neck and hoisted herself up, wrapping her legs around his hips.

Her action obviously surprised him; for a moment his whole body stilled. Then he made a fierce sound low in his throat and wrapped an arm beneath her to brace her, lifting her higher and deepening the kiss.

She felt the broad tip of his staff nudge against her at the same time his tongue stabbed possessively into her mouth. Excitement, anticipation and need went from bud to blossom, deepening the ache pulsing at her center. "Kaj. Yes. Oh, yes." Loosening her hold on his neck, she sank down and felt him slip shallowly inside her.

"Catherine, darling, slow down. I don't want to hurt you."

"You won't," she assured him breathlessly. "You couldn't. I want you, Kaj. Inside me. Now." Trembling, she wrestled the tie out of his hair, thrust her hands into the thick, inky locks and dragged his head to hers. "Please." Copying his action of a moment earlier, she breached his mouth with her tongue and mimicked the slow thrusting motion that had set her own blood on fire.

He made a strangled sound of protest. Or was it surrender? The answer came as he abruptly tightened his hold on her and flexed his powerful hips.

Catherine felt a brief, unexpected flash of pain as he slid deeper, then a stinging discomfort as her body stretched to accommodate him. The latter was more than bearable, however, offset as it was with other sensations: the drugging warmth of his lips plying hers, the delicious friction of her nipples rubbing against his hard chest, the unexpected sense of security she felt being in his arms. "More," she urged impatiently.

A shudder passed through him, shaking them both. Then he bent his knees and pushed.

The slow slide of him inside her seemed to last forever and left them both out of breath and trembling. Fully buried, he dragged his mouth away from hers to brush kisses over her cheeks and eyes. "Are you all right?" he murmured.

"Mmm," she answered, her focus inward. "Don't stop."

"No. I won't." Shifting his hold on her, he pulled back slightly, then rocked his hips.

It was like dragging a match over a strike strip. Heat flickered, expanded, flared. It was only a tiny flame at first. Until he repeated the motion. And then she caught fire. "Oh!"

Again he moved, settling into a steady pumping rhythm that soon had her rocking back.

"Kaj."

"What?"

"It's not—" She sucked in air, her voice shaking. "It's not enough. I want…I need…you. Deeper. Harder."

"Aw, Catherine. Sweetheart, you're killing me." Tightening his grip on her to keep them joined, he walked toward the bed, where, the muscles bulging in his upper arms, he slowly lowered her until her upper body rested on the high mattress.

Bracing his legs, he pulled back until he was almost out of her. Automatically she tightened the lock of her legs on his waist. "Kaj, please—"

"Shh." To her disbelief, instead of immediately acquiescing to her plea as she expected, he shifted his hands so that one supported her bottom while the other slid over the top of her thigh. Then one big finger skated sideways, zeroed in on the swollen seat of her need and rubbed. She cried out in shocked pleasure, and that was when he drove forward.

For one mind-altering moment the world ceased to exist as she knew it. Her stomach hollowed, her skin flushed, her back bowed, her every muscle clenched as she was swept by a monumental explosion of pleasure.

Powerless against such hot, mindless delight, she felt herself tighten around Kaj as he pumped full into her. He gave a guttural shout, then she too was again crying out as a second, even stronger explosion rocked her.

Catherine gladly bore his considerable weight when he collapsed on top of her moments later. And she knew, even as he wrapped his arms around her, keeping her close as he rolled onto his side, that nothing in her life would ever be the same.

Kaj lay sprawled in the center of the bed, one hand tucked beneath his head, watching with lazy interest as fingers of sunshine reached through the window tops to paint shimmering golden stripes on the ceiling overhead.

He felt boneless. Satiated. Beyond content. But then hours and hours of incredible sex with an incredible woman could do that to a man.

He shifted to look at Catherine. She lay nestled against him, her head cradled on his shoulder, her arm draped across his chest, her fingers lightly tracing the path from his ear to his collarbone. Although she'd stirred awake some twenty minutes ago, they had yet to speak. There was no need since their shared silence was so comfortable they might have been lovers for years.

Kaj had never experienced anything like it. Or like the night they'd just shared. His hunger for her had seemed to grow as the hours passed. Their every kiss, every touch, every joining had only made him want to hold her closer, thrust himself deeper, feel her shudder and cry out yet another time. And though he'd managed to cling to some semblance of control, to leash his strength so he wouldn't hurt her, he hadn't been able to stop. He doubted they'd slept an entire hour altogether.

Which might have concerned him far more were it not for the fact that, as often as not, it had been Catherine who'd initiated another round of lovemaking. She was definitely unique, a jewel to be treasured, he thought, idly rubbing his thumb over the silken skin of her hip. "Good morning, princess."

Her fingers stilled and she angled her head up toward him. "Good morning yourself," she said softly.

"How do you feel?"

"Tired. Marvelous." She gave a small, delicate yawn. "What about you?"

"Me?" He considered. "As if I just ran the world's longest marathon." He smiled. "And won."

She smiled back, and he realized she looked different. For the first time since they'd met she'd lost her usually guarded expression.

The discovery made him feel even more protective and territorial than usual, and he gathered her even closer. "I've pictured you here, in my bed, you know. I imagined the way you'd look against these very sheets, with your white skin and Titian hair. But my imagination didn't begin to do you justice."

"Oh." Pleasure colored her cheeks, but she glanced away from him and ran her hand over the exquisitely soft fabric that draped their hips. "*I* never imagined black velvet sheets. I always thought satin sheets would be the preferred choice for…worldly pursuits."

He shook his head. "No. Satin feels either too hot or too cold. Plus it's slippery."

"Ah." She considered a moment, then nodded thoughtfully. "No traction. A definite drawback."

His lips twitched at her serious tone. "My, aren't you a quick study."

"I suppose I am." She shifted to look at him. "Is that a problem?"

"Absolutely not. Your intelligence is one of the reasons I chose you to be my wife."

For a long moment she was silent. Then she said with a touch of amusement as well as something else he couldn't quite identify coloring her voice, "Do you know, sheikh, I remember agreeing to a lot of things last night. But a marriage proposal wasn't one of them."

He twisted a lock of her hair around his finger. "I rather imagine that's because I was too busy with other things to ask. But I will. And when I do, you'll say yes."

You'd better. Because you're mine, sweet Catherine, in every way that matters. And I intend to keep it that way.

The sudden violence of his emotions caught him by surprise, and he felt an abrupt stab of uneasiness.

He promptly shrugged it off. After all, he'd already acknowledged she inspired a host of unique feelings in him: possessiveness, protectiveness, an unprecedented tenderness. Just as he'd admitted that, though he didn't love her, he cared about her in ways he'd never cared about another woman. The fact that he wanted to please her, to make her happy, was a miracle all by itself.

A miracle that should help ensure that theirs would

be a successful marriage. "Trust me, *chaton*. We're meant to be together."

Her face softened, but to his surprise all she said was, "I'll think about it."

As responses went, it was totally unacceptable, and for one very long moment he was tempted to press the issue, to do whatever it took to bend her to his will. He hadn't a doubt that if he put his mind to it he could make her give him the answer he desired.

Yet, after a bit more thought, he realized such a power play was unnecessary. Given what had occurred between them in the past twelve hours, it was obvious she had deep feelings for him. All he had to do was be patient and she was bound to come around to his way of thinking and see the advantages of a union between them.

The realization sent a surge of energy through him. "Very well. In the meantime—" gently shifting her off him he climbed out of bed "—it occurs to me there's someone you should meet."

"You can't be serious."

"Oh, but I am."

Yawning again, she made a shooing motion. "You go ahead. Visit whomever you like." She snuggled deeper into the bed. "I'll stay here. I'm afraid I'm not in the mood to make conversation."

"That's quite all right. My friend isn't big on talk."

"Kaj—"

He held out his hand. "Please?"

Her gaze touched his proffered hand, took a leisurely dip lower, then slowly rose to his face. She chewed her full bottom lip. "Would we shower first?"

Given that he was once again as hard as a rock, it seemed like an excellent idea. "Yes."

"In that case..." She tossed off the covers and reached for him.

Nine

"So?" Kaj stood next to his friend, one hand resting on the big fellow's muscular shoulder. "What do you think?"

"Are you serious?" Catherine stared in awe at the huge orange tiger, who from whiskers to tail had to measure over nine feet long. "He's incredible. And utterly beautiful."

Kaj cocked his head. "You sound surprised. Did you think I was making things up that day at the orphanage when I told the children about him?"

"I wasn't sure," she admitted.

He made a faint tsking sound. "You need to have more faith in me, *chaton*. Although I've been known to withhold information during business negotiations on occasion, I don't lie. And certainly not to children."

"Yes. I know that. Now."

"Good. Now come say hello to Sahbak. Like me, he has a penchant for beautiful, red-haired women."

She didn't hesitate to do as he bade. Partly because she'd been raised to always show courage when confronted with a challenge. But also because she trusted Kaj not to put her in danger. Moving forward to stand at his side, she offered her hand to the big cat to be sniffed.

"Have you known that many?" The words popped out of her mouth before she could stop them.

"What? Redheads?" He gave her a lazy smile that made her feel warm all over. "Personally, just one. Sahbak, however, is acquainted with a number of such ladies. Although the captive Amur tiger population is considered to be stable, his genes are still very much in demand."

"I've never heard of Amur tigers."

"You've probably heard them referred to as Siberian tigers."

"I thought Siberian tigers were white."

"No, those are actually Indian tigers."

She rolled her eyes, and without warning, Sahbak took a friendly swipe at her hand with his long pink tongue. It was not unlike being stropped by a damp emery board and she gave a slight start. "Oh!"

"He likes you." There was no mistaking the satisfaction in Kaj's voice. "Good."

"You make it sound as if I've passed some sort of test." She tried not to sound as pleased as she felt as the cat licked her again.

"I'd say you have." Kaj scratched behind the animal's rounded ears, and the beast promptly began to make a low rumbling noise that was clearly the tiger version of purring. "After all, we've known each other a long time, he and I. I was just seventeen and he was a mere cub when he was given as a gift to my father. He's usually quite a good judge of character."

Unable to help herself, she rubbed her hand over the ruff of white fur that encircled the tiger's neck. "Then perhaps you won't be offended if I tell you I'm not sure I approve of an individual person, rather than a zoo, having this kind of animal. In Altaria, trading or owning any sort of endangered species is illegal."

"As it should be everywhere, since there are less than a thousand Amurs left, wild and captive. But the man who acquired Sahbak as a cub has never concerned himself with legalities, no matter the country, much less cared about wildlife conservation. And my father always believed *he* was a law unto himself. It took me several years just to convince him to have Sahbak's name entered in the International Tiger Studbook, and he only agreed then because he knew no one could force him to give the tiger up."

"Your father sounds rather difficult."

"My father was impossible," Kaj said simply. "He could be charming when he chose, and he did have some qualities I admired, but the majority of the time he wasn't an easy man to be around, particularly in the latter years of his life. He had to be in control, and he was willing to do whatever it took to get his own way."

Catherine reached out and touched her hand to his arm. "I'm sorry."

The strain on his face abruptly vanished. "Yes, I know you are. And while it's not very noble of me, it's a relief that you understand. Which is another example of why we're so well suited."

"Now, sheikh," she admonished, amused by how quickly his mood had turned around, "let's not ruin a perfectly lovely afternoon by bringing that up again. I told you I'd think about us. And I will."

With a wry smile he squeezed her hand. "Very well. But in an attempt to redeem the family image, allow me to at least explain that, except for a female with cubs, tigers are by nature solitary creatures. They don't do well in groups, which can put a real strain on zoos and other captive habitats. Because of that, and because I have the resources to provide a very large and customized enclosure, Sahbak is better off here than he would be any number of other places."

"He certainly appears to think so." She watched as the tiger, apparently tired of all their talk, leaned against Kaj and nudged the sheikh with his large head, clearly impatient to be petted again.

Ever dutiful, Kaj again began to scratch between the animal's ears, although he had to strain to stay on his feet as the contented beast slouched more and more against him.

"How much does he weigh?" Catherine asked curiously.

"Six hundred sixty pounds. And at the moment—" with a grunt, he gave the tiger's shoulder a shove that seemed to affect the placid Sahbak not at all "—I'm feeling every one of them. Lazy bounder."

"Pardon, Mr. Kaj." They both looked over as the younger of the two men Kaj had introduced as the tiger's caretakers spoke up from just outside the enclosure gate. "You have a phone call. Mrs. Siyadi transferred it from the main house to the office here. She says to tell you it's the call you've been expecting."

"Thank you, Jamal," Kaj answered. "I'll be right there." He motioned to Saeed, the other handler, who'd been quietly standing vigil several yards away, poised to intervene if the big cat made any unexpected moves. "If you'd be so kind as to take over. Sahbak seems to have a number of itches that need to be scratched."

"Certainly, sir." Walking slowly, Saeed went to stand opposite Kaj and began to knead the animal's neck. Snuffling happily, Sahbak shifted his weight toward the source of this new pleasure, barely taking note as Catherine and Kaj made their way out of the enclosure.

Clasping Catherine's hand, Kaj interlaced their fingers as they walked up the slight hill toward the airy stone structure that housed Alf Ahkbar's stables. "Praise be for phones," he said dryly. "Another few minutes and Sahbak would have been on top of me. An experience I've had previously and would prefer not to repeat."

"Did he hurt you?"

"Only my dignity. But being a tiger's doormat is not the image I want you to have of me."

There was slight chance of that, Catherine thought wryly, her pulse racing merely from the innocent contact of their fingers.

But then, where Kaj was concerned, she seemed to be ultrasensitive in all sorts of odd places—the backs of her knees, ears and neck, the inside of her wrists, the bottom of her feet—that until last night she'd never considered erogenous zones.

Even more confounding, her lips and breasts, as well as the inside of her thighs, actually ached. And not from being tender or tired as might be expected. No, they ached for *more*.

For the first time in her life she understood what it was to hunger for a man. To hunger for Kaj.

Coming on the heels of last night, it surprised her. She'd just assumed that once they made love the sharpest edge of her desire for him would be dulled. That she'd feel relaxed and fulfilled. That the compulsion to be close to him would ease and that the little things like a warm look from him or a husky tone in his voice would lose their power to affect her.

Clearly that hadn't happened. And didn't seem likely to in the immediate future.

Kaj let go of her hand and motioned for her to precede him into the large, air-conditioned office just inside the stable block. "This should only take a second," he promised, giving her arm one last, proprietary squeeze. Moving across the well-appointed space, he propped a hip on top of a large, curved desk, turned the phone around, put the receiver to his ear and punched a button. "Russard."

She looked around, taking note of the state-of-the-art computer workstation, the floor-to-ceiling stainless steel file cabinets, the inviting seating area that occupied the room's near corner. But it was the display of framed photos on the far wall that drew her. To her delight, a closer inspection proved that although most of the pictures were of horses, Kaj also appeared in some of them.

In one he couldn't have been more than two or three. Nevertheless he sat proudly atop a lovely dapple gray mare, a smile of unabashed delight warming his small face. Even then he appeared to have a light grip on the reins.

In another he was perhaps five years older. His face was thinner, his body long and rangy, his expression oddly guarded for someone his age. All of the joy that was so evident in the first photo was gone.

In the next several shots there was again a jump of several years. But to her relief, in these he appeared happy again, something she attributed to his company—a smaller boy with gilt hair and an impish smile who could only be his cousin Joffrey.

Smiling, she admired a teenage Kaj and his horse done up in full native regalia, caught her breath at a shot of him in formal English hunting attire atop a big bay taking an enormous cross-country fence, nodded her approval as he was caught leaning down to accept a blue ribbon and silver plate atop the same horse.

Next on the wall were several snapshots of him as a tall, elegant youth on the cusp of manhood, a tiger cub that had to be a young Sahbak in his arms. There was also a larger, more formal picture, this one with a man who had to be Kaj's father, and the cub. Boldly inscribed across the bottom in black ink was an inscription.

''My dear sheikh. May my humble gift to you grow to be as noble and fierce as his new master. Your servant, The Duke.''

She frowned, disturbed but not certain why. Something about that last seemed almost familiar....

"Catherine? Is something the matter?"

With a start, she realized Kaj was standing beside her. "No. I don't think so."

"Then why are you frowning so?"

"It's just that this picture..." She trailed off, feeling silly. Surely the use of that title was just a coincidence. Lord knew there were lots of dukes in the world.

"What about it?"

"Do you know the man who wrote this?" She indicated the inscription.

"I know him, yes. His name is Georges Duclos. The other is an appellation I'm sure he gave himself."

"He's not a real duke?"

He grimaced. "No."

"What does he do?"

He gave her a puzzled look. "Why do you want to know?"

"I just do."

He considered her a moment longer, then sighed, no doubt at the determination that most likely was stamped on her face. "Very well. If it's important to you. The duke is a middleman of sorts. He made a vast fortune as an illegal arms broker in the 1980s, then retired and did his best to become part of the so-called jet set, befriending a number of influential European and Arabic royalty.

"Because he still had criminal contacts and a total lack of scruples, he gained a reputation as a fixer, if you will. He was—and is—someone who can provide a prominent, married friend with the name of a person willing to put a scare into an ex-girlfriend who threatens to go to the tabloids, for instance. Conversely, he's also been known to connect a wealthy crime lord who wishes to see a certain law watered down or eliminated altogether with a down-on-his-luck but still-well-connected aristocrat.''

Catherine turned to stare blankly at the photo as she digested what he was telling her. "I see."

Kaj laid his hand on her shoulder. "Now tell me why he's of interest to you."

"It's probably nothing, just a coincidence. But a few weeks ago I used my father's computer to check his e-mail. I was trying to see if he'd read my message, the one I told you about. More to the point, there was another e-mail. I don't remember the exact wording, but in essence it assured my father that things were in order and that as long as something continued to go on unhindered, a loan he'd taken out would be retired.

"I honestly didn't think much of it at the time, since my father often did favors for people and I'd only recently learned he owed a great deal of money, and I had...other things on my mind. But I do remember it was signed exactly the way your photo is: 'Your servant, The Duke.'" Ignoring the sick feeling twisting through her stomach, she forced herself to meet Kaj's gaze without flinching. "The more I consider it, the more likely it seems that your duke and mine could be the same man."

"Yes." Kaj's voice was unexpectedly gentle. "I think you're right."

They both fell silent, considering.

Catherine was the first to speak. "Given this Du-clos's reputation and the kind of people he knows…" She swallowed. "Do you think he could have any-thing to do with what happened to Grandfather's boat? Or the attempt on Daniel's life?"

Kaj shook his head. "Doubtful. Or at least, not personally. Remember, he always acts merely as a middleman. As for the third party he was represent-ing, if you're accurately remembering what was in that e-mail, it sounds as if everything was under con-trol. Why would anyone commit murder if they didn't have to?"

"Yes, I suppose that's true."

"In any event, when we get back to Altaria we can make a hard copy of the e-mail and let the king and his people take it from there. That is, if that's all right with you?"

"It's fine." It was more than that, really. Having someone she could confide in, whose judgment she trusted and who treated her like an intelligent partner, was a rare and precious gift.

"Now, quit worrying." Wrapping an arm around her shoulders, Kaj drew her toward the door. "This will all work out, I promise you, although it may take some time to get all the answers."

They stepped into the stable aisle, and as if there to provide a distraction, a good two dozen priceless Arabian horses, their necks extended over the bottom halves of their stall doors, nickered as they caught sight of Kaj.

Catherine raised her eyebrows. "My, you're pop-ular. Let me guess—these are all mares."

"Of course not." He gave her a smug, supercilious look that was so unlike him she had to choke back a laugh. "Such is the strength of my appeal that I'm appreciated by all of my horses."

She did laugh then. "Oh, really? I don't suppose it could have something to do with the carrots you were handing out earlier?"

"Certainly not." Pulling her close to his side so they were pressed hip to thigh, he urged her toward the end of the corridor. "Now enough of this nonsense. We're falling behind schedule."

"We have a schedule?"

"Yes."

"I don't suppose you'd be willing to share it with me?"

"But, of course. First we're going to eat the lovely late lunch Mrs. Siyadi has prepared for us. Then I think we could both use a nap so we'll be well rested for tonight."

"What are we doing tonight?"

"Now that, *chaton,* I can't tell you. After all—" he swung her around, planted a kiss on her lips, then pulled quickly away, a devilish glint in his smoky-gray eyes "—if I did, it wouldn't be a surprise."

Kaj pulled the blindfold loose from Catherine's face and took a step back.

He watched with a now familiar combination of tenderness, expectation and lust as she made a slow circle, her long legs flexing in her high, spike heels, her body slim and supple beneath her thin blue sheath. She took her time, examining every detail of her surroundings.

The tiny oasis, with its handful of palm trees and its deep crystalline pool. The pair of glossy-coated horses and the stacks of supplies he'd had brought in so he and Catherine might stay as long as it suited them.

The airy pavilion, draped with silken hangings, lit against the night by dozens of hanging brass lanterns. The priceless jewel-toned carpets piled to create a floor over the soft sand. The large *dawashak,* or mattress, covered in dozens of pillows.

And surrounding everything, for as far as the eye could see, the desert. Empty. Mysterious. Eternal.

By the time Catherine's gaze finally came to rest on him, her beautiful green eyes were wide and awestruck. "I feel as if I've stepped into a dream," she said softly.

"You're not disappointed we didn't go into Akjeni to sample the nightlife, then?" He'd been afraid after he'd assisted her into the Land Rover instead of the limo that, blindfolded or not, she'd guess they were headed somewhere more remote than the capital.

"Don't be silly. Although—" she did her best to shape her lips into a pout "—when you told me to pack an overnight bag I did think it was possible I'd get a chance to see your apartment there. Or do you call it a love nest?"

Damned if she wasn't always surprising him. Every time he started to think of her as sweet and malleable, she drew a line, threw in a little spice and reminded him that she hadn't been referred to as the Ice Princess for nothing.

And he was glad. The occasional tartness of her tongue coupled with her refusal to worship at his feet pleased him. Immensely. "I can see I'm going to have to speak to Mrs. Siyadi. Sarab talks too much."

"Don't you dare."

"Very well. If you feel that strongly." He closed the space between them and cupped the back of her neck. "But I'm afraid my cooperation will come at a price."

She tipped her head up. "Blackmail, sheikh?"

He leaned down and lightly kissed one corner of her mouth. "I prefer to think of it as taking advantage of an irresistible opportunity."

"Lucky me." She turned her head and captured his lips with her own.

Their kiss was tender, teasing, full of mutual understanding and silent promises about the night to come. Kaj had never experienced a kiss quite like it, and while his body reacted predictably, his mind marveled. *This is what you've been waiting forever for. This closeness, this silent communion, this sense of rightness.*

Out of nowhere, unease slithered down his spine. Irritated, he brushed it away, telling himself it meant nothing, that it was simply the result of his lifelong habit of limiting whom he trusted. Given that he intended he and Catherine would be together for the rest of their lives, it was clearly time he started letting down a few barriers. As for the rest, they'd just have to see. Maybe with time…

He ran his hand down the silken valley of her spine. Urging her closer, he savored the slowly accelerating drumbeat of desire pounding through him. She was so very lovely. And he was so intent on exploring the sweetness of her mouth, it took him a moment to register that her hands were pressed against his shoulders, pushing him away.

He released her instantly. "Catherine? Sweetheart? What's the matter?" Even to his own ears, his voice sounded ragged.

She drew in a shaky breath of her own. "Nothing."

"Then why—"

"I have a surprise for you, too."

"Trust me." He reached for her. "Whatever it is, it can wait."

"It could, but that would also ruin it." She stepped back out of range.

"Catherine—"

"Indulge me, Kaj. Give me a minute and allow me to change into something more comfortable. Before I punch a hole through your carpets or break an ankle in these shoes."

"Take them off. Better yet, take everything off."

She smiled. "Try to be patient. Now, where did you put my bag?"

He took a firm grip on his temper and reminded himself that every woman he'd ever known had certain idiosyncrasies. If Catherine didn't want him to see her in her pantyhose, or something equally ridiculous, he supposed he could live with it. It wasn't as if he were some randy youth, after all; he was a grown man who for good reason prided himself on his self-control.

Still, he couldn't resist a small, long-suffering sigh. "Your bag is in the back of the tent, behind the partial wall."

"Thank you. You may not believe it now, but I think you'll appreciate the delay." Going up on tiptoe, she bussed his lips, then turned on the balls of her feet and headed inside.

Determined not to add to his own torture by watching the sway of her hips, Kaj resolutely turned away. Yet he couldn't seem to get Catherine's "surprise" completely out of his mind. What could she possibly have planned that was worth delaying their mutual satisfaction?

Clasping his hands behind his back, he walked over to where the supplies were stacked and made sure everything was in order. Next he checked the horses, who, unlike some people, seemed to welcome his company. Finally he walked back to the entrance to the pavilion and, desperate for a diversion, raised his face to the clear night sky and began to count stars, alternating between Arabic, French and English in a last-ditch attempt to keep from turning and walking inside.

Wahid, deux, three, *arba, cinq,* six…

He'd gone all the way to *sitten*—sixty—when Catherine's soft voice saved him. "Kaj?"

He turned. And looked. And looked some more.

Gone was his modern, sophisticated princess. In her place was a barefoot siren in diaphanous emerald-green trousers that clung to her hips and a matching jeweled bra that appeared to be at least one size too small for her full, high breasts. Her sleek, pale midriff was bare, exposing the shallow indentation of her navel. In sharp contrast, her hair and face were modestly veiled, leaving visible only her kohl-rimmed eyes, the lashes demurely downcast.

"Allah save me." He fell silent, forced to swallow

as he discovered there was no moisture left in his mouth. ''Where did you get that outfit?''

''Mrs. Siyadi. According to her, Sarab's mother once flirted with the idea of being a dancer.''

''You're not serious.''

''I am.''

''What about you? Do you also have aspirations to dance?''

''Oh, no. I thought we might explore more of the pleasures we shared last night. That is, if the idea pleases you…master.'' She finally lifted her eyes to him and he saw the hint of challenge in them, so at odds with the rest of her meek, harem girl mien.

It fired his blood the way nothing else could have. To his shock, he realized his hands were shaking. ''Oh, it pleases me, woman. It pleases me mightily.''

''Good.'' She closed her hand around his. ''Then come.''

He didn't require much urging. His breath was already labored, his body hot, tight and ready.

He let her lead him under the tent awning to the mattress. He reached for the buttons of his shirt, but when she brushed his hands away he allowed her to undress him. He even managed to keep his hands to himself when she stepped back to look at him in all his naked glory.

''I didn't know,'' she said softly, her gaze once more demurely downcast.

''What?''

As light as a feather, she traced a line from his throat to his navel with her finger. ''That a man could be so beautiful.''

He closed his hand around his erection, already so hard he almost hurt. "Even here?"

She reached out and nudged his hand away, replacing it with her own. "Especially here."

She gripped him, too gently. He parted his lips to tell her so, only to shudder with an overload of sensation as she tightened her hand and stroked her thumb over the broad, swollen tip of him.

It was clearly time to take control. Before she did him in.

He carefully unclasped her hand, eased down onto the mattress and stretched out on his back. Looking up, he held out his hand. "Come here."

"Do you want me to undress?"

"No." Executing an effortless stomach curl, he came up, caught her around the waist and pulled her down so she was straddling his lap. "Not yet. Or rather—" he reached around and deftly unfastened her glittering top "—not completely."

Her breasts spilled free as he tossed the jeweled fabric away. With a groan of pleasure, he cupped the soft, firm globes in his hands, then rubbed his smoothly shaven cheek over one taut, supple nipple. "Ah, but you're perfect. So soft. So very soft."

Sinking back, he propped his head on a pillow. He tugged her forward and down, pushed her face veil out of his way and began to suckle, first lightly licking just the tip of her nipple, then sucking gently, then working the erect bud with his teeth, carefully increasing the pressure until she began to rock against him in a tight little circle, chasing release. "Kaj—"

"Shh. There's no reason to hurry." He turned his head to her other breast, filled with an almost primitive satisfaction as he found that nipple already swollen and tender, just waiting for his mouth.

Catherine whimpered. What he was doing felt so very, very good, yet at the same time with every tug of his mouth she felt a growing tension. Pressing against him, she felt her warm center become slick with need.

With a faint smacking sound, he released her breast, gently gripped her shoulders and eased her up. "Such beautiful eyes you have, princess," he murmured, his thumb coming up to touch the corner of one above her veil. "Do you have any idea how exotic you look with your bare breasts and your veiled face?"

She shook her head.

"Well, you do." His hand dropped away from her face and he slid his warm palms beneath her arms. His thumbs brushed her nipples, then his hands drifted down even further, coming to rest just above the feminine swell of her hips. She held her breath as he spread his right hand and his thumb slowly stroked her silk-covered dampness. "No panties?"

She swallowed, feeling her pelvis begin to sway as the throbbing inside her grew. "No." Her voice was a mere whisper.

There was no mistaking his satisfaction. Or that the heat pouring off his golden skin seemed to originate in his silver eyes. "Good." With carefully calculated strength, he gripped the flimsy fabric between his fingers and yanked, splitting open the trousers cleanly at the crotch.

"Kaj!"

Ignoring her startled protest, he took a long look at

the dark auburn curls now framed by the emerald silk. "Ah, Catherine, you're like a picture of paradise. Come to me, *chaton*. Come to me now."

Her throat too tight to speak, she nodded. Then she came up on her knees, moved him into position and sank slowly down, exulting in the way he filled her like a broadsword sliding into a sheath. Biting her lip in order to stay focused, she waited until he was buried in her as far as he could go. And then, guided by an instinct she didn't question, she rotated her hips.

Kaj's control snapped.

Clamping his hands around her waist, he dug his heels into the mattress, lifted her up, then guided her back down as he thrust.

The pleasure was intense. Arching her back, Catherine braced her hands on his thighs and closed her eyes. So intent was she, she barely noticed when he rasped, "I want to see you. I want to see you when your pleasure comes," and reached up and tugged the veils from her hair and face. Instead, her entire being was focused on the quickening inside her as he drove in and out, slowly picking up speed like the piston of some great steam engine.

Again and again, they rocked together. Then Catherine felt him stiffen, felt his hands spasm against her hips, heard the low choked sound of exultation coming from his lips. She felt the hot, wet surge of him inside her, and her own body answered, contracting around him and rocking in wave after wave of pleasure.

When the storm finally passed, she fell bonelessly against his heaving chest, fairly certain she'd never be able to move again.

It was a long time before either of them spoke.

"Have I told you you're incredible?" Kaj murmured.

His breath tickled her cheek. "Umm. I can't really remember." She stroked his hair with her fingers, feeling drowsy, peaceful, replete. "Have I told you that I love you?"

He went very still. A second later he rolled to his side, propped himself up on an elbow and gazed down at her. "Do you mean that?"

She gazed steadily back at him. "Yes."

Just for an instant there was something in his expression—a twinge of sadness, a flicker of regret?—and then it vanished, replaced by a look of absolute resolve. "Then make me the happiest man on earth. Say you'll marry me. Please, *habibi*."

Habibi. She knew the word meant beloved, and her heart lifted. It might not be the declaration of undying love she longed for, but it was early yet. And it was obvious he cared. Plus she couldn't imagine her life without him. "If I did say yes, when would you want the ceremony?"

He didn't hesitate. "Next week."

"What?"

"Why wait?" He clasped her hand in his and pressed it to his heart. "I'm not some callow schoolboy. I know my own mind and I want you to be my wife. Not next month or the month after that. And just so we're clear, there's still half a year before my father's deadline, so it's not that."

She looked into his eyes and he looked steadily back. "Marry me, Catherine."

The last of her resistance crumbled. "Yes. Yes, Kaj. I'd be honored to be your wife."

Ten

"**D**arling, you look exquisite," Emma Rosemere Connelly said to Catherine, her gaze sweeping approvingly over her niece's ice-pink ball gown with its strapless beaded top and full tulle skirt. She paused the barest instant. "Exactly as a Royal should."

Catherine smiled fondly at the older woman. "Compared to you, Aunt Emma, I feel like a child playing dress up. You look perfect, as always."

It was true. The former Altarian princess, who'd shocked her parents and the world more than three decades earlier when she'd renounced her title to marry an upstart American businessman, had the sort of classic beauty that was timeless. She also had impeccable taste. Tonight she was wearing an elegant, plum-colored Chanel gown that was the perfect complement to her dark-blond hair and willowy figure.

Framed in the entrance to the suite of rooms that were now always kept ready for her at the royal palace, she looked at least a decade younger than her sixty years.

"I realize I'm here early," Catherine said. "But I wanted to see you and Uncle Grant for at least a few minutes without half the kingdom in attendance."

"And I'm glad you did." Putting an arm around Catherine's slender shoulders, Emma drew her inside. "Grant should join us in a moment. He's on the phone with Elena, your cousin Brett's new bride." Motioning her niece toward one of a pair of chairs grouped cozily together in the lavish sitting room, Emma sat down on the other. "They've been trying to connect with each other for the past two days."

Catherine made a face. "It has been hectic, hasn't it? I keep telling myself I'll get some sleep after the wedding."

Emma laughed softly. "From the way your sheikh looks at you, I wouldn't count on *that,* darling. As for all this feverish activity, you have only yourself to blame. First you call out of the blue from Walburaq to announce you're getting married. Then you ask Grant to give you away. And *then* you reveal you intend to hold the ceremony in barely more than a week!"

Catherine did her best to look contrite. "I know, and I am sorry. But as I believe I've mentioned, Kaj was quite insistent."

"Yes, and from the little I've seen of him, he's a very persuasive man. I must say, he reminds me more than a little of my Grant."

Catherine's gaze met her aunt's and for a moment the years between them fell away and they were simply two women discussing the men they loved. "I can see how he might. And not because they both have black hair and gray eyes."

Emma shook her head. "I should say not. What they share is an air of command, coupled with an indefinable something that proclaims they're all man." Her voice softened. "Not to mention that way they have of looking at you as if you're the only woman in the world."

"Are you two ladies talking about how wonderful I am again?" Still dynamic and vigorous at sixty-five, Grant Connelly strode into the room, instantly making it seem half its previous size.

Emma gave her husband a chiding look. "Did I also mention a healthy ego?" she inquired.

Grant winked at Catherine. "Of course I have a healthy ego." Pouring himself a brandy from the sideboard, he walked over and sat down on the sofa across from them and stretched out his tuxedo-clad legs. He took a shallow sip of his drink. "It takes an exceptional man to catch and tame an Altarian princess."

"Really, Grant," Emma protested. "You make Catherine and me sound like bucking broncos."

"Never, sweetheart." Grant's eyes twinkled. "I was thinking more along the lines of Thoroughbred mares. Spirited, headstrong and totally without equal. As I believe I mentioned to Catherine's young man at lunch today, he's marrying into exceptional stock. Just look at us. Thirty-five years and eight children later and I still think you're the most beautiful woman on earth."

His wife's smooth cheeks flushed with pleasure.
Yet as Catherine knew, Altarian princesses of the old
school had been raised to observe a very strict protocol, one that didn't allow for making intimate conversation with a man in public—even if that man was
one's husband.

True to form, her aunt demurely changed the subject. "How was Elena?" she asked Grant. "Is she
still feeling well?"

"Yes. Except for a slight case of exasperation. She
claims that by the time the baby comes, Brett will
have cornered the market on childbirth books and in-
fant supplies."

Emma smiled. "Good for him. I hope you told her
to take it easy."

"I did."

"And?" There was a brief silence as the two
locked gazes. Finally, sounding faintly vexed, Emma
elaborated. "Did she learn anything more about Ms.
Donahue?"

Grant's expression abruptly sobered. "I'm sure
Catherine has better things to concern herself with
than our family problems, Em."

"Nonsense," his wife replied. "I know she'll want
to hear about this since it concerns Seth. The two of
them have always been particular friends. Haven't
you, dear?" She glanced at her niece for confirmation.

"Yes, we have." And for good reason, Catherine
thought. Seth was the third Connelly son, but he
wasn't Emma's child; he was the product of a brief
affair Grant had had early in his and Emma's marriage, when the conflicting styles of his driving am-

bition and her royal upbringing had resulted in a short separation.

Like Catherine, Seth had also been given up by his mother. And though he hadn't come to live with the Connellys until he was twelve and Catherine just four, an unlikely but very real bond had formed between the two cousins.

"So what did Elena say?" Emma asked.

Grant gave his snifter another swirl. "She finally managed to locate Angie and talk to her. Angie," he added for Catherine's benefit, "is Seth's biological mother. And though Elena didn't say so straight out, it's obvious she has some misgivings about her. Apparently, not only did the background check Elena did on Angie turn out too good to be true—Elena's words, not mine—but when they talked, Angie reportedly told Elena more than once how much she now regrets giving up Seth to us."

Emma's spine straightened. "You're not serious," she said, not even trying to hide her disbelief.

"I am."

"Well." For a moment Emma simply sat there. Then she lifted her chin just a fraction and said with obvious conviction, "Let us hope, for Seth's sake, that she's sincere."

"Yes. Let's." Grant looked at his wife with obvious admiration. "Have I mentioned lately how lucky I am to have you, Emma?" he said softly.

Emma Rosemere Connelly smiled at him, and for a moment they might have been alone, so thoroughly absorbed did they appear to be with each other.

And then Altaria's former princess seemed to remember who and where she was. She turned toward

Catherine. "Now, enough Connelly family drama," she said briskly. "Let's talk about you, darling. After all, that's why we're here."

"Your aunt's one hundred percent right," Grant chimed in. "I like your sheikh, but I can't say I'm wild about this hurried-up affair. You're not going to give me a grandniece or nephew in eight months, are you?"

"Uncle Grant!" Catherine protested.

He looked at her indignant face and chuckled. "Well, somebody had to ask."

There was a solid knock on the door. "I'll get it," Catherine announced, springing up and hurrying toward the entry. Briefly pressing her hands to her warm cheeks in an attempt to cool them, she took a breath, then opened the door.

She gave a start of surprised relief. "Kaj! What on earth are you doing here?"

Her fiancé, looking tall and dashing in exquisitely tailored evening wear, gave her an appreciative, all-encompassing look. "I came up to escort you downstairs, and your maid said I'd find you here. And from the look on your face, I'd say my timing is perfect as usual."

"Happy?" Kaj asked her as he expertly navigated a path for them through the crush of other dancers.

Catherine gave her head a slight shake. "No. Not really."

As she'd imagined he might, he instantly raised an eyebrow. "Pardon me?"

The waltz they were doing was one of her favorites, a fast step-step-whirl done while revolving around the floor. She smiled at the way the skirt of her dress billowed around her as they danced. It gave her almost as much pleasure as the sight of the large square-cut emerald and diamond ring glittering on her finger.

But neither meant as much as the solid weight of Kaj's hand against her hip, or how safe and protected she felt being in his arms. "Happy is far too tame a word to describe how I feel. Ebullient? Ecstatic? Deliriously thrilled? None of those are exactly right, either, but they come closer."

His gaze skated over her. "How about exquisite?" he said, tightening his hold as they twirled toward the far end of the ballroom.

"If I'm exquisite, it's merely reflected glory from being close to you." The cool air from the open French doors washed over them and she gave a soft sigh of appreciation.

"Hardly. There isn't a man in this room tonight who doesn't envy me. And for excellent reason."

"Are there other men here?" she asked. "I hadn't noticed. While you…I've missed you the past few days," she said softly. "I wake up during the night and wish you were beside me."

He gave her an indecipherable look. Then to her surprise, he abruptly altered course and danced them right out through the doors and onto the terrace.

She gave a gasp of laughter. "Kaj!"

"Hush. I wanted to do this that first time we danced, but controlled myself. I'm not about to give up a second opportunity." Without missing a beat, he led the way around a corner and backed her up against a short section of balustrade hidden by an enormous planter. "You're a menace to my peace of mind. You know that, don't you?" Pulling her flush against him, he found her mouth with his own.

Their kiss was mutually hungry, fueled by the past several days of deprivation. Although they'd managed a few other stolen kisses, it seemed they'd only served to heighten their desire for each other. Now, tongues tangled, hands feverishly searching for any available patch of bare skin, they clung together, desperate to touch and taste.

When finally they eased apart, Kaj tipped his head back and blew out a frustrated breath. "Three more days until the wedding," he said with disgust. "We should have eloped."

"I know." Smoothing her hands over the back of his jacket, Catherine rested her cheek against his black satin lapel. "Sometimes I don't think I can wait, either."

His concern immediately shifted to her. "Just how are you holding up to all this craziness? Every time I call you on the phone, that tyrant of a palace operator says, 'I'm sorry, sir, the princess is unavailable.'"

He sounded so insulted she had to smile. "I'm fine. Between Erin doing all the planning for tonight and Aunt Emma arranging the wedding, all I've had to do is say yes or no when they've asked my opinion. Although it's time consuming—"

"That's an understatement," Kaj muttered into her hair.

"—everything has gone far more smoothly than I expected. Except for missing you. And being unable to show you and Daniel that e-mail..." Although she did her best to keep the regret out of her voice when she got to that last part, Kaj wasn't fooled.

"I've told you, it doesn't matter that the e-mail was erased. It's the connection you drew between it and the photograph at Alf Ahkbar that's important. And now that you've told Daniel about it, he'll pass it along to his investigators who'll be sure to look into it. You needn't worry about that."

"I know. It's just...sometimes it doesn't feel right that I should be so happy, while Father and Grandfather—" She broke off, chiding herself for being negative on such a special night. "I'm sorry."

As he so often did, Kaj seemed to understand perfectly. "There's a reason the old cliché Life Is for the Living is an old cliché," he said gently. "I know you and your father had your differences and that King Thomas wasn't terribly demonstrative, but I don't think either one of them would begrudge you a chance at personal happiness. Do you? Truly?"

"No. I suppose not."

"Good. Now come here and let me help you forget your troubles."

He didn't have to ask again. Linking her arms around his strong neck, she leaned against him, heat instantly rising through her as his firm, warm lips moved over hers. Kissing him was better than drinking the headiest champagne, she thought. It made her feel bold and brave, hopeful, incredibly alive. It made her believe that anything was possible....

When they finally came up for air, Kaj gave a raspy chuckle. "Sweet, sweet Catherine. I'm afraid we'd best go in...while I still can."

She sighed, reluctantly released her hold on him and stepped back. "I suppose you're right."

They took a moment to straighten their clothes. "Ready?" he murmured, reaching for her hand.

"Yes."

Hand in hand they strolled from their trysting place across the terrace and on inside. They'd barely cleared the door when a familiar male voice said, "Ah, there you are."

Materializing out of the throng, Grant Connelly smiled at them. "I've been looking for you, Catherine. Do you think I might steal my niece for this next dance, sheikh?"

"As much as I hate to give her up, I suppose I must," Kaj said with a gracious smile, "seeing as we're soon to be family. Speaking of which, I need to see if my cousin's finally arrived, anyway. He was catching a late flight in. So if you'll excuse me?" Giving Catherine's hand a brief kiss, he nodded at the other man and strode away.

Grant watched him go for a second, then turned to Catherine, held out his hand and gestured to the dance floor. "After you, Your Highness."

Her smile, which had been feeling slightly strained, became genuine. "Thank you, Mr. Connelly."

With the ease of years of training she went easily into his arms, gracefully following his lead as the music started up again. "I believe I owe you an apology, Catherine," Grant said seriously. "I didn't mean to insult you earlier. Or imply that I don't have the highest regard for your character—"

"No, Uncle, please. Not another word. I know you

were kidding and trying to look out for me. It's all right, truly. It's rather nice to know that you care.''

''Of course I do. You're a special young woman, my dear. I hope you know how proud your aunt and I are of you.''

Touched, Catherine squeezed his hand. ''Thank you.''

Comfortable with each other, they danced without speaking for several turns of the floor. ''Did your aunt tell you about the twins?'' Grant finally inquired.

''Drew and Brett? What about them?'' Her twenty-seven-year-old cousins were the only twins she knew.

''No. Douglas and Chance Barnett. Soon to be Barnett Connelly.''

She felt her eyes widen. ''You and Aunt Emma are adopting?''

He smiled ruefully and shook his head. ''No. Of course not. The boys—men, actually, I guess—are mine. They were conceived by a woman I knew in college, before I ever met your aunt. Their mother chose not to tell me she was expecting. Or to tell them my identity. At least not until she fell mortally ill, and by then they felt they were old enough to take care of themselves.''

''Good heavens.''

''Yes. Oddly enough, it was all the publicity about Daniel coming here, to Altaria, that made them decide they might like to get to know me and the rest of the family.''

''I'm not sure what to say. It all seems sort of fantastic, like something out of a movie.''

''I couldn't agree more. It's been hard on your

aunt—hard on us both, really. But the good news is from what I can see, in addition to having the Connelly good looks—'' that faint rueful smile flashed again ''—they're both hardworking and resourceful young men. Chance is a Navy SEAL and Douglas is a doctor. We're having a big party to welcome them to the family once Emma and I get home. Jennifer is taking care of everything.''

Jennifer was Emma's social secretary, a blond, pretty, single mother about Catherine's own age whom she'd liked very much the one time they'd met. ''Are Tobias and Miss Lilly going to be there?'' Grant's parents were two of her favorites.

''Yes, they are. For once they're actually interrupting their annual Palm Springs hiatus—can you believe it?''

She shook her head. ''I'm sorry I'll have to miss it.''

''Now, none of that. You'll have plenty of time to see everyone some other time,'' Grant said easily. ''While with any luck, you'll only get married once.''

Catherine smiled.

And then, out of all the myriad conversations floating around them, a laugh from overhead arrested her attention. Looking over her uncle's shoulder, she caught sight of Kaj and Joffrey standing upstairs on the balcony.

Pleasure exploded like champagne bubbles through her veins at the sight of her fiancé, and she had a sudden urge to be with him, to touch him and share her overwhelming happiness with him. It was all she could do to uphold her end of the conversation for the remainder of the dance, and she could only hope the manners that had been drilled into her since birth stood her in good stead as the music came to an end.

She hoped she thanked Grant for the dance, but she couldn't be certain.

Then she dismissed the concern. And picking up her skirts, she turned and headed for the stairs.

"They may be a tad on the formal side, but these Altarians do know how to throw a party," Joffrey said, gazing admiringly down at the crush below. "This is quite the impressive affair."

"Don't forget the new king and queen are Americans," Kaj said. "And in case it's somehow escaped your notice, I happen to be quite fond of Altarians. At least, one in particular."

"Yes, I know. I've been meaning to talk to you about that."

Kaj groaned. "Spare me, Joff. I assure you I already know more than you ever will about the birds and the bees, nor do I need you to lecture me on the responsibilities of marriage. Particularly when you yourself are in possession of neither a wife nor even a significant other, as I believe they're called. As for love, you don't have any more experience with it, dearest Joffrey, than I do."

"One does not need to be a poet in order to understand great verse," the Englishman said with dignity.

Kaj made a deliberately rude noise. "Please. If I remember correctly, your last prediction—something to the effect that I'd have a difficult time making a certain princess aware I was alive—didn't pan out."

The other man made a vague, dismissive gesture.

"One slight miscalculation hardly disqualifies me to speak my mind."

"One? In case it's slipped your mind, it is currently March 26, my ring is on the aforementioned princess's finger, and you'll simply have to take my word as a gentleman that I fulfilled the third requirement of our wager. Speaking of which, when should I expect to receive my new Renoir?"

Joff grimaced. "I've been wondering when you'd be ill-mannered enough to bring that up. And I can't help but point out that you're being incredibly shortsighted. That painting clearly belongs in my drawing room. You yourself are always saying how perfect it is for the space. Think about how much you'll miss seeing it there when you come to England to visit."

"I'll survive. We had a wager, I won, and now—" He narrowed his eyes as Joff's gaze drifted to something beyond him. Accustomed to Joff's tendency to try to distract him whenever his cousin felt he was on the verge of losing an argument, Kaj pretended not to notice when the other man stiffened in seeming alarm. "Now I expect you to pay up. Just as I haven't a doubt you'd be pressing me to ship you Tezhari if the tables were turned."

"Kaj, shut up."

Damned if Joffrey didn't sound genuinely distressed. He stared at his cousin curiously. Then, with a faint shrug, he turned to see for himself what, if anything, was causing Joff's odd behavior.

Catherine stood no more than ten feet away, her gaze riveted on him, her face whiter than his shirt.

He swore under his breath. "Would you excuse us, Joff?" he said, never taking his eyes off his betrothed.

"Certainly."

He felt Joff withdraw. And then it was just Catherine and him.

This, Catherine thought, as she stood frozen in place, must be what it felt like to be struck by lightning.

She could hear the blood rushing through her ears, feel her pulse pounding, taste the metallic flavor of crushing hurt on her tongue. Her skin burned, but at her core she felt colder than death.

As for her heart... She couldn't feel it at all.

"Catherine, don't look like that," Kaj said sharply. Striding close, he reached out and clasped her cold hands in his own. "I'm sorry you had to hear that, but I assure you it meant nothing."

"You—" She stopped and wet her lips, which felt bruised and stiff. "You and your cousin had a bet? About me? About us?"

"Yes. But I promise it was made well before I got to know you, and was nothing more than the sort of stupid posturing that men are prone to."

"I see." And she did. She believed he was telling the truth. Unfortunately, that wasn't what had her rooted in place, feeling as if she'd had her soul torn out. It was what he'd said so casually to Joffrey before the bet had even come up:

"As for love, you don't have any more experience with it, dearest Joffrey, than I do."

She took a deep breath, then swallowed, trying to dredge up the courage to ask what she was very much afraid she already knew the answer to. "Do you love me, Kaj?"

Just for an instant he seemed taken aback. Then his expression cleared. "I want to spend the rest of my life with you, Catherine," he said persuasively. "I want you to be my wife, the mother of my children—"

"That's not what I asked you. Do you love me?"

"I care for you more than I've ever cared—"

"So the answer is no."

"Catherine, sweetheart, you're not listening—"

She jerked her head up at that. "Oh, no, you're wrong, Sheikh al bin Russard. For the first time I really *am* listening. And I'm hearing what you're saying. Or perhaps to be accurate, what you're *not* saying.

"And it's not your fault. You told me right from the beginning that you intended to marry me. I was just foolish enough to delude myself that, like me, somewhere along the way you'd fallen in love." Somehow she managed a slight shrug. "I love you, Kaj. And because of that, and what we've shared, for the first time in my life I feel worthy to be loved."

She pulled her hands free of his, slipped the beautiful emerald and diamond engagement ring he'd given her off her finger and pressed it into his hand. "So while you might be willing to live in a loveless marriage, I'm not." She looked him straight in the eye. "As of now, this engagement is off."

Then, not giving him a chance to respond, she turned and walked away.

Eleven

"So, are you going to go after her? Or are you just going to stand up here all night like some sort of lovelorn statue?"

Joff's ultrapolite voice punched through Kaj's paralysis. Slowly, feeling not unlike he had when he was fifteen and a spooked stallion had tossed him to the ground and stomped on him, he turned and addressed his cousin. "Go to hell."

Whatever he saw in Kaj's face chased every trace of amusement from Joff's expression. "I very likely will. Someday. In the meantime, why don't you tell me what happened?"

"What do you think happened? Catherine overheard our conversation and decided she'd prefer not to marry me."

"Because of the bet?" Joffrey said in amazement.

"You can't be serious. I mean, it was obvious she was upset, but I was sure once you explained and assured her how much you love her—" He broke off, his eyes abruptly narrowing on Kaj's face. "You *did* tell her you love her, didn't you?"

Confronted with his cousin's probing gaze, Kaj set his jaw and looked away.

There was a thunderous silence. And then Joff said carefully, "Would you care to tell me why you didn't?"

For a moment Kaj considered just walking away. Only the knowledge that his cousin would hound him clear to Walburaq and beyond until he had an answer prompted him to reply. "Because I care for her too much to lie."

There was another silence. This one, however, was much shorter, shattered as it was by Joff's snort of disgust. "Bloody hell! If that's not the most ludicrous thing you've ever said, I don't know what is!"

Kaj stiffened. "Spare me, please. I find I'm not presently in the mood for your opinion."

"Fine. But at least let me ask you this—if you don't love her, why the big rush to get married?"

"I beg your pardon. Apparently you've had so much to drink you've already forgotten our wager."

"To hell with the wager. It had nothing to do with this wedding, and you know it. All you had to do was be engaged by month's end. So I'll ask again—why the hurry?"

"Does it really matter?"

"Yes."

"Then my answer is, I don't know," Kaj said impatiently. "I suppose I wanted to get it over with."

"Ah. This from a man who's been dodging every beautiful, intelligent, eminently suitable woman intent on tossing herself at his feet or any other body part for longer than I can count? A man who could have married any female he ever dated with just a snap of his fingers? Who in the past decade became so well-known for his avoidance of the altar that his own father felt he had to blackmail him into wedding to ensure the family bloodline?" He sniffed in the particularly contemptuous way that only the English could really pull off. "Sorry, old boy, but I don't buy it."

"Then that's your problem."

"Hardly."

"And just what's that supposed to mean?"

"Just that if you're any kind of man, you'll also consider your princess. Because it's obvious she loves you. Just as it's also obvious—at least to me—that for the first time in your entire always-in-control-of-yourself life, you're in love as well."

"Really? And on what do you base your conclusion, if I might be so bold as to ask?"

"That's easy. Every sense you possess has been engaged by her from the very start. I've never seen you so single-minded about a woman, much less feel free to be your real self the way you are with Catherine. Most telling, just being with her clearly makes you happy. And I think all of that is because you fell in love with her that very first night, in this very palace, on that dance floor down below, when you first held her in your arms."

"Are you finished?"

"No. I also think you're scared. Scared because for

some reason you think if you acknowledge your feelings, things will go sour. That Catherine will turn into a tease like your mother and you'll become like your father—jaded, selfish, embittered.''

''I believe I've heard more than enough. If you value our friendship at all, Joffrey, you'll drop this now.''

''Very well. But my leaving isn't going to change anything. Whether you admit it or not, your feelings aren't going to vanish merely because you want them to. And by refusing to face them, by insisting on basing your life on your parents' past, you'll get none of the joy you so rightly deserve—only misery. And that *will* make you like your father.''

Back rigid, face set, Kaj refused to respond, simply stared at the other man until Joffrey gave a slight, regretful shake of his head and retreated. Then Kaj swiveled back around and resumed his unseeing contemplation of the ballroom below.

Joffrey was wrong, he thought mutinously. Dead wrong. He was not in love with Catherine. Nor was he afraid—of anything. And he was most certainly not worried that he would ever turn into someone as empty and cut-off from real life as his father.

Really? So why, for the first time in your life, does the thought of going home to Alf Ahkbar bring you absolutely no pleasure? And why does the mere thought of living out the rest of your years without seeing a certain smile, hearing a particular laugh, having the right to touch and watch out for one special individual leave the taste of ashes in your mouth? As if you just burned down the only bridge that ever mattered—or ever will?

The future suddenly seemed to stretch out before him like a barren wasteland.

Unable to stop himself, he slid his hand into his pocket and drew out the ring Catherine had returned to him. On her slim, graceful hand it had shone, full of life and brilliance. Now, without her warmth, her fire, her vibrancy to define it, it seemed dull and lifeless.

Just like his heart.

In that moment he knew that somehow, some way, no matter what it took, he had to get her back.

Catherine sat huddled on the edge of the mattress in the dark sanctuary of her bedroom. Although she couldn't seem to stop shivering, she felt too listless to bother with a cover for her bare arms and shoulders. In much the same way, she couldn't summon the energy to reach over and switch on the bedside lamp.

Soon, she promised herself. Soon, she would pull herself together. She'd stop this ridiculous shaking and turn on a light. She'd climb to her feet and make her way to the powder room, where she'd smooth her hair and retouch her makeup. Then she'd lift her chin, plaster a smile on her face, go back downstairs and find Daniel or Erin or Emma or Grant and inform them the wedding was off. Surely they would then make some sort of announcement. One that would preclude any but the vaguest of explanations.

Because while there would no doubt be endless speculation, despite her brave words to Kaj she didn't think she could survive the whole world knowing that he simply didn't love her.

If she didn't hurt so much, it would almost be funny. Consider: after years of believing there was something about her that prevented the people she loved from loving her back, Kaj hadn't even had to dupe her into believing he cared. She'd done a more than adequate job of deceiving herself.

She made a small hiccuping sound. To her horror, it sounded almost like a sob. Clenching her teeth, she choked back the emotion threatening to spill out. She was not going to cry. She was *not*.

A sharp rapping sound momentarily startled her from her misery. For a second she couldn't imagine what she was hearing. Then, as she realized someone was knocking on her sitting room door, she nearly gave way to panic. She wasn't ready to face anyone yet. Not her maid, not her family. She needed more time, time to lick her wounds, to gather the cloak of her composure around her.

As abruptly as the knocking had started, it stopped. She held her breath as she heard the doorknob briefly rattle, and then the distinct memory of herself turning the lock surfaced in her mind. She sagged in relief, only to jerk to her feet at the violent sound of splintering wood.

There was a sudden flash of light as a lamp in the other room was snapped on, and then the carpet-cushioned thud of a long-legged stride she would have recognized anywhere.

"Catherine?" Kaj stood in the doorway, outlined by the light behind him. She couldn't see his face.

She didn't want to. Nor did she care for him to see hers.

Not now. Not like this.

"That locked door was a signal, Sheikh al bin Russard. It indicated my profound desire to be alone." Miracle of miracles, her voice sounded deceptively strong, even if her stride was unsteady as she made her way toward the balcony doors. Hugging her arms to her chest, she stopped before the tall panes of glass and pretended to gaze out. "In plain words, I don't want to see you. So please go away." She shut her eyes, praying he'd do as she asked.

"You're shaking." It was a statement, not a question.

She managed a shrug. "It doesn't concern you."

"Catherine—"

"*Go away.*"

"What a stubborn woman you are."

Something marvelously soft and warm slid around her icy shoulders. With a start, she realized it was Kaj's evening jacket. And that he must be right behind her. She frantically reached down and fumbled for the door handle. If she could just get out onto the balcony she could escape—

Too late. Reaching around her, Kaj caught her gently by the arm and turned her around to face him. "No doubt that's one of the reasons I love you."

She stared blankly up at him, telling herself she couldn't possibly have heard him right. "I'm sorry. I must have misunderstood. What did you say?"

"I'm a fool, *chaton.* And a stubborn one, at that. I've spent so many years determined never to repeat my parents' mistakes that somewhere along the way I lost sight of the truth. I blamed love for the failure of their marriage. But the reality is that what they had wasn't love at all.

"I know that now. Because of you. Right from the start you made me feel more alive than I ever had. You challenged me, you beguiled me, you infuriated and moved me. Most of all, you made me want more. Of your temper and your laughter, your passion, your insight, your heart. For the first time ever, I want to share my life. With you. I love you.

"Marry me. Be my wife. I can't promise it will be perfect—nothing ever is. But I swear you'll never again doubt how much I love you. Please, Catherine. Give me another chance."

She searched his face, the strong lines and planes starkly illuminated by the moonlight pouring in. He looked unwaveringly back at her, his chin firm, the curve of his mouth resolute. But it was the sight of his eyes, usually so steady, so direct, so forceful, that stole her breath and mended her aching heart.

They were sheened with tears, filled with uncertainty, alight with hope. For the first time they were totally open to her, nothing hidden, nothing held back.

"Yes." She reached up and cupped his lean cheek in her hand. "Oh, yes."

His thick, inky lashes swept down for an instant as a shudder of relief went through him. Then he leaned down and captured her mouth with his, kissing her with a sweet tenderness that was totally new.

Catherine didn't know how long they stood there, holding each other, exchanging kisses. All she knew was that when the first flash of brilliant light filled the room, for a second she thought it was just a reflection of her happiness.

Then another blazing burst lit up the grounds outside, and they turned just in time to see a pinwheel of colored light explode above the very cliffs where they'd shared their first passionate embrace. Another barrage followed and then another and another until the entire sky was painted with shimmering fireworks.

"Oh, I had no idea! How beautiful," Catherine breathed.

"Not half so beautiful as you, *habibi.*"

And with that Kaj took her left hand, pressed a kiss to her palm and slipped her ring back on her finger where it belonged.

Epilogue

The first bell began to peal as Catherine and Kaj stepped out of the ancient chapel where Rosemeres had been getting married for more than two centuries.

A cry went up from the waiting crowd. Old ladies wept, the working men removed their caps, children waved, matrons called out their blessings. Then more bells began to ring, until the chiming seemed to stretch the entire length of the Kingdom of Altaria.

It was, Catherine thought, a joyous sound as much as one of thanksgiving. But it didn't compare to the sweetness that filled her every time she looked up at the tall man beside her.

Her husband.

She supposed that to anyone else, this moment right now—with Kaj in his formal gray cutaway and her in her pearl-encrusted satin gown, her long sheer veil held in place with a tiara of diamonds and flowers, their hands clasping each other's—would seem like the perfect fairy-tale ending.

But not to her. She knew this was just the beginning. That they had a whole life ahead of happily-ever-afters. And she couldn't wait to get started.

Kaj's fingers brushed her cheek. "Are you ready?"

"Yes. Absolutely."

He smiled. "Then let's go."

Her right hand held safely in his, she picked up her skirt with the other. Together they began the dash down the steps toward the waiting limousine, laughing as a shower of rose petals fell all around them.

* * * * *

THE SEAL'S SURRENDER

by
Maureen Child

MAUREEN CHILD

was born and raised in Southern California and is the only person she knows who longs for an occasional change of season. She is delighted to be writing for Silhouette Books and is especially excited to be a part of the Desire line.

An avid reader, Maureen looks forward to those rare rainy California days when she can curl up and sink into a good book. Or two. When she isn't busy writing, she and her husband of twenty-five years like to travel, leaving their two grown-up children in charge of the neurotic golden retriever who is the *real* head of the household. Maureen is also an award-winning historical writer under the names of Kathleen Kane and Ann Carberry.

To Sandra Paul, Barbara Benedict, Angie Ray and Michelle Thorne: Thank you for the ambush and for my tiara. You guys are the best.

One

He hated parties.

Give Chance Barnett a machine gun, and he was a happy man. Tell him to mingle, and you got a mean dog on a short leash.

But, Chance told himself, sometimes a man just had to bite the proverbial bullet. And this was a big one, in his humble opinion. Hell, it was damn near a mortar round.

He clutched his bottle of imported beer in a tight fist and made his way around the periphery of the party. His gaze narrowed slightly as he silently assessed his new family. A hell of a way to meet the relatives, he told himself, yet couldn't think of a better way to handle it.

There probably wasn't a *good* way to introduce
him and his twin, Douglas, to the rest of the Connellys. Though to give them their due, they'd all
taken the news of the twins' existence a lot easier
than they might have. After all, it wasn't every day
you met thirty-six-year-old illegitimate twin relatives, was it?

Though he had to admit that none of the Connellys had treated him and his brother as though
they were somehow not good enough to be part of
the family. Hell, even Miss Lily and Tobias had
come home early from Palm Springs just to meet
him and Douglas. Chance's gaze shot to the older
couple. Correction, he told himself silently, his
grandparents. Weird. He smiled as he watched Tobias trying to slip past his much smaller wife, but
Miss Lily, cane or no cane, was too fast for her
husband and snatched that glass of whiskey from
his hand.

Interestingly enough, the big man just gave her
a smile and a peck on the cheek. What would it be
like, Chance wondered, to spend your life with one
person? To love that one person so much that some
fifty-odd years later, the stamp of it was still clearly
on your features?

Those two old people had somehow managed to
raise a dynasty. Amazing really, if you stopped to
think about it. Sure, the Connellys were practically

American royalty. But they actually were *real* royalty as well.

And Chance and Douglas Barnett were a part of it.

He shook his head and moved on, drifting through the crowd like a finger of fog. A strident female voice caught his attention, and he slowed his steps, listening.

His half sister, Alexandra, a tall woman with raven-black hair, a too-important manner and sharp green eyes was center stage, where she seemed most comfortable. "I'm *so* sorry you won't have a chance to meet my fiancé," she was saying, "but Robert was called away on business."

Everyone in her audience nodded sagely, but all Chance could think was, Lucky guy. At least the missing Robert had gotten out of attending this party. He moved on, turning a bit too fast and feeling the pull of the stitches in his side.

A reminder of the reason he was able to be here at this party. If he hadn't been wounded on his last mission, he'd have been happily out trooping through a jungle somewhere. And as soon as he was healed enough, that was just what he'd be doing. Hell, he kept his duffel bag packed and ready to go.

Man, was he ready to go. He needed to get back to his SEAL team. Needed to get back where he belonged. He scowled to himself. He caught a glimpse of Doug, chatting it up with a few of their new relatives, and almost wished that he was half as at ease with people as his brother. Hell, he'd even heard his twin talking to one of their new cousins about his ex-wife and how the reason they'd broken up was because she hadn't wanted the children Doug wanted so badly. Yeah. Chance's brother was sliding right into this and didn't seem to have any trouble at all stringing the name *Connelly* behind the Barnett they'd grown up with. But then, Doug always had been the reasonable twin. Which was probably why Chance had grown up to be a fighting man and Doug had become a doctor.

Okay, he thought, way too philosophical.

"Excuse me, sir." A low-pitched voice came from right behind him and Chance spun around to face a tuxedo-clad waiter. "May I get you something from the bar?"

Chance held his beer aloft. "No thanks," he said, shaking his head at the realization that these people probably dealt with in-house waiters and butlers all the time. "I'm covered."

Maybe it was the military training and maybe it was just his own innate need to be in control at all times, but Chance rarely had more than one beer at a party. Even one like this, where he felt more out of place than a pauper in a palace.

The waiter moved off soundlessly into the milling crowd and Chance shook his head again. How had he wound up here? he wondered. And just how soon could he make a polite exit? He moved off into a corner of the room, kept his back to the wall and let his gaze slide across the people filling the cavernous room.

A SEAL in a Lake Shore mansion? He chuckled inwardly at the absurdity of it. Hell, nobody would buy that. He stood out from the elegantly dressed crowd. His U.S. Navy whites were startling in a sea of bright colors and black tuxedos. But for the first time in his life, he was also in a room filled with people he was actually related to.

He and Douglas had grown up alone, raised by a single mom who'd done her best. But she hadn't been able to provide enough of her own presence to satisfy her boys—let alone provide relatives. So here he stood, a thirty-six-year-old man suddenly meeting cousins and half brothers and sisters for the first time.

Weird.

He took a sip of beer, swallowed it and silently admitted that family wasn't necessarily a bad thing. It was just going to take some getting used to. From across the room, Douglas caught his eye and gave him a "Do you believe this?" look and a half smile. Instantly, Chance felt more at ease. He and his twin had pulled each other through plenty of scrapes over the years. And as long as they could count on each other, then tacking the name *Connelly* on after the Barnett wouldn't change much.

Still, he could do with some air.

Instinctively, he moved toward the sliding glass doors that led onto a balcony. The muted noise of conversation and softly-played piano music followed him as he skirted the crowd. But as he neared the glass partition, his plan for solitude fell apart.

A woman stood on the balcony in the late-afternoon sun, her short, light-blond hair tousled by the wind. He knew her. Jennifer Anderson, Emma Connelly's social secretary. They'd met a couple of times in the last few days. She wasn't very tall, but every inch of her looked to be packed to perfection. She wore a deep-green dress with a flippy sort of hem that stopped just short of her knees, displaying to their best advantage what looked to be excellent legs. Her breasts were high and full and her waist was narrow enough that he figured given a chance, he could span that distance with both hands. Her back was straight as she stared out at Lake Michigan, but he frowned as he noticed she kept one hand clapped across her mouth and couldn't quite hide the droop in her shoulders.

Instantly, something inside him stirred to life. The protective instinct was strong and he felt it push him outside. He slid the glass door open, and the wind off the lake tried to shove him back into the party. But SEALs didn't give up that easily.

Chance ducked his head, stepped quietly onto the stone balcony and soundlessly closed the door behind him.

"Get a grip, Jen," the woman muttered to herself before he had a chance to announce his presence. "Crying's not going to help. It's only going to make you look like hell."

Well, he couldn't resist responding to that.

"Lady," he said softly, "all the tears in the world would have a hard time pulling that one off."

She turned quickly, her body language letting him know that she wasn't pleased at having been found giving in to tears. But she recognized him right away and the Keep Out sign in her eyes blinked off.

"You surprised me," she said, lifting one hand to swipe away the telltale track of tears on her cheeks.

"Sorry," he said, though he really wasn't. "Old habits. I'm used to moving quietly."

One blond eyebrow lifted into an arch. "This isn't exactly the jungle, Commander," she said. "Around here, most people knock."

"Ah," he said, walking closer, "but you knock when you want to come *in*. I was coming *out*."

"Great," she muttered thickly, turning her face back into the wind. "Semantics."

Jennifer stared out at the horizon, deliberately ignoring him in the hopes that he'd go away. She couldn't very well *order* him off. Not one of the long-lost sons for whom this party had been arranged. So either he left of his own accord, or she'd be forced to go back to the party and pretend everything was all right.

Please God, let him leave.

Apparently though, God wasn't listening.

Chance Barnett Connelly moved up right beside her and curled his hands over the wrought-iron balcony railing. She glanced down at those strong, tanned hands and noticed that his knuckles whitened with his grip. Obviously, he felt as tense as she did. But their reasons, at least, were very different.

"So," he said, keeping his gaze locked on the wall of clouds hanging just at the horizon, "what seems to be the problem?"

"Problem?" She straightened up. The last thing she wanted or needed was sympathy. Especially from a man she didn't even know. Besides, he was a Connelly. If she told him, then soon everyone would know and she'd like to put that off for as long as she could. At least until she'd had a chance to talk to Emma Connelly first.

Along with being her boss, Emma was as close to a mother figure as Jennifer could claim. Her own parents had died years ago, and but for her daughter, Sarah, Jennifer was alone in the world. Which had never really bothered her. Until yesterday.

"Yeah," Chance said, shifting her a glance, "when I see a beautiful woman alone and crying on a balcony while there's a party going on not five feet from her…well, I naturally figure there's a problem."

She inhaled sharply, taking the cold wind inside her, needing the bracing strength of it. Then, she forced a cheer she didn't feel into her voice. "Thanks for asking, but I'm fine. Really."

"Uh-huh."

"I mean it."

"Yeah, I can see that."

She looked at him from the corner of her eye. "But you don't believe me."

"Nope."

"Well," she said, pushing away from the balcony railing, "that's not my problem, is it?"

He reached out and grabbed her forearm. "Don't go."

His touch felt warm and strong and seemed to wrap itself not only around her arm, but around her bruised heart, too. Jennifer stopped short and lifted her gaze to look into amber eyes the exact color of fine, aged brandy. Her heartbeat stuttered slightly. His jaw looked as though it had been carved of granite. His nose had obviously been broken at least once sometime in the past. His brown hair was military-short, but even at that, there was a slight wave to it that made a woman want to stroke her fingers through it.

And good Lord, he was tall. With shoulders broad enough to balance the world. Today she could surely use a pair of shoulders broad enough to lean on. But Jennifer was too used to standing on her own two feet to take advantage of a near stranger in a weak moment.

As if he could read her mind though, he said, "I didn't mean to intrude, but now that I'm here, why not let me help if I can?"

Tempting, she thought. Oh, so tempting. But no. She shook her head. "I appreciate it, but—"

"I'm a stranger."

"Well," she said, "yes."

"Sometimes that's better." He kept his grip on her forearm as if he expected her to scurry for the door. Which she would have done, given half a chance. Then he smiled and her stomach flipped over. "Telling your troubles to a stranger is like talking to yourself. Only you don't have to answer your own questions and run the risk of being locked in a padded room."

A return smile tickled the corners of her mouth and she had to fight to keep it from blossoming. Which was a good thing actually, since she hadn't had a thing to smile about since talking to her daughter's doctors yesterday. And that stray thought was enough to wipe the beginnings of humor from her face.

A cold, empty well opened up inside her and she felt her heart slide into it.

"Hey," he said, letting his hand slide from her forearm up to her shoulder, where his fingers squeezed gently. "Come on. Talk to me. Maybe I can help." He dipped his head a bit and gave her another half smile. "I'm a SEAL. Trained to be a hero. So let me ride to the rescue here, okay?"

Jennifer glanced over her shoulder at the party just beyond the glass doors, then turned back to look at him again. What the heck, she thought. She *could* use a shoulder at the moment. And his were certainly broad enough to hold up under her assault.

"It's my daughter," she blurted before she could change her mind.

His gaze darkened slightly. "You have a daughter?"

"Yes." Just the thought of Sarah brought up her image in Jennifer's mind and she smiled to herself. Big brown eyes in a round little face that was usually smudged with dirt. Pigtails that were really no more than tiny wisps of light-brown hair caught up in barrettes at either side of her head. Small, pudgy hands and short, sturdy legs. Butterfly kisses and sticky-fingered hugs. Tickle bugs and belly laughs.

Doctors in white coats, long, dangerous-looking needles and Sarah's tears.

"Oh, God," Jennifer half moaned and clapped her hand to her mouth again, not sure if she was going to be sick or start screaming.

It was all just so damned unfair.

"Come here," Chance said, turning her as he spoke, shifting to hold her, wrap his arms around her.

And because she needed a hug so badly, she went.

Nestled against that wide chest, she hung on for a long moment, wrapping her arms around his waist and drawing on the strength he so casually offered. She felt him awkwardly patting her back and for some silly reason, it helped. Though she knew it didn't actually change anything, the physical act of being comforted soothed the frayed edges of her soul, and just for an instant, the world didn't seem as terrifying as it had only minutes ago.

"Tell me," he said, his voice a gruff whisper coming from somewhere above her head. "Tell me what's wrong."

"Sarah," she said, saying the words aloud for the first time since the doctor had so clinically outlined the trouble the day before, "my baby. She needs an operation. On her heart. There's a small hole in it."

"Aah…" A comforting sound, more of a deep breath released, maybe, but it too helped. She felt his sympathy in the gentle tightening of his grip on her. "How old is she?"

"Eighteen months," she whispered, looking past him to the lake, but really looking at her mind's-eye picture of Sarah. "She's so small. So tiny. This shouldn't be happening."

"No, it shouldn't," he said softly. "It sucks."

Jennifer nodded. "Yes," she said, grateful to hear someone else say what she'd been thinking, "it does."

Two

Chance wasn't a family kind of man by any means. But he felt Jennifer's fear as if it were his own. It rattled through her small body with the force of a freight train and shook him to his bones.

His every instinct told him to rush in and defend. Protect. But none of his training would do a damn sight of good here. And that realization was a bitter pill to choke down.

Hell, he couldn't even think of something helpful to say. It sucks? Real eloquent, Chance.

He continued to hold her though, hoping his silent support helped in some way. Strange, a few days ago, he hadn't known or cared that any of these people existed. Now he was standing on the balcony of a *mansion,* for Pete's sake, holding a weeping woman.

"What am I doing?" Jennifer muttered as she pulled back out of his arms and took another step away from him just for good measure. "I'm going to rain mascara all over your white uniform."

No she wouldn't, he thought, looking into those forest-green eyes of hers. They were big and wet and sad, but there was no smudge of dark makeup around them. Just the remnants of tears she was fighting to control. Damned if he didn't admire her for that, too.

She could be wallowing in the fear that was close to strangling her, but she wasn't. Instead, she was holding herself together through the force of her will. Hell, she didn't even want sympathy. So what exactly was it he could do for her?

"Do you want to go back inside?" he asked.

"God no," she said, shaking her head and moving back to the railing. Keeping her face averted from both him and the sliding glass doors behind them, she said, "I don't want them to know I've been crying. I just couldn't take the questions right now."

Privacy. Something else he could understand. Well, if he couldn't escort her through the maze of party-goers, he could at least make her eventual trip inside a little easier. "Okay. Just wait here, then. I'll be back."

Before she could say anything, he opened the sliding glass doors and stepped back into the party. Noise assaulted him and he instantly missed the relative peace and quiet of the balcony.

Focused, Chance paid no attention to the people around him. He moved through the crowd as if he were on a mission. He kept his goal in mind and went about accomplishing it as quickly as he could. Which wasn't as easy as he'd expected. There were just too many people.

He cast one quick, nearly wistful glance at the front door, then forgot about leaving and went on with his quest.

When he walked into the kitchen, the folks in there looked as surprised as they would have if lightning had struck the butcher-block work island in the center of the massive room.

"Can I help you, Mr. Chance?"

Grateful, he looked to the woman on his right. Mentally, he scrambled for her name and came up with it an instant later.

"Ruby, right?" he asked.

"That's me," the housekeeper said, giving him a nod sharp enough to shake loose a graying red curl from her topknot to lie askew in the middle of her forehead.

In the few days he'd been in town, Chance had

seen this woman running the Connelly household—
and family, for that matter—with an iron fist. Grant
and Emma might think they were in charge, but the
truth was, Ruby was the brass around here.

The short, slightly rounded woman with kind
blue eyes had the ability to get things done, and
Chance appreciated that. Even while keeping under
radar, staying unnoticed himself. He'd seen how his
half brothers and sisters scampered when Ruby
gave an order. Hell, even his father, Grant, didn't
argue when she laid down the law.

Clearly, she'd been in charge so long, she never
even considered the possibility that people wouldn't
obey her without question. In the military, she
might have made it to the Joint Chiefs of Staff.
Here, she ran the Connelly household like a well-
oiled machine and wouldn't accept anything less.

"Now, how can I help you?" she asked, snatching his attention as she would have the hand of a
child inclined to wander off.

Chance glanced around at the others clustered
within hearing distance, reluctant to speak up with
so many eager ears nearby. The housekeeper noticed and clapped her hands sharply. "What are you
bunch staring at? Get about your business. Don't
you have drinks and canapés you could be serv-
ing?"

They scattered like windblown leaves, and, in

seconds, he was alone in the room with Ruby. "I'm impressed," he said.

"For running them off? Don't be. I am sorry about them, though," the woman said, with a shake of her head. "They're day help for the party and their mamas apparently forgot to teach them any manners."

He smiled. "I have a feeling you'll take care of that."

She straightened up and puffed out her chest. "I'll do my best in the short time I have them," she assured him. "So what is it you need, Mr. Chance?"

He winced a little at the implied title. Now, people calling him "Commander," he'd earned. He could even live with "Hey, sailor," but "Mr. Chance"? No way. That was just way too highfalutin. "Just, Chance, all right?"

One corner of her mouth twitched, but she only nodded. "Chance it is, then." She studied him for a long minute, then said, "You know, you've the look of your father around the eyes. More so than your brother does."

Chance shifted uncomfortably. He didn't necessarily want to be reminded that he looked like the man who'd managed to ignore both him and his brother their whole lives. What was he supposed to say to that, anyway? Thank you didn't seem appropriate somehow. So he ignored the comment entirely.

After all, it wasn't as if he'd come here looking to find family. He already had his family. Douglas. With the death of their mother, all they had left was each other. And that had always been enough before.

The only reason he was here at all was as a favor to Doug. And if he hadn't been shot by that sneaky little terrorist on his last mission, he wouldn't have had to put up with any of the pomp and circumstance surrounding the Connellys. But then, he wouldn't have been here to ride to Jennifer's rescue, either, would he?

And that thought returned him to why he'd come to the kitchen in the first place.

"Any chance I could get a glass of water and a box of tissues?" he asked.

Ruby narrowed her eyes thoughtfully as she looked at him. "Feel a crying jag coming on, do you?"

Chance played along. "Yes, ma'am. I'm feeling real emotional."

She snorted. "Yeah, I can see that." But without another word, she bustled around the room and came back with just what he'd asked for. As he turned to leave the room, though, her voice stopped him. "You tell Jennifer for me that everything's going to be all right."

He looked at her. Shouldn't be surprised, he thought. He'd already discovered that nothing much went on around here that Ruby didn't know about. "What?"

"I've been with the Connellys for more years than I care to admit. Not much gets past me. I know there's something wrong."

Nodding, he told her, "You would have made a good admiral."

"Phooey," she said, waving one hand to dismiss him. "Admirals are small stuff. I'd have made a good president."

"You know something?" he said, giving her a wink, "I believe you." Then he slipped from the room before she could give him any orders he'd be too afraid not to follow.

"Oh, this is good," Jennifer told herself aloud as she clutched the balcony railing and stared out at Lake Michigan. "Way to ensure your employment, Jen." Shaking her head, she blinked back tears that still threatened and solemnly vowed they wouldn't fall. She'd already screwed up big-time.

What had she been thinking? Crying on the shoulder of the guest of honor at her employer's party. The one time she indulged in a good old-fashioned pity party, she had to be caught by Mr. Tall, Dark and Dangerous.

"For goodness' sake," she grumbled, tightening

her grip on the cold iron railing. She lifted her face into the wind sweeping in off the lake and told herself that if she was very lucky, the newest addition to the Connelly family would keep her embarrassing behavior to himself.

Although, for all she knew he was inside now, trying to get Emma to come out and comfort her, readily handing off the crazed secretary to someone else. She could almost imagine him, stalking through the party, heading for the front door as fast as he could. And she couldn't really blame him, either.

What man wanted to be a human tissue for a weeping woman? Especially one he hardly knew.

Behind her, the glass door slid open, allowing a brief pulse of conversation and piano music onto the balcony, and in an instant, the door closed again, sealing off the intrusion.

She didn't turn around. She didn't have to. She knew who it was. She *felt* his presence almost as an electrical charge. Her nerve endings hummed and the hairs at the back of her neck stood straight up.

Probably not a good sign.

"Sorry I took so long," he said and darned if his voice didn't scrape along those already tense nerves.

Get a grip, Jen. He's your boss's stepson. He's a stranger. He doesn't give a damn about your problems and there's nothing between you but an embarrassing crying jag.

So why was her stomach suddenly in knots and her breath coming fast and hard?

Because you're an idiot, she told herself just before turning to look at him.

Well, that didn't help any. He was just too darned good-looking, that was the problem. He looked like a poster boy for navy recruiting. Or like one of those navy lawyers on that television show. His uniform shone a bright white against the backdrop of the blue lake and shimmering April sky. The ribbons decorating his chest drew her eye as did the SEAL pin he wore proudly. Then she looked farther up, into his eyes, and saw...concern. And that nearly did her in on the spot.

Darn it.

"You okay?" he asked.

"Oh, dandy," she told him and sniffed.

He held out the box of tissues and she gratefully snatched one free of the dispenser. She wiped her eyes, blew her nose and still didn't feel better.

"Here, drink this." He offered the tall, pale-blue glass he carried.

"What is it?" she asked as she reached for it. "Hemlock?"

"Nothing so deadly," he said with a half laugh. "Just water."

She took a drink, letting the liquid soothe her

tight throat before trying to talk again. Lifting her gaze to his, she said, "Thank you. For the tissue and the water."

"Here to serve, ma'am," he said.

"But I bet you didn't expect to have to go above and beyond the call at a party."

He shrugged. "Hey, a party, a terrorist situation—the SEALS can handle it all."

"Good to know," she muttered, then, still clutching her glass of water, turned around again to stare out at the lake. She couldn't keep looking at him. That just wasn't good for her equilibrium. Way better on her nerves to stare out at a lake the size of an ocean, its choppy waves slapping toward Lake Shore Drive.

"Tell me about your daughter," he said quietly and Jennifer's eyes closed briefly on a twinge of something as painful as it was tender.

But she supposed she owed him this, for crying all over him.

"Sarah's so smart," she said, and though her voice started out thin and trembling, talking about her pride and joy strengthened it. Shaking her head, she continued, "She started talking before she was a year old and now she's already arguing with me." Jennifer chuckled, and the sound grated against her throat. "When she's a teenager—" *when* not *if,* she told herself silently "—we'll probably lock horns all the time."

"Probably," he said agreeably. "God knows Doug and I drove our poor mother nuts when we were teenagers. Of course your Sarah most likely won't be into drag racing, so that's one worry you won't have."

She flicked him a glance, not at all surprised by his little admission. He was a SEAL, after all. And clearly he loved his job. So it naturally followed that as a kid, he would have sought out dangerous pastimes.

Just like Mike, she thought with an inward acknowledgment of old pain. The two of them would have gotten along great together, no doubt. Then, as if he'd sensed what she was thinking, the man beside her spoke up again.

"Your husband must be just as proud of her as you are," Chance said.

"My husband's dead," she said, tasting the words it had taken her so long to get used to saying.

"Oh. I'm sorry," he said.

"You didn't know," she said softly. "No reason to be sorry. He's been gone almost two years now." She sighed heavily. "He never even knew Sarah."

A long uncomfortable minute passed before he said, "I was raised by a single mother," he said. "I know how hard it is."

She looked up at him, into those whiskey-colored eyes and read understanding there. And darn it, she appreciated it. Though Emma was beyond kind and a good friend as well as an employer, she couldn't really appreciate what it was like to be the sole person responsible for raising a child. Not when she had Grant, as much in love with her today as he had been years ago.

Then he said, "If you don't mind my asking, how did your husband die?"

"Mike was a police officer," she said, lifting her chin just a bit. "He was killed in the line of duty. I was still pregnant with Sarah when he died. He never even *saw* her."

"Maybe he did," Chance said and she looked at him. "Maybe he sees her every day."

"I'd like to think so."

"I've seen enough things over the years to convince me that anything's possible." He paused for a long minute, then said, "I never knew my father, either." Then he stopped and laughed shortly. "At least, not until a few days ago."

She shook her head in sympathy, though she was glad to turn the subject away from Mike. "I can't even imagine what that must be like," she said, choosing her words carefully now. "Finding your blood father after so many years…"

He nodded, lifting his face into the cold, sharp wind. "I know what you mean. I'm not real sure how I feel about it, either. But," he said, giving a quick look over his shoulder, "it meant something to Doug, so here I am."

"You only came here for your brother's sake?"

"Why else?"

"To get to know your family?"

"Nah. My mother's gone now, so my family is Doug. The rest…" He shook his head again as if he didn't know quite what else to say.

"The Connellys are nice people," Jennifer said, wanting him to know that this new family of his was ready and willing to welcome him.

"Seem to be."

"They've been wonderful to me and Sarah."

He gave her a slow smile. "If your daughter's anything like you, I can't see that that would be a hardship."

Oh, that smile was just as dangerous as the man, she told herself, taking a mental step backward. She didn't need this kind of complication right now. Her world was Sarah. Her attentions had to be devoted to making her little girl well again. And to help her keep her attentions focused, she knew the best thing to do was to keep her distance from this man.

"I, uh—" She glanced at the sliding glass doors with real regret. Though she knew she had to leave the balcony, she wasn't looking forward to making small talk while her heart was aching. Still, this party was a big deal for Grant and Emma. Hadn't Jennifer and her employer been planning it for weeks? No, heartache or not, she had to do her job.

"I'd better get back inside," she said and even she heard the reluctance in her voice.

Chance straightened away from the railing and looked from the doors to her. She wasn't ready to go back in there and face the chattering mob. He could see it in her eyes. The vulnerability was still there, etched deep.

It was none of his business, of course, but still, he felt a kinship of sorts with her. She was a single mother, as his own mom had been. Her husband had served the public, his country, as Chance did, only *he* had paid the ultimate price. A rising wave of protectiveness filled him and before he could think more of it, he said, "I think the party can get along without either of us. So why don't you let me take you home instead?"

She thought about it for a long minute, and he could see in her eyes just how much she wanted to get out of here. The question was, would she?

"As much as I'd like to," she said, "I don't think I should—"

"With that crowd in there, no one will even miss us."

"Emma would."

He acknowledged that with a brief nod. "Okay, then, we'll stop and tell her we're leaving. I should say thanks, anyway."

Now that her objections were taken care of, all that was stopping her from taking him up on his offer was the fact that he was a virtual stranger—long-lost relative of her employer or not. "You can trust me," he said softly.

Her lips twitched slightly. "It's not that," she said.

"Then what? I'm just offering you a ride home, not a weekend trip to Jamaica." Why was he trying so hard to convince her? He wasn't sure. All he knew was that suddenly he needed to be the one to see her safely to her door.

She looked beyond the glass doors again to the party, and he saw her shudder. She really didn't want to go back in there. And damned if he could blame her. He had no interest in rejoining the mob, either.

And playing on that feeling, he said, "You'd be doing me a favor."

"What?"

He smiled. "You'd be rescuing me from mingling."

Her lips twitched. "A fate worse than death?"

"Oh, definitely."

She nodded, and he knew this battle was won. "Well," she said, her decision made, "I suppose I shouldn't turn down my one chance to be a hero."

Three

A thick wall of noise welcomed them back inside the Connelly mansion, and for one brief moment, Jennifer thought about turning tail and disappearing again onto the balcony. But it wouldn't do any good. She had to make it through the minefield of the party to make good her escape at some point anyway. Better to do it now, when she had a tall, imposing man striding beside her, subtly clearing a path.

Faces flashed past as Chance steered her through the crowd with one strong hand at the small of her back. His touch felt warm, comforting, somehow. Strange, but she hadn't experienced that little nicety since Mike's death and she hadn't realized how much she had missed it. But then, she'd realized over the last couple of years that it was the small things that, once they were gone, left the biggest holes.

Now there was no one to hold her chair out for her at a nice restaurant. No one who knew how to whistle for a cab loudly enough to gather up a regular cluster of them. No one to kill a spider in the bathroom in the middle of the night. No one to warm her feet on, or to whisper to in the movies. No one to care for, to cook for, to worry about.

A wistful smile crossed her face. Of course, any self-respecting women's libber would have a heart attack if she could read Jennifer's mind. But she didn't care. She had always considered herself pretty liberated, but when it came right down to it, she'd *liked* being married. She'd *liked* being half of a team. And sometimes she missed that feeling so much, a slow, deep ache wrapped itself around her heart.

But then all it would take was one sweet smile from Sarah and everything was all right again. Silently, she reminded herself that she would never be alone again, not really. Not as long as she and Sarah had each other.

And that thought made her think of the heart operation her baby needed, and tears welled up in her eyes. It didn't seem to make a difference that the doctors all assured her that it would be a simple thing, as operations went. That though any procedure carried risks, Sarah had an excellent chance at a full and complete recovery.

Because no matter the kind words and assurances, Sarah was her baby. Her family. And the thought of losing her was simply too much to contemplate. She couldn't even imagine a world without her little girl in it—so she didn't. Jennifer blinked frantically, slammed a mental door on the dark, worrisome thoughts and hurried her steps. All she wanted now was to get out of here before she could be bombarded with concerned questions.

"There they are," Chance muttered, bending his head close to her ear.

Her gaze shifted to the right and she saw Grant and Emma Connelly, having what looked to be a very involved discussion with Seth. None of them looked very happy.

Jennifer slowed down instinctively, not wanting to intrude on what was obviously a strained moment. Shaking her head, she shot a glance up at the man beside her. "It looks like they're busy. Maybe we shouldn't interrupt."

He took her upper arm in a firm, but gentle grip and gave her a smile. "We won't interrupt them for long. Then they can go back to whatever it is that's got them all frowning so."

As they approached the threesome, Jennifer overheard Seth saying, "I just have to go and see her. I don't want to hurt you, Mom," he said to Emma, "but Angie Donahue is my birth mother. And I have to know why she suddenly wants to see me." He reached for Emma's hand and gave it a squeeze. "I'll be fine. I promise. And I'll be back."

Through teary eyes, Emma glanced at Grant, who kept his gaze focused on the young man in front of him, as though, if he studied him hard enough, he'd be able to pull the thoughts from Seth's mind. Finally, though, the elder Connelly said gruffly, "You do what you have to do, son. We're behind you all the way. Just like always. And we'll be here waiting for you when you come home."

Whatever the boy might have said in response was lost when Emma noticed Chance and Jennifer approaching. She smiled in welcome and made shooing gestures at Seth with both hands.

"And what are you two up to?" she asked as they came closer.

"I just wanted to say thank you, ma'am, for your hospitality," Chance said, then added, "and to say goodbye."

"Goodbye?" Grant asked abruptly. "Already?"

Jennifer's gaze flicked from father to son and though she knew Chance probably wouldn't be happy to hear it, she privately acknowledged just how much he looked like his biological father. But it wasn't just their features they shared. Both of the men had an air of self-confidence about them that people naturally gravitated toward.

It was part of the reason Grant had done so well in the business world—and why Chance would inevitably continue his rise through the ranks. No doubt one day he'd be an admiral. Men like the Connellys were born conquerors. All that differed were the prizes they sought.

"Jennifer's not feeling well," Chance was saying, "so I offered to take her home."

"Aah…" Grant nodded thoughtfully as his gaze flicked from his son to Jennifer and back again.

Jennifer felt her cheeks warm up at the knowing gleam in Grant's eyes, so she spoke up quickly. "I, uh—" think fast, Jen "—have a headache," she finished. Well, that was brilliant. But she didn't want to go into Sarah's medical problems now. Not at the party. "Commander Barnett was kind enough to offer me a ride."

"Barnett?" Grant stared at the man who was his son.

A touchy subject, Jennifer knew. Chance quite naturally wanted to keep the name he knew. The name his mother had given him. Grant, just as naturally, wanted his sons to use his name.

It would be interesting to see who eventually won this little tug-of-war.

"Sir," Chance said, holding his right hand out to his father, "thank you. It was a nice party."

Grant harrumphed. "You hated it."

"Pretty much," Chance acknowledged.

"Knew you would. Too much like me."

Chance nodded shortly. "Maybe."

Grant dropped one arm around his wife's shoulders. "Emma's the party-giver around here. Loves the hustle and bustle. She just tells me when to show up."

Emma gave his broad chest a playful slap, before looking at Chance. "It's true, you know. He'd much rather be out taking over small companies or sailing, or…well, just about anything."

Jennifer watched as a small smile curved Chance's lips, and to her surprise, a curl of something delightful spiraled through her in response. Oh, that probably wasn't a good sign.

"Then maybe we are more alike than I'd thought," Chance allowed as Grant took his outstretched hand and gave it a firm shake.

His father smiled. "I'll settle for a maybe. For now."

"Seems fair," Chance told him.

"All right, then," Emma spoke up. "Jennifer, I hope you're feeling better tomorrow. Why don't you take the day off?"

"Oh, that won't be—"

"A day off's not going to bring the world to an end," her employer told her firmly. Then she shifted a look at Chance. "You drive carefully.

Without Jennifer, I'd never get a thing done around here.''

"Yes, ma'am,'' Chance said, and in seconds he had Jennifer turned around and headed for the front door. They skirted the edges of the party and avoided being stopped again. Their steps clicked on the cold marble of the main staircase, then echoed as they moved into the grand entry hall on the main floor. Here, the marble gleamed and shone in the spill of late-afternoon sunshine slashing through the wide front windows. Chance left her just long enough to grab their coats, and once she was bundled up, he ushered her outside into the bite of the cold Chicago wind.

"I'm parked just up the street,'' he said. "Why don't you wait here and I'll go get the car?''

"Thanks, I'd rather walk.''

"Suit yourself,'' he said smiling, then offered her his arm.

Arms linked, they took the short flight of steps to the sidewalk below, crossed the narrow strip of lawn and turned onto Michigan Avenue.

"I can't believe you found a place to park around here.''

He grinned at her and Jennifer sucked in a breath. That really was a devastating weapon he had tucked away. Thankfully, her defenses had been strengthened over the last two years.

"I'm a SEAL, remember? We excel at the impossible."

"I'll keep that in mind."

While they walked, he talked, as if somehow sensing that she wasn't in the mood to discuss her problems anymore tonight. She listened to stories of his and Doug's childhood, heard the pride in his voice when he talked about his mother and what she'd managed to accomplish all on her own. She hoped that one day Sarah would be as kind when talking about her.

God knows, she tried to be both mom and dad. But it wasn't easy. Despite having a great job with the most understanding employer in the free world, Jennifer was pushed every day, wondering how to get everything done. She had no idea at all how women with less going for them managed to survive.

"It must have been so hard for her," she finally said, looking up at him. The wind blew strands of blond hair across her face and she plucked them out of her way so she could see him clearly.

He stared off into the distance as if looking into years past and nodded. "Yeah, it was," he said, "but we didn't know that at the time. She made it look so easy. Mom wasn't the kind to sit around and whine about finding herself. Or wishing that things were different. She used to say that the only thing you could change in life was yourself. So do the best you can.''

''Smart woman.''

''Oh, yeah.'' He turned his head to look down at her and gave her yet another of those great smiles. ''She would have liked you.''

''Really? Why's that?''

''Because your daughter's so important to you.''

Something clutched at her heart, but Jennifer only said, ''She's everything to me.''

''I can see that.''

''That easy to read, huh?''

''Does the phrase *an open book* mean anything to you?''

Jennifer laughed in spite of herself. She'd never had much of a poker face. ''Mike used to say the reason I was so honest was because I just couldn't pull off a lie.''

''Good a reason as any,'' he said and stopped alongside a cherry-red SUV.

''This is yours?'' she asked and wondered why she was even surprised. If this wasn't a guy's car, she'd eat it.

''Rental,'' he said and opened her door. Holding it for her as she got in, he added, ''I'm just in town for a while.''

She automatically reached for the shoulder harness. ''Where do you go when you leave here?''

''Back to my SEAL team.''

"And then?"

"Won't know until just before I go."

He slammed the door, walked around the front of the car, then opened the driver's-side door. Sliding onto the front seat, he latched his seat belt, stuck the key in the ignition and turned it. The engine leapt into life with a muffled rumble of sound.

Shifting slightly in his seat, he winced and Jennifer asked, "Are you okay?"

"Yeah," he said. "I just keep forgetting to move slow. Think I pulled a few stitches is all."

Stitches? The question must have been written on her face, because he gave her a shrug and an it's-no-big-deal look before saying, "Took a hit on my last mission."

"A *hit?*" she asked, her gaze dropping to his side as if she could see right through his uniform. "You mean you were shot?"

"It's nothing major," he said. "Just cut through the meat."

"Ah," she muttered, with a sage nod. "A *minor* gunshot wound. And did you actually call it a flesh wound at the time, in the finest John Wayne tradition?"

His brows drew together as he watched her. "What's the problem here?"

"Oh, not a thing," she said and gripped her hands together in her lap as she turned her head to stare out the windshield. Just like Mike, she thought. They were cut from the same cloth. Dangerous jobs. Dismissive of hazards. No big deal. How could any sane person think it was no big deal to face the possibility of death as a matter of course? What was it that drove men—and some women—to take jobs that threatened their lives?

"Jennifer," he said, over the low roar of the engine, "you want to tell me what's got you so tense all of a sudden?"

She swiveled her head to look at him. The planes and hollows of his face stood out in stark relief. He looked hard and dangerous—but for the gentleness she could still read in his eyes.

"I don't get it," she finally blurted. "What is it about you guys?"

"Us guys?" he repeated, a half smile on his face. "Care to be more specific?"

"Men like you. And Mike."

"Your husband."

"My *late* husband," she corrected, then muttered, "I don't know why that phrase is used. It's not like he's going to be on time somewhere. He isn't late, for heaven's sake. He's dead."

"Jennifer—"

"No, I want to know," she said, meeting his gaze and holding it. "What is it that makes you deliberately seek out the kind of profession that endangers your lives? Is it for the thrills? The rush of constant peril?"

His mouth tightened briefly. "I've spent years in training to do my job, and I'm guessing your husband did, too. You don't put in that kind of effort just for the thrill of it."

"Then why?" she asked, knowing he was right. Mike had worked hard at being a police officer. He'd loved it. Had lived, breathed and eventually *died* for it. She couldn't ask him why now, so she wanted an answer from this man who lived his life the same way.

"To serve," he said softly, simply. "To help. To fight for my country. Sounds corny, huh? But that's the plain truth of it."

His words seemed to echo in the enclosed space as he went on.

"Military or cop, we do what has to be done. It's not for some rush," he said and added, "and I think you know that. It's not an easy life, but it's the only one I know. Or want. And I'm guessing it was the same for your husband."

Jennifer drew one long, shuddering breath and released it. Watching him, listening to him, she knew he was right. Felt it. And a part of her even agreed with him. But admitting that brave men were necessary and actually living with one were two different things. She'd put in her time in the trenches. She'd worried every time Mike left the house. And it hadn't kept him alive.

She wasn't interested in living with that kind of fear again.

No. There was only one person in her life now. Her daughter. And thoughts of Sarah were all she had time for. Anything else would just be a distraction right now. A distraction she didn't need.

Even if it was six feet two inches of solidly packed muscle encased in a snow-white naval uniform.

Four

"Turn right here," she said and watched the familiar neighborhood pass as Chance steered the SUV down her street. Oak Park, Illinois, came by its name honestly, she thought, not for the first time.

Ancient oaks lined nearly every street, stretching long, leafy arms across the avenues to form what in summer, were cool green tunnels that blunted the steamy heat. Now the first of the new leaves were just beginning to sprout, and the skeletal trees rattled their limbs together in the wind as if clamoring for their new spring outfits.

Jennifer smiled to herself as she noted the sidewalks that rolled up and down like cement waves.

Unlike other big cities, where the slightest bump in a sidewalk meant death to the offending tree, here city workers just slapped fresh cement atop the protruding roots. They protected their trees and the city was the better for it.

"It's a nice street," Chance said and she gave him a quick glance.

"Yes, it is," she agreed, and inwardly cringed. Well, one sure way to discourage him was to bore him to tears. But in her own defense, with thoughts of Sarah constantly simmering in her mind, it was hard to try to make conversation.

So instead of even trying, she looked at the houses as they passed. Some were like hers, old, with wide front porches supported by stone pillars. Others were brand-new, boasting lots of glass and sharp angles. Not too long ago the neighborhood had been dying, but in recent years young professionals had discovered the beauty of Oak Park and had infused it with new life. It was practically trendy now, and if Mike hadn't inherited their house from his late aunt, they never would have been able to afford to live there. "Frank Lloyd Wright's house is just around the corner."

"The architect?"

"Uh-huh," she said. "It's a lovely place even if it is a little on the modern side for me."

He slanted her a long glance. "Just an old-fashioned girl, are you?"

She shifted in her seat and folded her hands in her lap. "About some things, I guess," she admitted. "Like these old bungalow-type homes. They're just cozier...warmer somehow. They've got character."

"I think I know what you mean," he said, and she turned to look at him. He gave her a half smile. "The older places have weathered the storms. They've earned the right to be here."

An interesting way to put it, she thought. But so true. "I guess that's it," she said. "Some of these places have been here more than fifty years. Sheltering families, withstanding tornadoes—and all they need is a little care. A part of me even feels sorry for the poor houses that are torn down to make way for some spanking new glass-and-chrome disaster."

He laughed then. "A romantic. Who would have thought it?"

Romantic? Nope. Not her. Maybe once, she thought, remembering how young and naive she'd been when she'd married Mike. She'd looked at the world through rose-colored glasses. When they'd moved into his late aunt's cozy bungalow on this street, she'd assumed that they'd still be sitting on the front porch together when they were eighty.

But that plan had been buried with Mike, and now she considered herself more of a realist than a romantic. No more believing in happily ever after

for *this* girl. Her fairy tale had ended. But there was
no point in explaining all of that to Chance Barnett.
He wouldn't be around long enough to care. He'd
made no secret of the fact that he was itching to be
gone. A couple more weeks and he'd be off living
his dangerous life—which was just as well, she
thought. Because she—she would still be here, trying to walk a minefield while carrying precious
cargo.

And just the thought of Sarah was enough to
bring her right back to the terrifying reality that was
now her life.

"The house on the left is mine," she said
abruptly, lifting one hand to point. "The blue one,
with the wagon in front of the steps."

Her heart seized briefly as she realized that there
was a very real chance that Sarah and her wagons
and toys—the same ones Jennifer complained about
being left all over—might not be a part of her life
much longer. But no. She wouldn't even entertain
the possibility. Hadn't the doctor told her this was
a relatively simple operation? Hadn't he assured her
that though there were always risks involved in surgery, this one was practically a cookie-cutter job?

Cookie-cutter.

How could anything requiring her daughter's tiny
chest to be opened be considered cookie-cutter?

Tears leapt into her eyes and she blinked them
back as Chance pulled into the driveway. Parked

directly in front of them was her own car, still listing to one side on its flat rear tire. She'd come outside that morning to find it like that, which explained why she'd been at the Connelly mansion with no ride home.

And why she was now sitting here beside a man whose very presence was a distraction she so didn't need at the moment.

He put the car into Park and turned off the motor. Instantly, a rush of silence filled the car and the only sounds came from a group of kids two doors down playing basketball against a garage. The steady thump of the bouncing ball felt almost like a heartbeat, and the minute that thought raced into her brain, Jennifer pushed it out again.

"Looks like your car had an adventure," he said quietly.

At his words, she smiled in spite of herself. "When I was little, I used to think that when their owners were asleep, cars would take off on their own. You know, go for drives along the beach, meet up with other cars at the garage to share a quart of oil."

He chuckled.

"Apparently," she said on a sigh, "*my* car took a bad bump somewhere along the road."

"So why didn't you fix it?"

"Gee," she said, giving her forehead a light slap, "why didn't I think of that?"

"Dumb question, huh?"

"No," she said, "not really." After all, since Mike's death, she'd had to take care of lots of things on her own. Like stopped-up sinks or blown fuses. "I should be able to do it, but I just haven't taken my tire-changing class yet."

"How about I do it for you?"

She flicked him a quick glance. A part of her longed to say, That'd be great. But the smarter side of her knew that she didn't need to be indebted any further to Chance Barnett Connelly. Actually, the more distance she kept between herself and a man who could start her blood simmering with a look, the better. "No, that's okay. Thanks, but you really don't have to."

"I know I don't have to," he said, snatching the keys from the ignition and palming them. "But it's no big deal."

"Right," she said, grabbing for the door latch, "and black grease would look great on those dress whites of yours."

A moment ticked by before he gave her a wide, sheepish grin.

Something inside her turned over with a loud thud and slapped hard against her heart. Good grief.

He shrugged and said, "Oh, yeah. Forgot about that. Guess I'm really not in my best mechanic's outfit."

No, she thought, but his heartbreaker outfit looked just fine. Too fine.

And on that thought, she spoke up. "Well," she said, unhooking her shoulder strap and reaching for her purse on the floor, "thanks for the ride."

He opened his car door and got out, then walked around to her side of the car. She watched him come with an inward sigh. Apparently he wasn't going to just drop her off and race away. And she wasn't entirely sure how she felt about that.

He wasn't good for her equilibrium. Oh, he seemed nice enough, but for heaven's sake, she hardly knew him. Yet in the last few hours she'd wept all over his uniform—and Jennifer *never* cried—plus, she'd felt...*stirrings* deep within her and darn it, she wasn't interested in stirring anything but a pot of soup.

So, it was time to tell the navy man to go for a long sail to...somewhere. All she wanted now was to get inside, alone, check on Sarah and make a cup of tea.

Chance opened her door for her and extended one hand to help her down. Jennifer looked at his open palm for a long minute, trying to decide if she should take it or struggle out of the oversize car on her own. Instantly, an image of herself, skirt riding high on her thighs as she slid inelegantly from the too-high car, shot through her mind and just like that, her decision was made.

"Thanks," she said and slipped her hand into his. Warmth skittered up the length of her arm and splintered inside her chest, sending shafts of heat dancing throughout her body. His fingers curled around hers and she felt his grip right down to her bones.

"My pleasure," he murmured, his gaze meeting and holding hers.

Uh-oh.

The minute her feet hit the driveway, she pulled her hand free, but it didn't help. She felt his touch anyway, as surely as if he was still holding on to her. Curling her fingers into her palm, she deliberately ignored the sensation and gave him her best, brightest, phoniest smile.

"Well," she said, then paused to swallow hard and lower her voice just a notch or two, "I guess I'd better go inside now."

"I'll walk you to your door."

"That's not necessary," she began but saw the determination in his eyes, and knew that she wouldn't be getting rid of him that easily. Nodding, she headed for the front door, listening to the sounds of his footsteps right behind her. And she couldn't help wondering if the *S* in SEAL stood for Stubborn.

Or maybe Sexy.

Oh, good grief.

She pulled the screen door open and walked quickly across the wide front porch.

Chance watched her. Hell, he couldn't *stop* watching her. The sway of her hips, the brush of her hair against the collar of her dress, the trim line of calf and ankle. And then there was the vulnerable shine in her green eyes. Damn, the woman was enough to bring the strongest man to his knees.

And he wasn't exactly in peak condition at the moment.

When she stopped at the closed front door, he took just a moment to look around the cozy little screened-in porch. Rag rugs dotted the cement floor that had been painted a glossy barn-red. Dolls had been plunked down at a tiny table set for an imaginary tea party, and he felt a tug of tenderness for the sick little girl he'd yet to meet.

Chance shifted his gaze back to the woman in front of him and admiration for her crowded inside him. He knew exactly how hard her life was. His own mother had worked herself to an early death taking care of him and Douglas. He remembered how tight money had always been and how tired his mother usually was. But he also recalled clearly what it felt like to be loved unconditionally.

Recalling the look in Jennifer's green eyes when she'd told him about her daughter's problems, Chance knew that whatever Sarah's medical situa-

tion was, she at least could count on her mother's
love.

But on the heels of that thought came other memories. Memories of the men his mother had dated
and the way Chance had felt about them as they
filed through their lives with numbing regularity.
He couldn't blame his mother for wanting to find
love. But he did blame those men for pretending to
care about him and Doug and then disappearing
without a backward glance when the relationship
ended.

He'd long ago made a vow to steer clear of single
mothers himself. He wasn't going to be one of those
guys who blasted through a kid's life leaving behind nothing but a memory and a string of broken
promises. And until today he'd kept that vow.

So what in the hell was he doing here?

Jennifer opened the door and stepped inside. Before he could ask himself too many more uncomfortable questions, Chance followed.

The first thing he noticed were the toys. Dolls
and coloring books and stuffed animals littered the
floor. The front door opened directly into the living
room and from where he stood, he could see everything. Well-worn, overstuffed furniture crowded
the small space and somehow managed to look inviting, rather than cramped. Doilies graced the tops
of the highly-polished tables and a small, tidy fire
burned in the hearth across the room. The walls

were a soft peach color and dotted with framed family pictures. A doorway off to the right led into what looked like the kitchen and to the left was a darkened hallway that probably branched off into the bedrooms.

"Mrs. Sorenson?" Jennifer called out as she walked into the living room and tossed her purse onto the closest table. "I'm home."

"In here." An older, female voice answered and Jennifer headed straight for it, moving toward the hallway on the left. She seemed to have forgotten all about Chance and he knew damn well he should leave. But he didn't. Instead, he walked along behind her, despite knowing that he had no business pushing into her life any further than he had already.

Somehow, for some reason, he just wasn't ready to leave yet. And he didn't really want to think about why.

Four doorways opened off the short hall, but Jennifer made right for the last one on the right. Looking over her head, Chance could see the pale-yellow paint on the wall and what looked like a mural of daisies. Then he was in the doorway, and there he stopped while Jennifer headed straight for the crib on the far wall.

"How is she?" she asked.

A short, round woman with gray-streaked red hair and deeply-etched laugh lines gave her a smile.

"She's fine now. Wanted to play, then tuckered herself out, poor sweetie."

Jennifer reached into the crib and smoothed one hand across her daughter's dirty forehead.

"Should have cleaned her up, I know," Mrs. Sorenson was saying, "but she was just so tired, I thought, why bother?"

"It's fine," Jennifer said. "I'll clean her up later."

"Well," the woman said, picking up her paperback book from the table beside the rocking chair she'd been occupying up until a moment ago, "if you need anything, you give a shout. Although," she added thoughtfully, "it looks as though you have all the help you'll need for a while."

Jennifer glanced at her and saw the speculative gleam in her neighbor's eyes as the woman gave Chance a slow once-over. Inwardly she sighed, knowing that sooner or later, her babysitter was going to want details about the tall, gorgeous hunk of sailor standing on the threshold. But not now.

"Eva Sorenson," Jennifer said, "Commander Chance Barnett Connelly."

The older woman gave him a quick grin. "I love a man with three names."

His grin matched hers. "Then I'll keep all three of them, for sure."

"Hmm," Eva mused, "cute and quick, too." She tossed a sidelong look at Jennifer. "Watch out for this one, honey. He's probably got a half dozen girls in every port.''

''Only half a dozen?'' Chance asked, his voice teasing.

''Quality, not quantity,'' Eva retorted.

''I'll remember that.''

Briefly, she inclined her head toward Jennifer, then warned not too subtly, ''See that you do.'' Then she inhaled sharply and said to no one in particular, ''Jim'll be wanting his dinner soon, so I'd better go. You know how that man is when he isn't fed on time.''

''Cheerful?'' Jennifer asked, since she couldn't ever remember seeing anything but a smile on Jim Sorenson's broad features.

Chuckling, Eva said, ''Hey, living with a perpetual optimist isn't all a picnic, you know.''

And then she was gone, slipping out the door and leaving Chance and Jennifer alone with the sleeping child. If he had any sense at all, Chance told himself, he'd be hot on the babysitter's heels, headed for his car and then his hotel.

But apparently his brain was on vacation, because he walked farther into the room and didn't stop until he was standing beside Jennifer staring down at the little girl lying beneath a flowered quilt.

He threw a quick glance at the woman beside him and noted the worry staining her eyes despite the soft smile curving her lips. She looked up at him briefly and said, ''Chance, meet Sarah.''

Love filled her voice and Chance couldn't help being moved by it. Then he shifted his gaze to the child with the dirty face and lopsided pigtails that weren't much bigger than the barrettes holding them in place. Her tiny, rosebud mouth was parted in sleep and as he watched, she lifted one grubby little fist and rubbed her eyes before rolling onto her side. Then she blindly groped around for a battered stuffed bear that was lying just out of her reach.

Chance moved the scruffy beast with one missing ear in closer and the little girl grabbed for it, latching on to his hand instead. Her tiny fingers clutched at him and held on tight.

A long deep breath rushed from his lungs.

And just like that, he fell in love.

Five

As that thought shot through his brain, Chance jerked back as if he'd been hit by a stray bullet. Absently, he watched the tiny girl's now-empty hand reach for and grab her stuffed animal. She pulled it close, buried her nose in its ratty fur and sighed in satisfaction.

Chance shoved his hands into his pockets and tried not to notice that he could still feel the toddler's surprisingly strong grip around his fingers.

"Are you okay?" Jennifer whispered, and he threw her a quick, wary glance.

"Yeah," he said, moving another uneasy step back from the crib. "Yeah, I'm fine."

Good job, Barnett, he told himself. Hell, he'd been in dozens of tight situations. Stared down the barrels of way too many guns. Slipped into and out of hostile nations without turning a hair.

And one soft stirring for a sick little girl had him ready to bolt for cover. He pulled one hand free of his pocket and scrubbed it across his face. This he hadn't counted on.

A pretty woman. A jolt of desire. Okay. But he hadn't planned on tenderness and wasn't at all sure what to do about it now that it had entered the picture.

"You don't look okay," Jennifer said and led the way quietly from the room.

Not surprising. A man suddenly slapped with feelings he'd never encountered before was liable to look as though he'd been hit in the head with a two-by-four. It was just that the girl was so tiny. So helpless. And damn it, a kid that small just shouldn't have to be sick. Scowling, he pushed those thoughts aside and concentrated on the woman in front of him.

He was only a step or two behind her and even with his thoughts churning, he managed to lower his gaze long enough to admire the sway of her hips and the shapeliness of her calves. Damn, but high heels did amazing things for a woman's legs.

And as dangerous as it was to be thinking about

Jennifer's legs, it was safer than dwelling on other, even more dangerous thoughts.

As soon as she walked into the living room, she stepped out of those heels and instantly became softer, more vulnerable somehow. And just as quickly, Chance's internal radar sent out a warning ping. Admiration for a single mother was all well and good. But did he really want another complication in his life? Wasn't dealing with a newly-inherited family enough at the moment?

"Hello?" she asked, prodding gently. "I asked if you were okay, remember?"

"I'm fine," he said firmly, silently congratulating himself on the fascinating conversation. Hell, what had happened to the glibness he was noted for with women? "Just tired, I guess. Not completely back up to speed yet."

Her features paled a bit, but she recovered quickly, he gave her that.

"How badly were you wounded?"

"Like you said before—just a flesh wound."

Jennifer folded her arms across her middle, dipped her head briefly then looked up at him again. "I'm sorry about that."

"Don't be."

"No, I shouldn't have said it."

"I'll live," he assured her and took a step closer. He couldn't seem to help himself. Everything about her drew him in. She touched something inside him and though he knew he should be fighting it, he surrendered to the feeling instead.

Her scent drifted to him. Her eyes looked wide, troubled, and for some damn reason, Chance wanted to do something—*anything*—to help. As he came closer, she shook her head in warning.

"Chance," she said, then corrected herself, "Commander Barnett—Connelly— Blast it."

A flicker of a smile danced across his face and was gone again, but in that instant, Jennifer knew she was in trouble. This man was pure, undiluted, top-grade sex appeal.

"Chance will do," he said and the amusement in his tone told her that he knew exactly what she was up to. Trying to put distance between them.

His amber eyes focused on her and it was like looking up into twin topazes. Her breath hitched and she wanted to back up, but there was simply nowhere to go. For the first time, she resented the fact that her living room was so darn tiny. A little maneuvering room was needed here and she was flat out of luck.

"Look, I appreciate you giving me a ride home, but—"

"But you'd rather I left now."

"Exactly," she said. "No offense, it's just—" Why couldn't she talk? Or think? He was too close, that was it. That broad chest. The startling white of his uniform against the deep tan of his skin. The cluster of medals and ribbons pinned above his heart.

Medals.

For bravery? For being shot?

For living the kind of dangerous life that had already robbed her of a husband?

Instantly, her heartbeat evened out, her breathing came just a bit easier and she felt control again. That's all she'd have to do. Remind herself continually of the fact that Chance Barnett Connelly was a man to whom life equaled danger.

And she'd had enough danger in her life already, thanks very much.

She lifted both hands, palms out, to stop his ever-increasing advance. It worked.

"What?" he asked, and he was so close, she felt the brush of his breath dust across her forehead.

A whisper of goose bumps raced along her spine, but Jennifer ignored them. She *had* to.

"This isn't a good idea at all," she said, "and I think you know it, too."

"Maybe," he said and his gaze moved over her features as surely as a caress.

She shivered, but shook her head. Steeling herself, she said, "I'm not interested in joining your group of 'girls in every port.'"

He actually looked offended. "Hey, I didn't say that. Your baby-sitter did."

"Yeah, but she was right," Jennifer muttered,

knowing it had to be true. No unmarried man who looked like Chance was hurting for company.

He took a half step back and she breathed a little easier.

"No, she wasn't," he said.

Jennifer looked up into his eyes and caught a glint of anger shining in those golden depths. Well, better anger than the desire that had been there a moment before. Much easier to deal with.

"It really doesn't matter, does it?"

"Yeah, it does," he said, his gaze locking onto hers. "There's something between us, Jennifer. Call it chemistry. Hell, call it lust."

"I'd rather not call it anything," she said.

"Ignoring it won't make it go away."

"Worth a shot," she quipped nervously and a moment later cringed to realize that by saying that, she'd actually admitted that there was something to ignore.

He nodded slowly and moved away. "I'm gonna go now."

Thank heaven.

"But I'll be back."

And as he walked toward the front door, Jennifer couldn't help wondering if that last statement had been a warning or a promise.

It turned out to be both.

The clatter of two small feet on the linoleum announced Sarah just a moment before that little voice shouted, "Chanz here!"

Expectation, excitement and dread all coiled together to form a knot in her throat that Jennifer dutifully swallowed back. Wrist-deep in soapy water, she looked back over her shoulder and smiled at her daughter.

"Tell Chance mommy's coming, all right?"

"'kay," the child said and spun around to run back the way she'd come.

"*Walk,* Sarah," Jennifer called out and was pleased to see the girl instantly slow down. Now shuffling her feet in obvious disgust, she left the room.

Chanz. Her daughter was nuts about Chance Barnett, and the feeling appeared to be mutual. He'd spent so much time here in the last three days that Jennifer now automatically set an extra plate on the table for him. Somehow, he'd managed to invade her life, captivate her daughter and send her own hormones on a white-water raft ride—all with very little effort.

Shaking soapsuds off her fingers, Jennifer grabbed a dish towel, dried her hands, then reached up to smooth her hair. Silly. She didn't *want* to look good for Chance Barnett, so what did she care if her hair was a mess?

Just a female reaction, that was all. It didn't mean anything. It didn't mean—

"Well, hi there, Chuckles!"

Chance's voice floated through the living room and into the kitchen where it raced up the length of Jennifer's spine and tickled the base of her neck. She hardly heard Sarah's delighted laughter over the roaring in her own ears. Her stomach took a nosedive and her breath came fast and hard.

For heaven's sake, she was acting like some teenager waiting for her prom date to pick her up. This wasn't a date, she reminded herself. And she sure as heck wasn't a teenager. So why couldn't she stop these ridiculous flutters of excitement that rippled through her whenever he was close?

Shaking her head, she muttered, "Quit stalling and get out there. Otherwise he'll think you're hiding from him."

She was, of course, but he didn't have to know that.

Chance sat on the couch, Sarah on his lap. The little girl held a book open and was stabbing at the pictures with one index finger.

"Tuttle."

"Turtle," he corrected gently and smoothed one hand over the back of the child's head.

"Yes," Sarah agreed, nodding sharply. "Tuttle."

Chance grinned and, as if sensing her presence, looked up directly into Jennifer's gaze. She felt the power of that stare right down to the soles of her feet. The man really packed a wallop.

"We're reading," he said.

"So I see." And darned if they didn't look like father and daughter. So cozy. So comfortable with each other. So— Don't go there, she warned herself even as she started walking toward the twosome.

"Momma come sit, too," Sarah announced, then shifted her gaze back to the book. "Doggie."

"Sure is," Chance agreed.

The little girl reached for his cheek and turned his face to hers. "Me wanna doggie."

"We talked about this, baby," Jennifer said, drawing Sarah off Chance's lap to sit with her. "You can have a doggie when you're all better."

"Me better," the girl insisted.

"Not yet," Jennifer said, past the aching knot in her throat, "but soon."

"Now. Better now."

She wished that were true, but looking into her little girl's face, Jennifer could see the dark violet shadows beneath her big brown eyes. Her skin was as pale as fine porcelain and just as fragile. Her little body might look sturdy, but it held a damaged heart, and until that was fixed, Jennifer would take no chances with her baby.

Her family.

"Wanna doggie," Sarah pleaded, leaning in and

tipping her head to one side for that extra special emphasis all children seemed to know instinctively.

"I'm sorry, honey, the answer is no."

Her bottom lip shot out and she folded her chubby arms across her chest. Then with as much dignity as an eighteen-month-old could manage, she stomped out of the room.

"No dog?"

Jennifer slanted the man beside her a look. "Not until she's well enough to play with one."

"It might help her to—"

"I know you mean well," Jennifer said, interrupting him before he could side with Sarah against her, "but she's my daughter and I have to do what I think is best for her."

"I'm not arguing," he said, lifting both hands in mock surrender.

"You were going to."

He looked like he might argue that, then gave it up and admitted sheepishly, "Yeah, I was."

"It's not easy saying no to her," Jennifer said on a sigh as she slumped back against the cushions.

"I noticed," he said with a chuckle. "I think she had my number from day one. All she has to do is look up at me with those big brown eyes and I'm her sucker."

Yes, Jennifer had seen that. He'd developed a special relationship with Sarah, and, though it worried her a little, she was also pleased. Sarah didn't have enough family in her life, and no close male relatives. It was good, wasn't it, to have Chance here, even for a little while? Or was she making a mistake in letting the two become friends? After all, when Chance left, as he would eventually, Sarah would miss him desperately.

And not, she thought with an inward twinge, just Sarah.

A crash from the other room shattered that train of thought.

"Sarah?"

Jennifer shot up from the love seat and raced across the room, her heart pounding in time with her hurried steps. "Sarah honey?" she called, "Are you all right?"

Dashing through the hallway, she rounded the corner and came to a sudden stop. Sarah stood in the center of the room, staring at the toppled doll-house, lying on its side on the floor. She must have collided with the little table it sat on when she ran into the room. But it didn't matter. All that mattered was that she was safe. Relief coursed through Jennifer's body with the strength and overwhelming power of a river bursting its banks.

Huge tears formed in the little girl's eyes as she looked up at her mother. Jennifer dropped to her knees, gathered the girl up close and held her tightly. "Are you all right, baby? Are you hurt? You have to be careful, sweetheart. You shouldn't run. Just walk, all right? It's okay, don't cry. Don't cry…''

Her soothing words flowed into a steady stream of comforting sounds and hums, and Chance stood in the doorway, watching. Morning sunlight poured through the gleaming windowpanes to fall like a golden spotlight on Jennifer and her child as the two of them clung together like the only survivors of a tragedy.

He felt distanced from them, left out of this tender moment, and it surprised him to note just how much that bothered him. Inhaling deeply, he leaned one shoulder against the doorjamb and kept his gaze locked on the two females who had some-how become too important to him. His own heart rate was just slowing down. Amazing how the sound of a crash could scare you when a kid was involved. Hell, he'd come through firefights with less of a reaction. Yet as the seconds ticked past into minutes and still Jennifer hadn't released the girl, he began to wonder.

He wondered if Jennifer had always been this protective of the child, or if it was as a direct result of the heart problem that she was so terrified.

Six

"**W**hat is he up to?" Jennifer stared across Emma's office at the soft, soothing Monet hanging on the wall opposite her. But neither the violin music drifting out of the stereo nor the filmy greens and blues of Monet's gardens were going to be enough to calm the nerves jangling throughout her body.

"Why does he have to be 'up to' anything?" Emma answered the question with one of her own.

Sliding a glance at her employer, Jennifer gave her a rueful smile and said, "You would have made a good psychiatrist. Get the patient to answer her own questions."

"Oh, honey," Emma said, leaning forward to place her hand atop Jennifer's, "you're not a patient and you sure as heck don't need a shrink."

"I'm not so sure," Jennifer muttered with a shake of her head. Then she took hold of Emma's hand and gave it a hard squeeze before releasing it to lean back in her chair. "Lately I feel like I'm losing my mind."

"Of course you do," the older woman said. "You're worried sick over your baby."

True, Jennifer thought, as Sarah's sweet little face appeared in her mind. Every waking moment and most of her dreams were filled with half-frenzied, panic-filled thoughts of a nebulous, dangerous future. But to be honest, if only with herself, Chance was taking up a lot of time in her thoughts, too.

Blast it.

Heck, blast *him.*

She hadn't asked for this. Hadn't wanted any more complications in her life than already existed. She didn't need this right now. He was a distraction. Oh, a gorgeous one, granted, but still a distraction.

And she couldn't afford to have her concentration scattered right now. It didn't have anything to do with him personally, of course. It was just a bad time for her to try to have a relationship.

Jennifer groaned inwardly. Heck, even *she* didn't believe that.

There wasn't another man alive who could distract her from her worries right now. It was only Chance. Him. That smile. Those eyes. The way his voice rippled across her skin and made her think of hot summer nights. The gentleness he always showed Sarah.

"Oh, for pity's sake," she muttered and clapped one hand over her eyes.

Emma chuckled softly and took a seat beside her on the small floral damask sofa. "He's getting to you, isn't he?"

Jennifer parted her fingers wide enough to be able to peer at her employer. "Do I have to answer that?"

"Ah, honey," the woman crowed, "you just did!"

Emma Connelly was more than Jennifer's boss, she was a friend—and the closest thing to a mother Jennifer had. Which was why the woman felt completely at ease offering her opinions, whether they were asked for or not. But to be fair, it wasn't nosiness prompting her. It was concern. Emma'd been nothing but kindness itself ever since Jennifer had started working for her. And Jennifer thanked heaven every day that she had a good job with excellent insurance benefits.

But that didn't mean she was going to bare her

soul and start confessing the legion of confusing feelings she had for Emma's stepson.

Apparently, though, she didn't have to.

"Face it, child," the woman was saying with a grin, "you never stood a chance. That man's got his daddy's charm, and add that to how good he looks in his uniform, and, well—" Emma shrugged good-naturedly. "He just plain outgunned you."

"Maybe," Jennifer admitted as a mental image of Chance filled her mind and caused her heartbeat to stagger drunkenly. It took every ounce of her will to combat that feeling, but she managed. "But, Emma, I just can't deal with him now. There's Sarah to worry about and—"

"Darlin'," Emma interrupted, "I won't tell you not to worry, you'll do that anyway. Any mother would. But we've got the best doctor there is to perform the operation. Her hospital bills are taken care of."

Jennifer opened her mouth, but Emma cut her off.

"And no arguments, either. I don't want you worried about meeting deductibles or filling out paperwork." She sat up straight, picked up Jennifer's hand and patted it gently. "As for Chance, I'm not saying you should throw caution to the wind here. But on the other hand, where's the harm in enjoying the company of a handsome man? Where's the harm in having a bit of something for yourself in the middle of a trying time?''

"Emma..." She didn't mean any harm, Jennifer knew. But Emma didn't understand that even if Jennifer was interested in a man right now, it wouldn't be Chance. All fire and danger, he wasn't exactly the home-and-hearth type. "Don't go building fantasies, okay? He's only here temporarily and—"

"Honey, I'm not booking the church," Emma said softly. "All I'm saying is that you should try to relax a little. If Chance wants to offer you a strong shoulder to lean on during a hard time, why not take him up on it?''

Jennifer shook her head and smiled. "You know, women's libbers around the country would howl if they could hear you."

"Twaddle," Emma blurted with a wave of one hand, effectively dismissing hordes of irate feminists. "There's a difference between being a strong woman and a hard one." Standing up, she ran the flat of her hands down the front of her meadow-green Chanel suit while she continued. "Men and women weren't meant to stand alone, sugar. We complement each other's strengths and weaknesses. That's the whole point."

"Sure, in a perfect world," Jennifer said on a sigh.

"Nothing's perfect, Jennifer," Emma said, "but

it doesn't have to be as complicated as you make it, either.''

''Maybe,'' Jennifer conceded, more to end the conversation than for any other reason. She knew Emma meant well, but she also knew that her employer, despite her logical mind and keen business sense, was a romantic at heart. And there was nothing Emma would like better than for Chance and Jennifer to strike enough sparks off each other to ignite an eternal flame.

But that wasn't possible. First off, there was no such thing as eternal. No happily ever afters outside of fairy tales. The world just didn't work that way. Yet Jennifer was pretty sure she'd never be able to convince Emma of that. So what was the point of trying?

''Now,'' the other woman was saying, ''it's late. Why don't you go on home to that baby of yours?''

Automatically Jennifer checked her wristwatch and then, frowning, looked up and said, ''It's only three, Emma. I work until five.''

''You work until I say you're finished for the day,'' her employer corrected gently. ''Now get yourself home.''

A little stab of guilt flashed within her briefly as Jennifer thought of the mountains of letters she still had to get signed and mailed. But in the next instant, she decided that if her boss wasn't worried about them, why should she be? Besides, it'd be fun to get home early and spend some time with Sarah. Nothing strenuous, of course, she couldn't risk that. But they could sit on a blanket in the sun and watch the clouds.

Just thinking about it made her smile, so she stood up and walked to her desk before she could change her mind. "All right, I will."

"Good. And don't you come back until after that baby's well and home again."

Swinging her purse strap over her shoulder, Jennifer turned and stared at her boss. "I can't do that. The surgery's not for a few days and then—" She shook her head as if to clear the mental picture of her daughter's ordeal. "There's too much to do. The correspondence alone—"

"Poo."

"I beg your pardon?"

"Poo on the letters," Emma said sternly, walking across the room to stand directly in front of her. Cupping Jennifer's cheeks in her hands, she said, "I can take care of myself for a while. You spend time with your baby—*with* pay. And I'll take no arguments here, honey."

Jennifer had seen that steely look in Emma's eyes before and knew it signaled the fact that her mind was made up and already set in concrete. Slowly, she nodded. "All right, then," she said and was rewarded with a smile. "Just don't discover that you can get along without me, okay?"

"Not a chance, honey. Your job'll be here waiting for you."

"Thanks, Emma," she said. "Thanks for everything."

"You're welcome. Now get going."

Jennifer did as she was told and headed for the door. Before she could leave the room, though, Emma's voice stopped her briefly.

"Say hello to Chance for me."

Jennifer glanced back over her shoulder. "He's staying here at the mansion. You'll see him before I will." She hoped.

"Uh-huh," Emma said.

"You're hopeless."

"Hope*ful,* honey. There's a difference."

Shaking her head, Jennifer headed down the hall and toward the staircase. At least with the time off she'd been given, she wouldn't be running into Chance at the mansion anymore. And that would be for the best.

So why wasn't she happier about that?

He'd had no idea it would be this much fun.

Someone should have told him what it was like to spend time around kids.

But, Chance admitted silently, if they had, he wouldn't have believed them anyway. Besides, maybe all kids weren't as terrific as this one.

He looked down into Sarah's big brown eyes and

felt himself go all soft inside. Like her mother, she had the ability to touch something within him that he hadn't even been aware of.

In the last week or so he'd spent so much time with Jennifer and Sarah that he almost couldn't imagine living any other way. How had he gotten along without fierce hugs from tiny arms? How had he managed to get through his whole life without seeing Jennifer's lips curve in a smile? Without seeing her eyes light up with pleasure or the way her hair seemed to damn near sparkle in the sunlight?

"Cha-anz," Sarah wheedled, somehow managing to make his name two syllables. "Sving, Chanz," she said, grabbing a tiny fistful of his pantleg and shaking it.

"Sving?" he repeated with a laugh. "What are you, Swedish?"

"Sving." Sarah's bottom lip jutted out and Chance laughed. Hard not to. But dutifully, he picked her up, set her onto the swing and locked her into the baby seat. Then moving behind her, he gave her a small push and listened to the musical sound of her laughter.

She was magic. Pure and simple. And some day this kid was going to have the boys lined up outside her door. But as soon as that thought hit, he realized that he wouldn't be around then. He wouldn't know about her first skinned knee, her first bike ride, her first crush, her first date. He wouldn't be there to threaten those hormone-charged teenaged boys. He wouldn't know if she was happy or sad or lonely or laughing.

Hell, she wouldn't even remember him.

And with his next breath, he wondered if Jennifer would remember him—or want to remember him. Strange, for so many years, he'd done his best to be forgettable. He'd never had a relationship that had lasted for more than a week or two. But that had been the plan. He hadn't wanted a woman waiting at home for him. Hadn't wanted to have to worry about anyone but himself.

Well, it had worked like a charm.

There was no one who gave a damn if he lived or died. Except for his brother, of course, and that was completely different. That fact had never bothered him before. But it did now.

Ever since he'd looked into a pair of eyes greener than the sea. Ever since he'd stood alongside a short, curvy woman whose scent was enough to open up every closed door inside him. His back teeth ground together and his mind filled with images of him and Jennifer locked in a full body embrace. Want coursed through him and he knew a desire he'd never known before. This woman had reached him as no one else ever had.

The way she moved, the way she talked, the way she loved her daughter—everything about her made him hunger for what he'd never wanted before. And he knew damn well she wasn't interested. Jennifer and Sarah were a unit. The two of them were a solid wall, shutting out everyone else—including him.

Something cold and empty opened up inside him and to avoid thinking about it, he slowed the swing, unhooked Sarah's belt and picked her up, cradling her against his chest. For one long moment, he enjoyed the sturdy weight of her in his arms and the feel of her soft cheek pressed to his. How was it possible to love so much, so quickly?

And how would he ever leave her and her mother?

Sunshine poured down from a clear April sky and spattered the backyard with dappled shade from the surrounding trees. It was a picture-perfect scene. All that was missing was Jennifer.

Easing back from the baby a bit, he looked her dead in the eye and asked, "So, you think Mommy's going to be mad about the swing set?"

"Mommy?" Sarah's smile widened.

"Yeah, she has that effect on me, too," he admitted. Then, walking around the edge of the newly-installed play gym, he held Sarah at the top of the slide, one arm wrapped firmly around her middle. "You ready?" he asked.

She nodded fiercely, sending her tiny pigtails fluttering in the soft breeze.

"No, don't!"

Startled at the unexpected voice, Chance tightened his hold on the baby and looked across the yard to the back door. Jennifer stood on the threshold and even from a distance, he read the anger in her eyes.

Well, hell. Not exactly the reaction he'd been hoping for.

"What are you doing?" she demanded as she marched across the patio and then the grass. She stopped alongside the slide, reached up and plucked Sarah from his grasp. Tucking her carefully against her body, Jennifer then did a quick check, making sure her daughter was all right.

Chance bit back his irritation. Did she really think he couldn't be trusted to take care of a child?

The baby, picking up on her mother's tension, instantly began to sniffle and cry. Jennifer soothed her with a rocking motion and a few pats on her back—all the while shooting daggers at Chance.

"You're home early," he said, hoping to defuse a situation he didn't entirely understand.

"Just in time, apparently."

"What's that supposed to mean?"

"Where's Mrs. Sorenson?" she asked, looking around the yard as if expecting the older woman to leap up from behind a shrub.

Chance shrugged. "I told her she could go home early and I'd watch the baby."

"*You* told her?" she repeated, swinging her gaze back to his.

"Well, yeah," Chance said, shoving his hands into his pockets and stalling a bit. This wasn't at all how he'd imagined her reaction. Hell, he'd worked his butt off, deciphering instructions that read like Greek and putting this playground together in a matter of hours. He'd expected a delighted coo of appreciation for his efforts and maybe even an enthusiastic kiss. Good thing he wasn't a man to disappoint easily. "I was here and there was no point in both of us watching one little girl, so…"

"You're unbelievable," she muttered, shaking her head and staring at him as though he had three eyes, all of them blind.

At the sound of her mother's upset tone, the baby started crying in earnest. Now she was beginning to hit notes only dogs would hear.

Chance winced in sympathy and tried to figure out where he'd gone wrong. Things had been fine a minute ago. But then, Pearl Harbor on December 6, 1941, had been a pretty quiet place, too.

Jennifer started in on him again and he figured the only sure way to keep from getting killed was to pay attention.

"Mrs. Sorenson is *my* baby-sitter. You don't tell her when to stay or leave."

"But I was here and—" Why was he defending himself? She was being totally unreasonable. Couldn't she see that? Hell, he'd spent all day putting together a child's fantasy of a swing set, complete with slide and sandbox. He glanced over his shoulder at the bright blue-and-green monstrosity and his earlier pride in his handiwork shot right down the tubes.

"Why?"

"Why what?"

"Why *any* of this?" she demanded. "Start with why are you here?"

He shoved one hand along the side of his head and just for a minute, wished that the military would allow longer hair. It would have given him something to grab hold of and yank.

"I had to put the swing set together, for one," he said and before he could elaborate, she cut him off.

"Speaking of that, who told you to buy that in the first place?" Her gaze quickly scraped over his prize before settling back on him again. "I can't afford a swing set."

Okay now. Enough was enough. He hadn't asked her for a dime and she damn well knew it. "I bought it. As a gift. For Sarah."

Jennifer's eyes flashed and he knew this was going to get worse before it got better. Damn it, what was the woman's problem, anyway? Couldn't a man do something nice without being thrown on the barbecue and roasted?

"What?" she asked, sarcasm dripping from the

words. "The store was all out of stuffed animals, so you had to buy a swing set?"

"Sving," Sarah cried, burying her head in the curve of her mother's neck.

"Hah!" Chance shouted in victory and pointed at the crying baby. "*She* likes it!"

"*She* likes ice cream for dinner," Jennifer pointed out. "That doesn't mean it's good for her!"

Sarah let out a wail that tore at Chance's heart.

"Wanna sving…"

"Not now, honey," Jennifer murmured. "You could get hurt. Besides, you have to rest."

"She won't get hurt," Chance said and couldn't quite hide the impatience in his voice.

Her gaze should have sizzled him on the spot. "You can guarantee that, I suppose?"

"No," he said, folding his arms across his chest in a defensive position he felt he needed. Actually, he wouldn't have minded a flak jacket, either. Still, he tried to be the voice of reason. Hell, somebody had to. "But, Jen, kids get hurt all the time. It's a normal part of childhood."

She drew her head back and glared at him through narrowed eyes. Twin spots of red stained her cheeks and her breath came so fast and furious, it was a wonder she didn't hyperventilate. "Sarah's not a normal kid, though, is she? She has a heart condition. She shouldn't be running around or swinging or sliding or whatever else thing you have set up here.''

"I wouldn't have let her get too tired," he said, offended that she would think he wouldn't be careful of the child.

"And are you a doctor? You know how much tired is good and how much is bad?"

"No, but—"

"She's *my* daughter, Chance," Jennifer said. "I have to do what I think is best for her."

"And that's what?" he asked. "Basically just sitting in her room?"

"If that's what it takes to keep her healthy, yes," Jennifer snapped.

"What kind of life is that?" he asked, remembering how only minutes ago, Sarah had been laughing and enjoying herself, and wondering how it had all ended so abruptly. And why was he fighting with Jennifer when all he really wanted to do was grab her to him and take her mouth in a slow, deep kiss?

"A safe one," she said.

"Jennifer," he said gently, moving in closer, laying one hand on her shoulder, "you have to let her be a kid, too."

The anger in her eyes flickered out, like a match in a windstorm, and just as quickly a sheen of tears rose up and she blinked frantically, trying to keep them at bay.

"I want to," she said, shaking her head as she looked up at him. "But I can't. I have to keep her safe. She's all I have." Her arms came around her baby and held her tightly. "She's sick. She has to be careful. I have to be careful for her. She depends on me. And I don't know what I'd do if I lost her..."

An invisible fist grabbed Chance's heart and squeezed it, hard. Reaching out, he gathered Jennifer and the baby and drew them into the circle of his arms. Cradling the two females who'd so captured his heart, he stood in the dappled shade and silently made a vow to do everything he could to protect both of them.

"You won't lose her," he whispered as he rested his chin atop Jennifer's head.

She snuggled in closer to him, wrapping her free arm around his middle. "Is that a promise?"

"You're damn right it is," he said and held her tighter, as if the strength of his arms alone could keep the three of them safe from any dangers the world had to offer.

Seven

The next few days flew by in a blur of worry and fear. Jennifer tried to hide her concerns from Sarah, but the baby was just too perceptive. Picking up on her mother's tension, the little girl was whiny and pretty much miserable. If it hadn't been for Chance, the two of them would have driven each other nuts, she was sure.

But Chance *had* been there—nearly every minute. He arrived right after breakfast and wouldn't leave until well after dinner. Since Sarah's medical problems had been discovered, there were any number of people in Jennifer's life who insisted she call them if she needed anything. And undoubtedly, they meant it. But Chance was different. He didn't wait to be asked—he was just there, doing whatever he could to help, even if it was just listening to Jennifer talk, or reading a story to Sarah.

He'd become a part of their lives and she wasn't even sure how it had happened. The cold, logical, reasonable part of her brain kept screaming at her to use caution. To keep a safe distance between them. And she knew darn well she should be listening to such solid advice.

But on the other hand...she looked across the room at the man sitting on her sofa, holding her sleeping daughter, and her heart lurched in her chest. Not easy to stand firm against a man who not only sent sparks of awareness skittering through your bloodstream, but also managed to show such tenderness toward your child.

It had been too long, she told herself firmly, as Chance stood up and smiled at her.

"I think she's down for the count," he whispered, and walked closer to her.

She's not the only one, Jennifer thought, thankful that the one thing Commander Wonderful couldn't do was read minds. "I'll take her," she said and scooped her arms beneath Chance's as he eased the baby into her care. Skin brushed over skin, heat shimmered, breath quickened. Jennifer pulled in a gulp of air and told herself she was being an idiot. She wouldn't make more out of this than there was.

"She's gonna be a heartbreaker one day," he whispered, and she wished he would quit doing that. When his voice was just a hush of sound, the word *sexy* didn't even come close to describing it. Then he added, "Like her mother," and Jennifer felt that odd rushing sensation coursing through her veins. It was as if every ounce of her blood was racing south of the border to pool in one achy spot that throbbed with every beat of her heart.

She swallowed hard, told herself *again* to get a grip and said, "One day's a long way off. Right now I'm just concerned with getting her through the surgery tomorrow and getting her well."

"She will be," Chance said and reached out to skim a lock of her hair behind Jennifer's ear. His fingertips brushed her skin, then slid down the length of her neck before falling away, and Jennifer shivered slightly in response. Heck, she couldn't help it.

A woman would have to be *dead* to not respond to this man.

"I'll be back in a minute," she muttered and escaped into the hallway, carrying her precious bundle. She walked into Sarah's darkened room, giving a quick glance at the butterfly night-light on the wall. Soft, muted colors strained through the butterfly's wings to lay patches of red and yellow and blue across the floor.

Sarah pulled in a breath and Jennifer's heart

caught. She was just so tiny. So helpless. And she was counting on her mother for so much. To keep her safe. And well. And happy. Jennifer was doing her best. Now she could only hope it would be enough.

She laid the baby down in her bed and pulled the blanket up to cover her. Smoothing one hand over her silky, fine hair, Jennifer hummed a series of low-pitched notes that didn't add up to a song and lost herself for a moment in the wonder of watching her baby sleep.

Which probably helped to explain why she didn't hear Chance enter the room until he was standing right beside her at the crib.

"You move too quietly," she said in a barely heard whisper.

"The government pays me to be sneaky," he said just as softly.

She turned her head to look up at him and caught the full effect of the smile he had aimed at her. Something inside her flip-flopped dangerously. Dozens of thoughts spilled through her mind, each of them scrambling to make themselves heard.

Jennifer knew darn well that the best way to a single mother's heart was through her child. How many men, she wondered, had gotten close to a kid in order to win over her mom? Certainly more than a few had tried with her. But she wasn't that easily fooled. Or charmed. Just as she'd seen through them, she was able to see that this man wasn't playing that game.

He genuinely cared about Sarah. It was in his every touch. His every smile. And her daughter was crazy about him in return.

Which only made this situation even more risky. Sarah loved him. That meant that he was already an accepted part of the little girl's life. And that, in turn, meant that he would be missed when he left. And he *would* leave.

Jennifer's heart did that weird little hip-hop again and she wished she could just for a moment reach in and still it. Didn't that flighty organ realize that caring about Chance Barnett Connelly was only asking for trouble?

"What are you thinking?" he asked, and she blinked, drawing herself out of the jumble of thoughts to face the predicament staring right at her.

She took a long, deep breath hoping to steady her voice, then said, "I'm thinking we should get out of this room before we wake her up." Giving Sarah one last glance, Jennifer turned and led the way out of the baby's room and didn't stop walking until she was in the center of the living room. Here, at least, there were bright lights and the radio crackling with the sounds of sixties' rock and roll. There were no patches of soft light, no need for whispers, no need to stand close together in the darkness.

Running her hands up and down her forearms,

she told herself that was a good thing. Too bad her body wasn't listening.

Chance walked directly to her and stopped just an inch or so short of actually touching her. Everything in her ached for him to reach out, grab hold of her and pull her into his arms—so to be sure that didn't happen, she backed up just a step.

"Are you all right?" he asked.

Concern rang true in his voice and she wanted to say, Heck no, I'm not all right. I'm scared. And lonely. And hungry for you. But she didn't. She couldn't.

"I'm fine," she finally managed to squeeze past the knot in her throat. "Just tired. That's all."

"And worried."

She sighed. "That, too."

"What time tomorrow does Sarah have to be at the hospital?"

Oh, God. Desire withered in the space of a heartbeat and was completely swallowed by fear.

"Ten."

"I'll be here at nine."

Her gaze shot to his. She read his determination in his whiskey-colored eyes and knew even before she started arguing with him that she would lose. "You don't have to do that."

"I didn't say I *had* to," he said softly. "I said I'd be here."

And she knew he would be. If there was one

thing she'd learned in the last week and a half, it was that when Chance gave his word, he didn't break it.

"I should try to talk you out of this," she heard herself say. "But I'm not going to."

"Good," he said and flashed his grin at her. "You'd lose."

"There is that," she admitted, since he was a pretty formidable foe. After all, she still had that swing set in her backyard, didn't she? "But that's not the only reason."

"Yeah?"

"Yeah." Okay, so she wasn't ready to admit that she wanted him as badly as a teenager feeling her first blast of hormones. But she could at least be partially honest. "I don't think I could stand taking her in by myself. I mean, I *could* take her, but then I'd be alone while they were getting her ready for—" Suddenly she didn't even want to use the word *operation*. Didn't even want to think about a team of doctors and nurses hovering over her baby's inert body.

Jennifer's eyes squeezed shut, blocking out the mental images that were always too near lately. And when she felt Chance's arms come around her, she simply leaned into his strength, giving quiet thanks that he was there.

"You don't have to be alone," he told her, and

she felt the brush of his breath across the top of her head.

His heartbeat hammered beneath her ear and she clung to the steady, sure beat of it. "I know. Thank you."

He pulled back a bit and when she looked up at him, she saw the slight frown tugging at his lips. "You don't need to thank me for being here for you, Jennifer."

"But—"

"I'm not here as a favor."

"I know that," she said, and swallowed hard. Staring up into his eyes, she watched desire, hunger and compassion flit across their surface and her insides twisted. "I really do know that."

He nodded slowly, keeping his gaze locked with hers. "Good. Because the only reason I'm here with you is because here is where I want to be."

"I'm glad," she said, needing to let him know just what his presence meant to her. She hadn't expected to care about him. Hadn't wanted to care about him. But those feelings were there. She could keep them a secret from him, but there was absolutely no point in trying to pretend to herself.

One corner of his mouth twitched up into a mere shadow of the full glory that was his high-voltage grin—and even that was enough to set off fireworks inside her.

He gave her a hard, tight hug, then let her go

before she could do something stupid like ask him to keep holding her. Good heavens what was happening to her?

For days she'd struggled successfully against these feelings, and now she was suddenly just a passenger on a hormone-driven train running out of control.

Reaching out, he trailed his fingertips down the side of her cheek, then let his hand fall to his side. "Try to get some sleep tonight, okay?"

She nodded.

"I'll see you in the morning."

She nodded again, her throat way too tight for words to slip past. So, in silence, she watched him walk across the room, open the front door and step out, closing it behind him.

Sleep? No way. There wouldn't be any sleep tonight. And it wasn't just fear for Sarah that would keep her wide-awake for hours. It was the desire pumping through her system and the knowledge that tomorrow she'd be with him again. Things were only going to get worse.

"Please try to relax, Mrs. Anderson," the doctor said in his most practiced, kind-to-the-family tone. "I have every expectation that the operation will go smoothly."

Smoothly.

Jennifer wrapped her arms around her middle and

tried to ease the chills that snaked through her bloodstream. But nothing helped. Knowing that her baby would, in just a few hours, be lying on an operating table was enough to give her bone-deep shakes.

"Can I see her again?" she asked and hated that her voice sounded so small and tinny.

The gray-haired doctor with the gentle eyes glanced from her to Chance and back again before he said, "I don't think that's a good idea." When Jennifer would have argued, he interrupted her neatly. "Sarah's being prepped for surgery and it's best if you just leave her with us until after it's over."

Over. An ugly, final word, Jennifer thought, shifting her gaze to the mint-green walls. Why mint green? she wondered absently. She'd always hated the color, and had come to loathe it during the time she'd spent in this hospital as Mike lay dying.

Oh God, *dying.*

She shivered and gulped in a breath.

"How long?" she blurted. "How long will the operation take?"

"Hard to say," Dr. Miller said. "Anywhere from two to six hours, usually."

Usually.

Another doctor's words swam to the surface of her memory and rattled around in her brain. *Just a cookie-cutter operation.* But there was nothing "usual" about this. Her baby was going into an operating room.

Jennifer's stomach pitched suddenly and she clenched her teeth together.

"Thank you, Doctor," Chance said into the silence and stepped up beside Jennifer, dropping one arm around her shoulder and pulling her up tight against him.

Grateful for his support, she leaned into him, and instead of worrying about her knees folding, forced herself to breathe and concentrate on the doctor's words.

"Just try to relax," Dr. Miller said, then winced as if he knew just how ridiculous that advice sounded. "I'll be out to see you as soon as we're finished."

"We'll be here," Chance assured him as the doctor turned and headed for a set of double doors behind which lay Sarah and operating rooms and too many other hazards to think about.

Chance kept one arm around Jennifer and guided her down a short hallway that smelled of antiseptic and fear and into a small waiting room.

A TV perched black and silent on a shelf in the corner of the room. Vinyl couches in appalling shades of orange and green dotted the linoleum floor. Scarred but clean tables held a scattering of magazines and newspapers and a coffee-and-tea-vending machine stood guard near the door. On the far wall, windows and a glass door looked out onto a small plant-filled patio.

He sat her down on the couch nearest the patio and took a seat beside her. They'd already spent hours here at the hospital. His gaze shot to the clock on the wall. One-fifteen. And there were still hours left to go.

Suddenly antsy, he stood up and shoved his hands into his jeans' pockets, looking for change. "Would you like some coffee? Tea?"

She looked up at him, and a cold, hard fist closed around his heart. Her eyes looked battered, terrified. And everything inside him wanted to help...*somehow*. Damn it. There had to be something he could do. At least when he was out on a mission, there were weapons to check and stow, battle plans to be made. Here, he was as useless as the outdated magazines.

"No," she said softly, her gaze sliding toward the doorway that led back to those double doors. "I don't think I could swallow anything."

"I know what you mean," he said and took a seat beside her again. "But we've got a long wait ahead of us."

She sat up straighter and stared directly into his eyes. "Oh, I'm sorry. You've already been here so long. You don't have to stay."

Chance sighed and ran one hand across the top of his head. "That's not what I meant. And I'm not going anywhere. Not till I know that you and Sarah are both fine.''

She folded her hands together and twisted her fingers back and forth nervously until he laid his hand atop hers. "Good," she said, letting her gaze dip briefly before meeting his again. "I'm glad you're staying. I really don't want to be alone right now.''

''You won't be,'' he said simply, sitting back and pulling her up close. Her arms slid around his middle, her head rested on his chest and it felt…right. Resting his head on the back of the couch, he closed his eyes and thought about the last time they'd seen Sarah. An IV dripping into her arm, her little eyes swollen from crying, she had looked entirely too small to be in that big bed.

But more than the misery of seeing Sarah lying there so helpless was the pain of having to watch Jennifer's terror for her child. He'd wanted nothing more than to ease that pain. To be the one she turned to. To be the one man who could hold her and help her through the worst moment in her life.

And that feeling had completely rocked him.

Opening his eyes, Chance stared up at the acoustical ceiling tiles. He'd never before wanted to be that important to anyone. He'd always prided himself on getting in and getting out. For years he'd kept his relationships shallow enough to make a puddle look deep. He'd figured it was safest that way. He wasn't like Douglas. He'd never wanted an ordinary existence.

He'd never wanted to matter.

To anyone.

And now that felt like the most important thing in the world.

Eight

An hour later, they sat opposite each other in the crowded cafeteria. Jennifer didn't feel like eating, but to placate Chance, she'd agreed to come downstairs and stare at a plate of very unappetizing food.

"You can't eat it through osmosis," he replied. "You'll actually have to put the food in your mouth and chew it."

Sighing, Jennifer dutifully picked up her fork and pushed a series of straight lines through her scoop of mashed potatoes. Then she quit trying altogether and laid the fork down again. Shaking her head, she looked at him and said, "I just can't. I'm sorry."

He nodded and gave her a long, understanding

look. "It's okay. Maybe later." Then he reached across the small table and moved the cup of hot tea closer to her right hand. "But at least drink this."

As a compromise, she took a long swallow, but knew she couldn't drink any more. Her stomach was tied up in knots. There was just no way to put anything in there and not have it turn into an acid bath.

Sitting back in her chair, Jennifer let her gaze drift around the crowded eating area. Doctors, nurses and other hospital personnel sat apart from everyone else. At a long row of tables, they laughed and talked and, in general, looked to be having a great time. To them, this place was just a job. Where they reported daily to work. Where they treated patients and handed out medications and still were able to remain distanced from the lives of the people they touched.

Quite a difference from the rest of the people clustered around the tables. Conversations were muted, strained whispers scraped the air and were interrupted occasionally by a choked-off sob or quiet weeping. Jennifer looked at her fellow prisoners and, noting the desperation in some of their eyes, realized she too looked haunted. By old fears? By new ones?

"What are you thinking?"

She shifted her gaze back to Chance with relief.

"I was...remembering the last time I was in this room."

"Tell me," he said simply.

Maybe he was just trying to get her to talk. To ease the slow passage of time. But whatever the reason, she went along.

"It was almost two years ago," she said and in her mind's eye saw it all again—only this time, she was an observer. "An officer had come by the house to tell me Mike had been shot. They brought me here, sat me down, gave me coffee and told me everything was being done." She could still feel the sympathetic glances thrown her way from the dozens of police officers lining the hallways as they waited for news about Mike's condition.

The police department really was a community. Not unlike the military, she supposed. When one of their number was hurt, the rest of them circled the wagons and did what had to be done.

She fiddled with the handle of her teacup and fixed her gaze on her fingers as she continued. "It was nearly an hour before one of the doctors came in." The memory took a hard jab at her heart and she winced with the remembered pain. "I knew even before he said anything." Her gaze lifted to Chance's again. "It was in his eyes. Grief, pity. He said he was sorry, but that there was simply nothing anyone could do."

Chance reached across the table to take her hand.

She held on to him tightly as if readying to take the big dip on a major roller coaster.

"They took me to him then," she said. "He was lying on a bed, still hooked up to a few machines that beeped along with his heart rate." She paused, then said, "He looked so tired. I even remember thinking that maybe all he needed was some rest."

Chance squeezed her hand.

She laughed shortly, but there was no matching spark of humor in her eyes. "I sat with him and stared at the green walls and counted the beeps and held his hand and told him that I would tell his baby about him." Still holding on to his hand, she sucked in a deep gulp of air and said, "There were two hundred and twenty-six beeps and then he died."

"I'm sorry."

"You have no reason to be sorry," she said, shaking her head gently. "It wasn't your fault."

"I know."

"It was Mike's fault."

"What?"

She saw surprise flicker in his eyes. Pulling her hand free of his, she folded her arms across her chest in an instinctively defensive posture. "Mike loved his job. He loved the rush of danger," she said, and couldn't completely hide the bitter tinge to her voice. "He wouldn't—or *couldn't*—give it up. Not even when I became pregnant and I asked him to. I never understood that about him. I still don't.''

''I do,'' Chance said softly. ''When the stakes are high, you're living life to the fullest.'' Shaking his head, he went on in a whisper meant only for her ears. ''You can't appreciate living until you've brushed up against death.''

She sucked in a breath, leaned in toward him and said simply, ''Bull.'' And before he could open his mouth to counter that, she went on in a rush of words fueled by her own panic. ''You and Mike are so much alike, you could have been twins. And neither of you makes any sense at all.'' Her voice dropped a notch as she pointed out, ''Sarah is upstairs in an operating room right now, 'brushing up against death' as you called it. Think she's appreciating life?''

''That's different and you know it,'' he said hotly. ''She's a helpless child. I'm talking about men. Men who need to test themselves and stand up to a job that needs to be done. If I could change places with Sarah, I'd do it in a heartbeat.'' His hands curled into useless fists on the tabletop as he went on. ''What I do—and what Mike did—they're necessary jobs. Jobs that mean something to thousands of people. Mike kept others safe at a risk to his own safety.''

''And died for it.''

''True,'' he said, ''and you know damn well he didn't *plan* on that.''

''Plan or not,'' she countered, ''it happened. And he left me alone and pregnant.'' Old pain reared up and with it came an anger at Mike she had thought long dead. Her gaze lifted to the ceiling and the floors above, where her baby lay on an operating table. ''And now I'm alone, waiting to hear if my daughter will live or die.''

He reached across the table to touch her arm, still tightly folded over her chest. ''You're not alone now, Jennifer.''

Her gaze locked with his. A tendril of awareness scuttled through her and she fought it down. He was here, with her, true. But not for long. And she'd better remember that.

Jennifer pulled in a long, shaky breath and released it again before saying, ''I appreciate you being here, don't get me wrong...''

''But...?'' He prodded her to finish that statement.

''But,'' she said, ''you'll be leaving soon.''

His mouth tightened into a grim, straight line.

''You're not really a part of this,'' she added, not unkindly and still felt a stab of guilt when she watched regret flash across his eyes. ''You'll be gone soon and I'll be alone again. The reality is, you're just like Mike. You're anxious to be off chasing risks—and in the end, life will go on as it has. Sarah and me against the world. Alone.''

With that, she jumped up, nearly overturning her chair as it scraped loudly over the scratched linoleum. She grabbed her purse and rushed for the doorway, never looking back. If she had, she would have seen Chance hot on her heels.

He caught up with her in the hallway, grabbing her upper arm and pulling her around to face him. A sheen of tears blurred her vision, but even with that, she had no trouble making out the fury on his features. Her heart hammered in her chest until she wouldn't have been surprised if it flew right through her ribcage.

His grip gentled, but was firm enough to tell her that he wasn't letting her go. ''Don't lump me in with your husband, Jen. I'm not him.''

''I know,'' she said, feeling her stomach jitter nervously. Oh, she knew darn well he wasn't Mike. Being this close to him, feeling his strength pouring into her, signaled a sweep of emotion that she'd never known before.

Jennifer had loved her husband. But it had been a comfortable, warm love. A straight road of affection and tenderness, with no highs or lows to interrupt the sameness.

When Chance touched her, fireworks went off in her bloodstream. Her emotions went on a swift, sure climb—but could plummet again at a moment's notice. Haze enveloped her brain and a pounding, throbbing need settled down low in her body, making her want and need things she knew she shouldn't.

No, he wasn't Mike.

He was far more dangerous.

"Just let me go," she said, though even she heard the unsure tone in her voice.

"Not yet," he told her and started for the elevator that would take them back to the third floor and the waiting room. Four other people joined them in the tiny cubicle, so neither of them spoke. Silence reigned until they'd reached their destination. Then Chance led her across the room and out onto the small patio. Only there did he finally release her.

Jennifer rubbed her arm, but could still feel the imprint of his fingers on her flesh. She looked up at him and watched a dizzying array of emotions chase each other across his face, until she wasn't sure what he was thinking, feeling.

Finally, though, he inhaled sharply and blurted, "I'm sorry. I didn't mean to upset you. Didn't want to give you more grief than you're already going through here today."

"I know."

"But, Jen," he went on as if she hadn't spoken, "don't confuse me with your late husband. We're two different men."

"Different," she said, "but so much alike."

"At least in one thing," he admitted, closing the space between them with a single, long step. "We both care for you."

Trouble, her mind screamed, but her body just plain wasn't listening.

He cupped her face in the palms of his hands and bent his head to hers. She stared up at him, like a deer caught in the headlights, and tried to brace herself. But she had no way of knowing what the impact of his mouth on hers would be like, so there was no way she could have prepared for the on-slaught of sensations that slapped at her.

A simple, brief, almost tender kiss. Just a brush of his lips across hers.

And the ground rocked beneath her feet.

When he pulled his head back and looked at her, she saw the same dumbfounded expression on his face that she knew was on her own.

"Wow," he said on an exhale of breath.

"Yeah," she agreed and leaned into his strength, grateful for the arms that came around her and held her steady. There would be time enough later to worry about that kiss and what it signified.

For right now, it was enough to know she wasn't alone.

"What's taking so long?" she demanded on her five-hundredth trip around the waiting room. "It's four o'clock. Shouldn't they be finished by now?''

Jennifer had nearly worn a path in the linoleum. She was making Chance tired just watching her. He understood the nervous energy, but he didn't like the wild look in her eyes. Or the pallor of her skin.

Standing up, he crossed to her and ignored the older couple sitting on one of the other couches. They'd been here for less than an hour and hadn't started getting impatient yet. Their time would come, he knew.

But for now he took hold of Jennifer's arm and steered her toward the glass door and the patio beyond. "Come on," he said. "Let's get some fresh air."

She threw a glance at the doorway behind them. "But if the doctor comes in—"

"He'll see us through the glass."

"Okay," she muttered, swiping one hand through her hair.

He opened the door and instantly a blast of cold, fresh wind slapped at them. Jennifer tipped her face into it, closing her eyes and inhaling deeply. Chance simply stared at her, captured by the picture she made. Blond hair tossed and tousled by the wind, her arms folded across her breasts, her chin tilted defiantly up, as if she was somehow challenging the gods themselves.

And he knew he would always remember this

moment and just how beautiful she looked despite the fear crowding her.

"God," she said softly enough that the wind nearly devoured her words, "I needed to get out of that room."

She turned her head to look at him. "Thank you."

"My pleasure," he said and meant it. Damn, it was good just looking at her. Her navy-blue sweater hugged her curves and her faded, worn jeans clung to her legs like a lover's hands. And even now, in this tense situation, she made his body hard and hot and ready for action.

Of course, remembering that too brief kiss they'd shared a few hours ago only fed the fires within.

"I've been thanking you a lot lately, haven't I?" she asked.

"I don't know. Are you keeping score?"

"Maybe I should," she said, and moved toward a bench in the corner of the patio. Studying him, she continued, "You've been great, Chance. Really. But what I'm trying to figure out is why?"

"Why what?"

"Why are you here?" she asked, pushing her windblown hair back from her face with a careless stroke of her hand. "Why are you spending an entire day sitting in a hospital, keeping me company?"

"I already told you that. I'm here because I want

to be here.'' And in fact, he added silently, couldn't imagine being anywhere else.

She shook her head gently and said, ''That's not telling me why, though, is it?''

''Does there have to be a reason?''

''Yeah,'' she said slowly, ''I think there does.''

He reached up and scraped one hand across the back of his neck. Uncomfortable thinking about— let alone *talking* about—his reasons, he managed to shift her attention just a bit. ''Emma stopped by earlier. Grant was here, too. Why's it so unusual to you that *I'm* here?''

She stood up and walked to stand in front of him. Tipping her head back, she caught his gaze with hers and didn't let it go. Chance momentarily lost himself in the green of her eyes and thought that in another time, another place, he just might try to drown in the depths of those amazing eyes of hers.

''What's unusual is,'' she said, ''I've known those people for a couple of years. And I know they care about me and Sarah. But still, they came, they visited and they left. You, though…I've known you less than two weeks and you've been right here beside me through most of this.''

Because he hadn't wanted to leave her. Would have done anything he could to stay with her. But on the other hand, if she'd rather he were gone…if it would make this easier on her, then he'd leave. It'd kill him to go, but he would.

"If you don't want me here," Chance said softly, watching her eyes, looking for a sign, "just say so."

Jennifer laughed shortly. "That is *so* not what I'm saying."

"What exactly *are* you saying, then?" he asked, torn between irritation and frustration.

"I guess I'm saying thanks. Again."

"Well, stop," he told her, his gaze moving over her features with a hungry touch, "I don't want to be thanked. I just want to be here."

Jennifer nodded and gave him a long, thoughtful look. Something flickered in her eyes, but he wasn't sure just what it was. And before he could find out, her gaze shifted slightly to look behind him and her face paled. "The doctor," she said on a tight gasp and headed for the door.

The doctor grinned and Chance felt the weight of the world slide off his shoulders. He dropped one hand onto Jennifer's shoulder in support and listened.

"Everything went fine," Dr. Miller said, looking directly at Jennifer, willing her to relax, believe. "Sarah came through like a trouper."

"Really?" Jennifer asked breathlessly. "She's all right? We can see her?"

The doctor then glanced at Chance before shaking his head slightly. "Not yet. She'll be in recovery for a couple of hours, but once we get her settled into ICU, you can both visit for a few minutes.''

''But she's fine,'' Jennifer repeated.

''She's fine,'' Dr. Miller said and reached out to give Jennifer's hand an understanding pat. ''She'll be as good as new before you know it.''

''Oh God,'' she whispered brokenly and lifted one hand to cover her mouth. ''Oh, thank you, Doctor,'' she said and gave the man a fierce, hard hug that clearly surprised the hell out of him.

He patted her back awkwardly, sent Chance a sheepish smile then stepped back. ''You're welcome. Now why don't you two go have some dinner and relax. I'll come get you when it's time to visit Sarah.''

Then he left and Jennifer turned around to look up at Chance. ''She's okay.''

''She's okay,'' he repeated, knowing she needed to hear the words again and again.

''Good as new.''

''Better,'' he told her firmly.

''My baby's all right,'' she whispered and threw herself at Chance, flinging her arms around his neck and holding on tight enough to cut off his air. But he didn't mind in the slightest.

''My baby's all right,'' she whispered, pulling her head back to look at him through teary eyes. ''She really is. And it's over.''

"It's over, Jen, and you made it," he said, lifting one hand to stroke his fingertips down her cheek.

"*We* made it," she corrected, then slanted her mouth across his in the kind of kiss he'd been dreaming about for days.

Nine

Lips, tongue, teeth, breath mingling, bodies touching; she gave him everything she had, everything she'd been holding back, everything she'd wanted to give since nearly the first minute she'd laid eyes on him. His hands moved up and down her back, scrubbing over her thick, cable-knit sweater until she swore she could feel the hard strength of his palms against her skin.

He devoured her, taking what she offered and returning it tenfold. He tasted of pulse-pounding excitement and dreams and soft whispers in the night. Her heartbeat thundered in her ears. Her stomach pitched and rolled. Her knees liquefied. She clung to him tightly, kneading her fingers into his shoulders, feeling the warm, solid strength of him surrounding her.

And when she finally broke the kiss and pulled her head back, she was struggling for air. She stared up into those whiskey eyes of his as her lungs heaved in breath after breath. Still dangling from his neck like an oversize pendant, Jennifer grinned up at him and said, "Now *that* was a wow."

"Honey," he murmured, "you ain't seen nothin' yet."

Something hot and rich and delicious coursed through her and she swallowed hard. Now that she'd kissed him, let him know just how badly she wanted him, there would be no going back. She knew that. She was counting on that.

Because now that she knew for sure that Sarah was going to be all right, Jennifer planned to take Emma's advice. She was going to grab a little something for herself in the middle of all of this. And if it hurt more when he left because of it, at least she would have the memory of being in his arms to hold on to.

"You're a man of your word, right?" she asked, letting go of his neck and dropping to her feet.

His eyes went dark and hungry. "Count on it."

"Oh, I am, Commander," she said. "I am." Then she snaked her arm through his and leaned into him. "But to make sure I'm at my best, I think I'd better eat something. Keep my strength up."

A slow, wicked smile curved his incredible mouth as he said, "Need strength, huh? Jen, I'm going to buy you the biggest steak in Chicago."

Two hours later, they were back from dinner standing in front of a familiar set of double doors.

ICU.

Jennifer took a deep breath, steadied her nerves and held on tightly to Chance's hand. How odd, she thought absently, that two weeks ago she hadn't known he existed. And now she was hanging on to his hand for dear life. She couldn't even imagine having to go into that room alone.

For two years now, she'd dealt with everything life had thrown at her. She'd been strong for Sarah and had tried to be both mother and father to her baby. It hadn't been easy. In fact, she'd been so lonely at times, she'd have given anything just to hear the sound of another adult voice in the house.

Now, having Chance standing beside her, lending her his strength, giving his quiet support—well, it meant more than she could have said.

"Ready?" he asked quietly, giving her hand a squeeze.

Not quite trusting her voice, Jennifer nodded and moved forward when he opened the door and held it wide for her.

The first thing she noticed were the sounds. A respirator whooshed noisily. And a steady series of beeps shot straight to her soul, reminding her all too clearly of that last night with Mike. But this was different, she reminded herself as she forced her feet to walk to the side of Sarah's bed. These beeps measured the strong, sure beating of Sarah's healed heart.

Jennifer looked down at her baby and a choked-off sob caught in her throat. Lifting one hand, she reached across the metal bars separating her from her child and gently, carefully stroked Sarah's hair. She was sleeping. Sedated, the doctor had said, until she didn't need the respirator breathing for her anymore. There was a tube in her airway, feeding to the respirator, and two IV lines hooked to her small arm for feeding and medication and several other tubes and lines that Jennifer didn't even want to think about.

"Oh, baby," she whispered around a knot of tears filling her throat.

"It looks bad, I know," Chance said quietly, placing his hands on her shoulders. "But she's going to be fine. The surgery's over and now all she has to do is heal."

"She's so tiny. So very tiny," Jennifer said.

"But tough," he reminded her. "Like her mother."

Jennifer reached up and covered one of his hands

with hers. While they stood there in silence, a gray-haired nurse with sharp, kind eyes came in, smiled and busily checked the tubes and machines, read the chart, then said, "Just another minute or two, Mr. and Mrs. Anderson."

"Oh," Jennifer said, startled by the nurse's assumption, "we're not—"

"I know," the nurse said, "you're not ready to leave your daughter yet. But she's going to be sleeping for the next couple of days. She won't know you're here and you could both probably use some sleep."

"Thank you," Chance said, and Jennifer shot him a quick glance.

"I promise," the nurse assured them, "I'll take very good care of your little girl."

"I—we— Can we come back in the morning?"

"You can come back and see her whenever you want to, Mrs. Anderson," the nurse said, before leaving them alone in the room. "You're allowed ten minutes with her every hour."

When the other woman was gone, Chance smiled down at Jennifer. "Didn't want to correct her and start up a conversation," he said, explaining why he hadn't told the nurse who he was.

Jennifer nodded and turned back to Sarah. For the first time since coming into the room, she tried not to notice the tubes and machines and instead, concentrated on Sarah's face. There was a flush of pink color in her cheeks and the ever-present shadows beneath her eyes were almost gone.

She *was* healing. Relief rushed through Jennifer, making her almost light-headed with the force of it. She'd lived with the fear of Sarah's heart problem and now her baby was on the road to real health. A future. She would grow up and get married and have babies of her own.

And Jennifer's own heart swelled with gratitude and joy. Leaning over the bars, she planted a kiss on top of Sarah's head and whispered, "I love you, baby. Sleep tight."

"Champagne was an excellent idea, Commander," Jennifer said as she held her glass out for another refill.

"We're celebrating, aren't we?" he asked and set the bottle down after topping off his own glass.

"Oh God, yes, we are," she said, taking a sip and laughing as the bubbly froth slid down her throat. "I swear, I feel light as a feather. I mean, I know she still has to recover, but she's *going* to recover."

"Damn right she is," Chance agreed and felt the rich, full swell of pleasure fill him. The baby would be fine. Jennifer was happy. And, he thought with a smile, well on her way to being just a little tipsy. But hell, didn't she deserve to be? She'd lived with a suffocating fear for too long and now the worst was over.

Moonlight streamed in through the lace curtains hung at the windows. Music drifted from the stereo on the wall and soft pools of lamplight dotted the floor. Jennifer lounged back against the sofa cushions, watching him with a soft, secretive smile on her face.

"What is it?" he finally asked.

"Just thinking," she said as she stood up and set her glass of champagne down on the coffee table.

"Well, this could be dangerous, then," he muttered, only half kidding. "Usually when a woman says she's been thinking, a man ends up in trouble."

She shook her head and her blond hair fell in gentle waves about her face. "Not this time."

"Really?" he asked, standing perfectly still as she approached him. "And why's that?"

"Because," she said, staring up into his eyes, letting him see the full force of her desire, "I'm thinking about that date we made earlier tonight."

"Is that right?" Everything inside him went hot and still. He wanted her more than he'd ever wanted anything or anyone in his life. And yet…Chance sighed and said what he had to say if he was going to be able to look himself in the mirror. "Jen," he started, "you've had a lot of champagne and—"

"Not that much," she argued, smiling up at him.

"Enough that it might make a difference in any decisions you make in the next couple of minutes." Damn it.

"You're the real deal, aren't you?" she asked and took yet another step closer until all that was separating them was the slender cord of desire vibrating between them. "An officer and a gentleman. Just like the movie."

Uncomfortable with that comparison, he shrugged it off. "I just don't want to take advantage of you when you're in a vulnerable frame of mind."

Jennifer laughed, a low, deep, throaty sound that rippled through the air and danced along every one of his nerve endings.

"What's so funny?" he asked.

"You," she said, taking his left hand in her right and putting her left hand on his shoulder. "For heaven's sake Chance, *I'm* the one making advances here."

"Yeah," he said, through clenched teeth. "I noticed that."

"Good. I was afraid you weren't paying attention."

"Oh, you've got my attention, honey."

"And I intend to keep it."

"No problem," he assured her.

"Dance with me," she whispered, tipping her head back and smiling up at him.

He arched one eyebrow. This he hadn't expected. "You want to dance?"

"Yes, I want to dance. With you. Now."

"Yes, ma'am," he said and pulled her closer. He was all in favor of anything that would keep her in his arms. Holding her tightly to him, he felt the press of her breasts against his chest and the warm grip of her hand in his. Her breath puffed across the base of his neck, starting a small fire that erupted in his bloodstream and quickly spread, sending heat to parts of his body that didn't really need the encouragement.

"You feel so good," she whispered a moment later.

"Not half as good as you do, Jen."

"I like that."

"What?"

"When you call me Jen," she admitted. "No one else ever has."

Something shifted inside him. Maybe it was the old loneliness sliding out of its familiar spot. Maybe it was the wall he'd built around his heart beginning to crumble. All he could be sure of was that he'd never been happier than he was at this moment, dancing in the soft light with Jen. He released her hand long enough to tuck his fingers beneath her chin and tilt her face up to his. Meeting her sea-green eyes, he said, "I'm glad I'm the first."

Then, still keeping their gazes locked, as if looking away might mean his life, Chance lowered his head and slanted his mouth across hers. The kiss began slowly, tenuously, as they rediscovered the magic they'd found only hours ago.

Electricity sizzled between them.

Heat exploded.

Hearts pounded.

And in seconds the gentleness was gone, replaced by a driving need that eclipsed everything else.

He couldn't get enough of her. That one thought slammed into Chance's brain over and over again. He needed her as badly as he needed his next fevered gulp of air. No, more. He needed her more. Breathing would mean nothing if he didn't have her.

His hands swept down her back to the hem of her sweater and then beneath it and up, up along the column of her spine, his fingertips tracing patterns on her silky flesh. She shivered in his arms and that tender response pushed him further, higher. With one quick, practiced flick of his fingers, her bra came undone and his hands shifted to take advantage. He cupped her breasts in his palms, never taking his lips from hers, never ceasing the greedy plunder of her warm, sensuous mouth. He tasted her and while his tongue danced with hers, his thumbs circled her rigid nipples, drawing a moan from the back of her throat that instantly set his soul on fire.

Chance groaned, too, knowing that she was drawing everything from him. Feelings, desires, things he'd banked carefully for years were scuttling to the surface and there was nothing he could have done to stop them, even if he'd wanted to.

One corner of his mind still shouted at him to throw up his defenses. To batten down the hatches and prepare to be assaulted. But it was too late. The years he'd spent alone were forgotten in the rush of desire.

He pulled his head back and, gulping in air, looked down at her. Her eyes were closed, and her mouth opened on a sigh as his fingers tweaked her nipples, tugging gently at the sensitive flesh.

"Chance," she whispered, her fingers digging into his upper arms for support. "Chance, that feels so good. So...wonderful."

His throat tightened. Just watching the play of emotions dart across her features was enough to swamp him. He felt stronger, braver, more sure than he ever had been before. And at the same time, his knees were weak and everything inside him was humbled, just to be given the gift of touching her.

"There's more," he promised, his voice low and deep, scraping against his throat. "So much more."

"Yes," she said, her eyes fluttering open to look up at him. "Give me more. I want it all. Everything there is."

''Everything,'' he promised and dropped to his knees in front of her.

Caught by surprise, Jennifer swayed into him slightly and he shifted his hands to her waist, holding her until she found her footing again. When her hands came up to his shoulders, he let his fingers glide along the waistband of her jeans, dipping just beneath the worn denim to dust across her flesh. ''So soft,'' he murmured, ''so smooth.''

Her quick intake of breath was the only response, but it was enough.

Chance unbuttoned her jeans, then slowly pulled the zipper down, revealing a tiny scrap of blueberry-colored silk panties. Blood rushed to his groin and a fog rose up in his brain. The haze dropped over his vision but he blinked it back, determined to see her.

She swayed again and he gripped her upper thighs before tipping his head back to look up at her.

''Chance?'' she asked, a world of questions wrapped in only his name.

''I promised you everything,'' he reminded her. ''And this is just the first step.''

Her hips rocked as she moved unconsciously into his touch. ''But I want to feel you inside me.''

Heat.

Pure, hot as the sun, molten lava, heat poured

through him. He tightened his hold on her thighs. "Oh, you will, honey. We *both* will. Trust me."

She nodded and gave him a half smile that reached down inside him and quickly turned him inside out. "I do, you know," she whispered. "Trust you."

Chance groaned again, tore his gaze from hers and turned his attention back to that scrap of silk. He needed it off her. Needed to see beneath it. To the treasures beyond. To the very heart of her.

He gave one strong tug and her jeans slid down her legs, leaving her standing before him with nothing between him and heaven itself but that small triangle of blue silk.

She gasped and his hands slid up her thighs again, along the backs of her legs until he was cupping her bottom in his palms.

Jennifer held her breath as his incredibly strong hands squeezed her behind with tender firmness. She was caught. Imprisoned in his grip. And she loved it.

The feel of his hands on her. The whisper of his breath as his mouth neared her body. The tension in the room. The pounding of her own heart that nearly choked the last breath from her.

She tightened her hold on his shoulders and looked down, wanting to watch him take her. Needing to see this man touch her in the most intimate way imaginable. And she wanted to remember it all. Everything about this moment was now chiseled deep in her mind. Every time she entered this room she would recall this moment. She would be able to see him, kneeling in front of her. His mouth nearing her body. She would feel his hands on her backside. She would experience the nearly paralyzing sense of anticipation.

And she would want to feel it all again.

But tomorrow would take care of itself, she well knew. And all of the tomorrows after it were yet to be faced. For now, there was him. His touch. His scent. His—

She sucked in a deep breath as his mouth covered her. He hadn't bothered to pull her panties down, but was taking her right through the silk fabric. She felt his hot breath. Felt the gentle scrape of his teeth as he explored her body. Felt the strength of his fingertips as he held her tightly and pulled her even closer to him.

His tongue scraped across the silk, creating a sensation unlike anything she'd ever known before. Wet heat surrounded her, tempting her, toying with her. She rocked in his hands, moving closer, but he continued his teasing. Again and again, he licked the damn silk that kept her from feeling him completely.

"Chance…" she whispered, her fingers clutching at his shoulders. "Please…"

He pulled away from her long enough to say, "Please what?"

Jennifer tossed her hair back out of her eyes, looked down at him and read the silent command in his amber gaze. He wanted her to say it. Wanted to hear her say how much she wanted it. How much she wanted *him*.

Body on fire, mind whirling, she gave him the absolute truth. "I want you to taste me."

Flames danced in his eyes, and, in the next heartbeat, he yanked her panties down and took her.

She gasped aloud and forced herself to keep her eyes open. She watched him take her. Watched his mouth claim her in a way that no one ever had before. His lips and tongue and teeth tortured her gently. He pushed her so high, she thought she would never be able to breathe again and she didn't care. All Jennifer wanted, all she could think about was his next intimate kiss. The next swipe of his tongue.

Her knees wobbled and she locked them, refusing to give in to any weakness that might deprive her of the rippling sensations already beginning to build within. His breath, hot and wild, brushed against her most sensitive flesh. He tasted and suckled and teased, and her world spun while fireworks exploded inside her, shattering what was left of her control, sending splinters of brilliant color flashing across her mind.

He shifted his grip on her and slipped one finger into her depths.

"Chance!" His name shot from her throat on a choked-off gasp.

He didn't answer. He only redoubled his efforts, using his tongue to send her higher, faster, further than she'd ever been before. He caressed her body from the inside as he tortured her on the outside and Jennifer wanted him never to stop.

If she could have found a way to spend the rest of her life like this, she would have signed up for it. But even as she thought it, she felt her muscles tighten, tingle, and knew her climax was near.

She rocked her hips, moving in closer. She shifted one hand to cup the back of his head, holding him to her, as if afraid he would stop and leave her unfulfilled.

When the first shattering wave of completion took her, she surrendered to it, gloried in it and knew she was safe in the circle of his arms.

Ten

Chance stood up, caught her as she leaned into him and swung her up into his arms. One-handed, he swept her jeans and panties off her legs and let them fall to the floor.

"Okay," she said on a sigh as she looked up at him, "was that SEAL training or just a natural gift? Because I'm here to tell you, I'm impressed."

He grinned, despite the fever raging in his bloodstream. Her eyes were glazed, her cheeks flushed and even in his arms, her body still trembled with the force of her release. And it wasn't nearly enough. Not even close.

"You think *that* was impressive?" he asked,

shaking his head. "I keep telling you, Jen, you ain't seen nothin' yet."

She reached up, entwined her arms around his neck and whispered, "Wa-hoo!"

"That's the spirit," he muttered and tightened his grip on her as he headed across the living room toward the hallway. He'd waited as long as he possibly could. He had to have her. Here. Now. Before he lost what was left of his mind.

"Uh-oh."

His steps faltered and he glanced down at her. "Uh-oh? Not exactly what a man wants to hear about now, Jen."

"I know," she said, tossing her hair back out of her face, "but better now than in a few minutes."

"Okay, you have my attention," he said, stepping into her bedroom and walking directly to her bed. His fingers stroked the soft skin of her thigh while he waited for whatever news was important enough to interrupt this.

And he hoped to hell she wasn't going to say something like she'd changed her mind. That piece of news might be just enough to kill him.

One of her hands slipped from his neck, and she trailed her fingertips down his shirtfront, and Chance swore he could feel her touch right through the fabric of his shirt. Oh yeah. If she'd changed her mind, he was a dead man.

"I don't have any, um..." She stopped, shifted

her gaze to one side and muttered thickly, "this is nuts. I can have sex and I can't say *condoms?*"

He threw his head back and let loose a short, sharp bark of relieved laughter. "That's it?" he asked. "That's the 'uh-oh'?"

"Isn't it enough?"

"You remember when we stopped on the way here to pick up the champagne?"

"Yeah…"

He shrugged. "I picked up a little something else, too."

"Really?" Her eyes widened.

"Oh yeah." Chance laid her down onto the bed, dug in his pocket for a small package and tossed it onto the nightstand, then stretched out alongside her.

"My hero." She turned her head to smile at him. "You're really something, aren't you?"

"I try."

"I didn't realize that 'Be prepared' was a SEAL motto."

"Hey," he said, pulling her closer, "I started out a Boy Scout."

Her hands skimmed down, to his waistband, then she grabbed his shirt and pulled it free of his pants. "Boy Scout, huh?" she said, sliding her hands up beneath the fabric to caress his skin, "then I guess that means you also know how to start fires?"

His smile widened as he gave in to the need pulsing within. With one hand, Chance caressed the length of her thigh, watched her shiver, then murmured, "And I won't even need two sticks."

She arched into him, lifting her leg to place it atop his. "No," she whispered, "you sure won't."

He took her mouth, plundering her, tasting her, their tongues mating in a tangled dance that tortured as well as pleased. Chance's hands scooped up the bottom of her sweater until he had to tear his mouth from hers long enough to rip it and her bra from her body.

Then finally, finally, she was naked to his gaze and he feasted on her. The lush curves and valleys, the smooth silkiness of her skin. His fingers moved to encircle her nipples and when her head tipped back into the mattress, he muffled a groan. So responsive. So eager for his touch. He dipped his head to claim first one rigid nipple and then the other. Back and forth, he divided his attentions, driving her higher and higher. He heard her soft, whispered gasps, felt her body tremble, delighted in the way she moved into him, silently offering more of herself. And he wanted it all. He wanted to bury himself within her, he wanted to feel her body welcome him, surround him and hold him captive for the next fifty years or so. He wanted—no, *needed* to be a part of her. To be linked so intimately that she would never be whole without him again.

As these thoughts and more raced through his

brain, Chance tried both to make sense of them and to ignore them. He'd never felt this before. This…connection. It was as if he could feel her pleasure as well as his own. She moved and it touched him. She whispered and his heart responded. She sighed and his soul went up in flames.

Too much, one corner of his mind shouted. Not enough came the answer.

It would never be enough. He knew it even as he pulled back from her, stood up and yanked his clothes off. He felt it in her hot gaze. Knew it in the rush of blood to his groin. Recognized it in his pounding heart. Eternity with this woman would never be enough. He felt as though he'd been waiting for this moment, this night, most of his life.

And now that it was here, he told himself as he covered her body with his own, he wasn't going to ruin it by thinking so damn much!

Her thighs parted as he came over her and he relished the welcome. He knelt between her legs, smoothing his hands up and down her body, exploring every inch of her, reveling in the soft, exquisite beauty of her skin.

She held up her arms toward him and breathlessly said, "Be inside me, Chance. Be deep inside me."

"That's just where I want to be, Jen," he told her and reached for the condoms. Tearing one free, he opened the foil envelope, rolled it on and then turned his attention back to her. His hands scooped down her body to the small triangle at the juncture of her thighs. Delicately, deliberately, he stroked her center and smiled when her hips lifted off the bed.

"Chance!"

"Let it come again, honey," he urged her.

"No," she said, tossing her head from side to side on the mattress. Breathlessly, she continued, "Not without you. This time it has to be with you."

He slipped one finger, then two, into her depths. The warm, damp heat of her nearly pushed him over the edge, but somehow he managed to hang on to his tattered and unraveling control. He wanted her in a frenzy. Wanted her desperate for completion. Wanted her to want him as badly as he did her.

Only then would he allow himself entry to her body.

Again and again he stroked her, caressed her, his thumb rubbing across the most sensitive spot on her body until she whimpered. She planted her feet. Her hips rocked into his touch. Her hands fisted in the coverlet. She bit down hard on her bottom lip and groaned as he quickened his gentle assault.

And when the first tremor began shaking through her, Chance pushed his body into hers. He felt her muscles clamp down around him, felt the contractions, felt her release quickening within her. And it almost undid him.

He moved, creating a rhythm that Jennifer instantly matched. Her fingers clawed at his back. Her heels ground into his waist. She cried out as the last of her climax crested, and a heartbeat later he followed after her, groaning her name as he found a peace he'd never known before.

An hour or two—or five, who was counting?— passed before Jennifer staggered from the bedroom. Every muscle in her body felt weak and soft and, she thought, extremely limber.

A smile curved her lips as she slapped one hand on the wall for support and kept walking toward the kitchen. In the living room, the lights were glowing softly and music still drifted from the stereo that had been set to repeat.

"Should turn those off," she muttered and thought about the few extra steps it would take to accomplish the task. "Nope," she decided, preferring to use what was left of her strength to get to the kitchen where she could find something to eat.

Chance was still sleeping, but who could blame him? After the third time they'd made love, he'd simply collapsed. Of course, so had she. It was only her growling stomach that had wakened her. And once it was fed, she'd stumble back into bed and cuddle up next to her incredibly talented lover.

"Lover?" she said the word out loud, trying it on for size, so to speak. But then, what else could she call him? He wasn't her boyfriend. Nor a fiancé. And he certainly wasn't a one-night stand. So, she told herself, *lover* was definitely the right word.

But how strange. She'd never thought of herself as the type of woman to take a lover. She'd always been the good girl. The obedient daughter. The loving wife. The dedicated mother. The brave widow.

Frowning at that thought, Jennifer hit the light switch over the oven, preferring its tiny bulb to a blast of overhead lighting that just might blind her at the moment. Brave. Hah. She hadn't been brave. It wasn't as if she'd had a choice. She'd simply done what she'd had to do.

Just as she had tonight.

Oh, she'd needed this night with Chance desperately. She knew darn well it wasn't going anywhere, but that didn't seem to matter. Tonight would be enough. She would make it be enough. And if her heart ached for him after he'd gone, then she'd salve it with the memories of this one incredible night.

She pulled the refrigerator door open, bent down and looked inside, as if waiting for an invisible hand to offer her something. Frigid air wafted across her naked body and she laughed to herself.

"Naked in the kitchen."

"Sounds good," Chance said from the doorway. "I'll have one of those."

She gasped and straightened up. "You scared me. I thought you were sleeping."

One dark eyebrow lifted. "I was resting my eyes."

She laughed. "Then you should have them checked, because your eyes snore."

He gave her a rueful half smile and reached up to shove one hand along the side of his head. Jennifer's gaze locked on to the play of muscles beneath his bare skin and something inside her went hot and achy.

Good heavens, she thought, surprised at herself. *Again?*

He must have seen the flash of desire in her eyes, because he walked toward her, leaned across the half door of the refrigerator and gently tweaked one of her nipples.

Her knees wobbled.

"I woke up and you were gone," he said, scraping the pad of his thumb across the tip of her nipple.

She swallowed hard, pulled in a shaky breath and managed to choke out a few words. "I was hungry."

"So'm I," he said, cupping her breast in the palm of one hand.

"Oh my," Jennifer whispered on a long exhale of breath.

He eased his way past the open refrigerator door and backed her up against the wall. His hands cupped her breasts, his fingers tugged and pulled at the tips of her nipples until Jennifer ached all over and felt as if her body was burning up from the inside out.

She flattened her palms against the wall behind her, instinctively looking for something to hold on to. Cold air sighed from the refrigerator and pooled around them, locking their heated bodies in a chilly grip.

"I want you again," Chance said, burying his face in the curve of her neck. His teeth nibbled at her flesh and goose bumps raced down her spine.

"I want you, too," Jennifer admitted as he straightened up to look down into her eyes. "What's happening to me? To us?"

"Who cares?" he asked, letting one hand slide down the length of her body to cup her hot center.

"Oooh, not me," she said. "Not at the moment, anyhow."

"That's my girl," he whispered and lifted her off her feet. Turning around, he sat her down onto the butcher-block cooking island in the middle of the room.

The cool, smooth wood felt weird against her behind, but Jennifer was beyond caring. All she knew was that she had to have him again. Had to feel him inside her. Needed to experience the wild rush of his body dancing within hers.

"Now, Chance," she whispered, grabbing his head and pulling him close enough to kiss. "Be a part of me now."

"Oh yeah," he muttered and kissed her, taking her mouth in a kiss that electrified her.

Parting her thighs, she took him inside her and wrapped her legs around his middle, holding him in place. He rocked against her and she arched forward, meeting his every thrust and countering it with one of her own. She'd never known such hunger before. Never known the need he instilled in her.

Heck, she'd never walked around naked in her own house before him. Now she couldn't imagine ever wearing clothes again—not if it would keep him from her.

Her arms went around his neck and she caressed his tongue with hers, gave him her breath, her soul, her heart. His rhythm set and familiar now, she moved with him as easily as though they'd been doing this for years. And when he clutched at her and spilled his body into hers, she held on tightly and rode the wave of pleasure that only Chance could create.

But a moment later, that mood was shattered by two little words.

"Uh-oh."

"That's my line," she whispered, leaning her forehead against his chin.

Chance lifted her chin with the tips of his fingers until she was staring up at him. "Where are we?" he asked gently.

She cleared her throat, blinked and gave a quick look around. "The kitchen?"

"Yeah. And where are the condoms?"

She thought about that for a long minute, then, "Uh-oh."

"Exactly." Chance disentangled himself from her and took a step back. Perfect Barnett, he told himself. Now that it's too late, keep your distance.

She scooted off the edge of the butcher-block island and reached out to close the refrigerator. "Well," she said in what he thought was a perfectly reasonable tone, considering the situation, "there's nothing to be done about it now, is there?"

"That's it?" he asked. Hell, any other woman he'd ever known would be either screaming at him or throwing something at his head. Something heavy and preferably sharp.

"What do you want me to do?" she asked, giving him a shrug. "Throw myself into a lake? Besides, you don't have to worry anyway. I started taking the pill six months ago to regulate my cycle. So, I'm safe." She looked at him, a silent question in her eyes. "As long as you're healthy."

"I am," he said quickly, at least wanting to ease her mind on that score.

She nodded. "Then there's no problem."

"But—" He shook his head. No way. No way did he deserve to be let off this easy. "Damn it, this was my fault. I should have kept my head. Should have been careful."

"We were careful," she told him, then gave him a brief, wry smile. "Well, mostly."

"I didn't say 'we,'" Chance said softly, "I said 'me.' I'm the one who should have been careful. I lost control. For the first time in memory, I lost control."

Jennifer inhaled sharply, let it out again and grabbed one of his hands. "You know, Commander, I think that may be one of the nicest things anyone's ever said to me."

"Most women would be yelling about now, you realize that, right?"

She shrugged bare shoulders. "I'm not most women."

"You got that right."

"And I'm just having too good a night to ruin it now."

She turned around then and walked to the counter. Lifting the top of the cookie jar, she reached inside, pulled out a chocolate-chip cookie and took a bite. After she chewed and swallowed, she said, "But since I'm safe and you're healthy, why stress about something that's over and done?"

"You're amazing," he said simply.

"Thanks," she said and took another bite. "Right now I feel pretty amazing."

He watched as her tongue swept crumbs off her bottom lip, and an instant ache of need splintered through him. Then she walked across the room again, opened the fridge and got out the milk.

Handing it to him, she dived back inside. "So? Are you hungry?" she asked. "Want to split a sandwich?"

"Sure," he muttered thickly, his gaze locked on the curve of her bare behind. Food was the furthest thing from his mind. Right now his brain was filled with jumbled images and thoughts.

He'd just dodged a bullet and he knew it. Thanks to birth control pills, he wasn't in imminent danger of becoming a father—so he should be happy.

The problem was, he wasn't. Well, not entirely. At any other time, with any other woman, he'd be doing a mental happy dance about now. But this was Jen. And a part of him he hadn't known existed before tonight was damned sorry he hadn't made her pregnant.

Eleven

The next week passed in a blur.

Jennifer had never been more grateful for an understanding employer. If she had worked for anyone besides Emma Connelly, she wouldn't have been able to spend nearly every waking minute at the hospital.

Of course, she told herself as she walked into the waiting room with two steaming cups of coffee, her gratitude wasn't limited to Emma. Her gaze went straight to Chance, sitting on one of the vinyl couches. Smiling, she silently admitted that no one had ever looked more out of place. His long, denim-clad legs stretched out in front of him and crossed at the ankles, he had his brawny arms folded across his chest and a thoughtful expression on his face as he stared out the glass doors opposite him. He looked too…powerful, too lean, mean and strong to be locked up in this room. He had an air about him that sang of danger and wild places.

A whirlpool opened up in her stomach, spinning, churning, as she realized the truth in that thought. He *was* danger. Somehow, over the last couple of weeks, she'd been able to put that little slice of reality out of her mind. But the truth was, Chance was a temporary situation. Any day now he'd be taking off, headed for God knew where—into heaven knew what kind of risk.

Her fingers tightened around the paper cups until she wouldn't have been surprised to find them plunging right through the flimsy barrier into the hot coffee. What had she been thinking? What had she allowed to happen here?

And how would she ever be able to stand his leaving?

He looked up, as if sensing the turmoil in her mind, and his amber gaze locked with hers. Even from a distance, she felt the slap of the heat simmering in those golden depths.

"Something wrong?" he asked, pushing himself to his feet. "Is it Sarah?"

"No," she said quickly, wanting to assure him that the baby was fine. They'd looked in on her only a few minutes ago and she'd been sleeping in her hospital-issue crib.

"Good," he said, giving her the slow smile she'd come to know so well over the last couple of weeks. "I was worried that maybe they'd taken her back to ICU."

"Nope," she replied, forcing a light tone she didn't feel into her voice. "Doctor's orders still stand. She can go home tomorrow."

"Then why the long face?" he asked, taking the cup she offered him.

"Nothing." It was a lie. And a bad one, apparently. She saw it in his eyes. He didn't believe her.

He reached out and stroked her hair back from her face. He flicked a quick glance at the couple on the other side of the room, but they were fascinated with the news program playing on the television. Still, he kept his voice low when he spoke, so they wouldn't hear.

"There's something bothering you, Jen. Tell me."

She sucked in a long, shaky breath and blew it out again. Then shifting her gaze, she studied the oil slick on the surface of her coffee rather than look into his eyes. He was just too good at this. He'd worm it out of her and she wasn't ready to say what she was thinking. Might never be ready.

Heck, she'd just figured it out for herself: Somehow, she'd let Chance into her heart and now she had to find a way to get him out of it again.

"I'm just thinking about Sarah and how long it will take her to recover," she said softly. "That's all." And instantly guilt pooled inside her. What kind of rotten mother was she, to use her sick little girl as an excuse to her lover?

Oh, good grief, this has gotten way out of control.

"Hell, honey," he said, accepting this lie and pulling her up close to him, "the docs say that a few days' rest and she'll be better than new."

Jennifer latched on to that and clung to it as if it were a bobbing life preserver tossed into a raging sea. "It'll take longer than a few days," she said, more to herself than to him. She'd done plenty of thinking about this. She had to be careful with Sarah. Make sure the little girl didn't do too much, run too fast or play too hard. She didn't want Sarah taxing her new strength. Better to take it slow. Easy. Shaking her head, she said aloud, "She'll have to be careful."

"Well, sure," he replied, then paused for a sip of coffee. "No playing football for at least ten years."

She heard the amusement in his voice and bristled. "I mean it. This was a serious operation. She'll need time to recover. To heal."

He frowned down at her, concern sparkling in

those amazing eyes of his. "Honey, she's been healed by this operation."

"The problem's been *fixed*," she said. "But she hasn't healed. Not yet."

Chance watched Jennifer and wished he knew what she was thinking. In the last week they'd grown closer. At least, he'd felt that they had. Every day they spent together at the hospital, and every night they were together in her bed. He'd found something with Jennifer that he'd never thought to find. A connection. A sense of belonging that he hadn't known since he was a child.

For so long now, his only family had been Douglas. His one tie to the world. And it had always been enough. Until recently. Now, though, he knew he wanted more. He wanted to matter. To count for something beyond his job. He wanted to be an integral part of Jennifer's and Sarah's lives.

And as that thought struck home, he knew he needed them to want him, too.

Jennifer gave him a smile that looked too distracted to be real. There was something going on here that she wasn't talking about. Something beyond worries over Sarah.

And it bugged the hell out of him that she obviously didn't want to tell him about it.

"Jennifer?" A soft, female voice cut into his thoughts and he looked up as Tara Connelly Paige walked across the floor toward them.

"Tara," Jennifer said, holding out one hand toward the woman, "it's so nice of you to come by."

"Well," Tara said, nodding hello to Chance before returning her gaze to Jennifer, "I just wanted to bring a little gift for Sarah." She held out a small teddy bear in a ballerina tutu.

"She'll love it," Jennifer said. "Thank you."

"You're welcome. Hey, we single moms have to stick together, don't we?"

"You bet," Jennifer said, casting a glance at Chance.

Tara checked the elegant gold watch on her wrist and rolled her eyes as she said, "I can't stay. But I did want you to know we're all thinking of you. Especially me. I know just how hard it is to take care of your baby alone. To do all the worrying yourself."

"I know you do." Jennifer gave the woman's hand a squeeze. "And I appreciate it."

"Kiss Sarah for me, will you? Chance, good to see you again." Tara turned for the door, her high heels clicking against the linoleum. Glancing back over her shoulder, she promised, "I'll come to see you both at home in a couple of weeks."

"That'd be great." Jennifer watched the woman walk out the door and disappear around a corner.

"That was nice," Chance said and his deep rumble of a voice set her insides to shaking.

"Yes, it was."

"Are you sure you're all right?" he asked.

"Fine," she murmured, staring down at the ballerina bear in her hand. But she wasn't fine. There were too many thoughts racing around in her mind for that.

Single mom. Those two words had struck a chord that was still echoing deep inside her. She hadn't realized it until just now, but the truth of the matter was that she hadn't been truly on her own since Chance had blown into town—and into her life. For the past three weeks he'd always been there. For Jennifer *and* for Sarah.

Heck, her baby daughter prattled constantly about "Chanz," even referring to him occasionally as Daddy. An ache settled around Jennifer's heart as she silently admitted just how important Chance had become in their lives. And how big a hole he was going to leave behind when he left. As he would, any day now. His wound was almost healed. Pretty soon, he'd be heading out to put himself in the line of fire again.

Darn it, she hadn't asked for this. She didn't want to care for him. She didn't need this kind of pain again. She needed someone safe. Someone boring. Someone who would be home every evening at 5:15. She absolutely *didn't* need another warrior.

Her fingers curled into the bear's soft stuffed body. It was a shame, then, wasn't it, that it was the warrior she loved?

* * *

Two days later, Chance pulled into Jennifer's driveway and thought to himself how much it felt like coming home. A strange sensation for a man who hadn't known a real home since he was a kid.

Strange…but nice.

He threw the gearshift into Park, turned off the engine and set the parking brake. Then he just sat there. Staring at the house. Picturing Jennifer and Sarah inside. And imagining himself, thousands of miles away.

Scowling, he grabbed the steering wheel with both hands and squeezed until he wouldn't have been at all surprised to see the damn thing snap in two. It didn't help.

He was leaving. He had his orders. Just that morning he'd spoken to his commanding officer. In just a few short days, he'd be gone, headed back out into the unknown—and Jennifer and Sarah would continue their lives without him. In time he'd be nothing more than a pleasant memory. And not even that to Sarah. She was too young. She'd never remember him. Pain sliced at him. Chance tried to ignore it, but this ache went far deeper than a simple bullet wound.

This pain would follow him for the rest of his life. He knew it. And damned if he was going to allow that to happen. He wanted Jennifer. Needed her. And he knew damn well that she felt the same way.

Opening the car door, he stepped out, slammed it, then headed for the house like a man on a mission. Mentally, he started going over all of the arguments she might make and coming up with counterpoints for each one. This was the most important battle he would ever engage in and he was determined to win.

He knocked on the front door as a matter of courtesy, but didn't wait for an answer. Opening it, he stepped into the house that held so many of his hopes and dreams. Sunlight streamed through the curtain to lie in lacy patches on the floor. Warmth reached out for him and dragged him close. Closer than he'd ever been to such coziness.

"Daddy!"

Instantly, Chance's heart swelled. His gaze shot to the fresh-faced toddler already pushing herself up from the floor to run to him. He went down on his haunches, held out both arms toward her and grinned as she ran toward him eagerly.

"Sarah, no!" Jennifer's voice sliced into the happy moment and shut it down.

The little girl stopped in her tracks and, frowning, looked from Chance to her mother, standing in the hall doorway. Her tiny bottom lip poked out into a full-fledged pout. "Chanz here."

"I see that," Jennifer said quietly, "but you mustn't run, baby. Walk. Slowly."

Impatiently, Chance sucked in a breath and stood up. Walking to Sarah, he scooped her up in his arms and gave her a kiss on the cheek that stopped her pout from becoming tears.

But it didn't solve the problem. His gaze followed Jennifer as she moved closer, coming to take her daughter from him. Once in her arms, she ran her hands up and down Sarah's body as if assuring herself the child was uninjured. And a flash of worried irritation swept through him.

"Jen, you've got to stop this."

"What?" she asked, not even bothering to tear her gaze from Sarah's flushed face.

"The doctor says Sarah's fine, but you're acting as though she's at death's door."

Sea-green eyes flashed up at him. "She's just out of the hospital," she reminded him hotly.

"Yeah," he said, agreeing to a point. "And I know she's still recovering. But," he added, reaching out to stroke the tip of his finger along Sarah's chubby cheek, "she's feeling pretty good now. Yet every time she tries to show her independence a little, you stop her and wrap her up in cotton."

Jennifer's head snapped back and she stared at him open-mouthed.

While she was speechless, he pressed his advantage. "If you coddle her too much," he said, keeping his voice soft, understanding, "Sarah will never get to enjoy the freedom and health the operation was supposed to give back to her."

"You don't understand," Jennifer said, shaking her head and tightening her hold on the baby in her arms.

"Yeah, I do," he said and meant it. He knew exactly what she was so terrified of. He'd seen it in her eyes since the moment they'd met. The thought of losing the daughter she loved so much had her frozen in fear. Yet now, the danger was over. Sarah could grow up healthy. Strong.

But Jennifer wasn't seeing that. She saw only the danger, not the gift.

"You couldn't possibly understand," she said, and he focused on her instead of his rampaging thoughts. "You weren't here for those months when walking across the room made her so tired she was gasping for breath."

"No, but—"

"And I didn't see you sitting up beside her crib at night, watching her little chest. Waiting for the next breath." Her voice broke and it ripped a hole in his own heart. "Hoping it would come."

"Jen," he interrupted, prodded by the pain in her eyes.

"No. No, I listened to you, now it's your turn." Keeping her arms wrapped around her daughter, Jennifer said, "You can't know how I feel, Chance.

You don't know what it's been like, living with this. Sarah is *not* your child.'' She paused, lifted her chin and inhaled sharply. ''You don't get a vote in this.''

The baby hiccuped and gave a little half cry and Jennifer instantly started bouncing her up and down in a doomed attempt to calm her.

Stung to the core, Chance just looked at her. ''No, you're right,'' he said softly, pushing the words past the knot in his throat. ''She's not my daughter. But we—the three of us—have been through a lot together in the last few weeks.'' His back teeth ground together briefly. ''And I thought we'd— Doesn't matter,'' he said after a second or two. She'd effectively pushed him out of their tight little circle, and that hurt more than he cared to admit, even to himself.

For damn sure he wasn't going to admit anything like that out loud to Jennifer. Still, there was more at stake here than his wounded feelings. There was Sarah's future to think about. And no matter what Jennifer thought, he loved that little girl, so he had to say something.

''Fine,'' he snapped, letting the pain inside flavor his words with a bite. ''I'm not her father. But I love her as though she were mine. And I'm not going to stand by and watch you smother her without speaking up.''

''*Smother* her?''

He heard the outrage in her voice, but he went right on. This was important and someone had to say it. "You can't protect Sarah forever, Jen. She has to run and fall. She has to scrape her knee and heal."

"Why?" she shot back, fury goading her words. "Why is it that you men think pain belongs in life? Why shouldn't I try to protect her from being hurt? Try to keep her safe?"

Frustrated, he argued, "If you wrap her up in velvet and tuck her away in a drawer somewhere, then she's not living. She's just existing. Is that all you want for her?"

Sarah's cries came in earnest now, but the two adults just talked right over them while Jennifer tried to soothe her.

"Living doesn't have to require taking chances," she said, shaking her head as she narrowed her gaze on him.

"Of course it does," he said, reaching out and grabbing hold of her shoulders. "Life *is* taking chances. Every morning when we wake up, we run the risk that this is it. This is the last day we get."

She blanched, but he plunged on. "That's life." Chance threw both hands high and let them slap back down against his thighs. "That's why it's so important how we spend each damn day. Bruises come with the territory. Everyone dies, Jen. It's how you live that counts."

Jennifer shook her head. She wouldn't listen. He could see it in her eyes. Frustration bubbled inside him. Hell, he hadn't come here to fight with her. He didn't want them squaring off against each other. Not when he had so little time left to be with her. Soon, he'd be back out in the field, and this cozy haven would be nothing but a memory.

And a sinking feeling in his guts told him that it was already sliding out of his reach.

"I want Sarah safe," Jennifer said tightly. "She's already run enough risks for a lifetime. She shouldn't have to know any more pain. Shouldn't have to grow up and be disappointed or hurt or left alone or…" Her voice trailed off into nothingness.

There it was, he thought. This was the real enemy he had to face. It wasn't worry for Sarah driving her. It was Jen trying to protect her heart. "This isn't just about the baby, is it?" he demanded, wanting the truth out where it could be faced—and conquered. "Who is it you're really trying to protect here? Sarah? Or yourself?"

Twelve

A deep, throbbing ache settled around her heart and pounded out a rhythm that ran in counterpoint to her heartbeat. It slammed home with the precision of a surgeon's scalpel and it was all Jennifer could do not to weep with the pain.

It didn't help to know that he was right about this, as he was about the rest of it. Logically, she knew she shouldn't treat Sarah as if she were made of glass. But she'd come too close to losing her. And now it was pure instinct to protect. Defend.

But it wasn't only Sarah she was bent on protecting. It was her own heart. If she allowed herself to love Chance and he were taken from her, it would destroy her. She'd lost Mike and survived, true. But what she felt for this man was so much more, it terrified her. And if she had to avoid crushing pain later by enduring slightly lesser pain now, then that was what she would do.

With that thought firmly in mind, she steeled herself and said, "You should go. Now."

"What?"

He looked incredulous, and she couldn't really blame him. This was coming out of nowhere, she knew. But it was better this way. For all of them.

She swallowed hard. "I mean it. Leave, Chance. Just go."

A harsh, humorless laugh shot from his throat. "You're kidding, right?"

"No," she said, shaking her head and holding on more tightly to the crying baby in her arms. "I'm not. I want you to leave."

"No way." He crossed both arms over his broad chest and planted his feet as if he was taking root.

"Damn it, don't you see that this is the only thing to do?"

"What I see is that you're using the excuse of an argument to chase me off."

She winced but didn't admit to a thing. "Why are you making this harder than it has to be?"

"*I'm* not doing this, you are," he snapped.

Sarah's cries notched higher in volume and Jennifer swayed, trying unsuccessfully to soothe the baby even while her own heart was breaking. She looked up at Chance, knowing this could be the last time she would ever stare up into those whiskey-colored eyes. Her soul cringed away from that truth, like a child hiding from the encroaching darkness. But she didn't have a choice. These things had to be said. Better now than later.

"Look," she began, pitching her voice to carry over Sarah's cries, "we both knew this was coming. You don't belong here, Chance."

"We," he said in a furious mutter, "belong *together.*"

Oh, God. Before she could do something really stupid like throw herself into his arms and beg him never to let go, Jennifer shook her head, tears and flying hair blinding her. "No, we don't. You're action-adventure man and I'm the home-and-hearth type. It would never work. This...thing we've shared was temporary. We both knew that."

Hurt flashed in his eyes and regret pooled in her stomach.

"Is that right? Funny, it didn't feel temporary to me," he said, and reached for her again, but she stepped back, determined to keep him at a distance. When he spoke again, anger colored his words. "Damn it, Jen, you're just ending it? Like this?"

Hot tears rolled down her cheeks as she whispered, "This is the only way it *could* end. Don't you understand?"

"No," he said tightly, shaking his head, "I don't. I don't get how one of the strongest women I've ever known can turn her back on something fantastic just because she's too afraid to take another chance on life."

She flinched as if he'd struck her.

"Don't do this, Jen."

"I have to," she said. "For all of our sakes."

"I *love* you, damn it."

He looked as surprised by the admission as she was. Her resolve wobbled along with her knees. She was loved. By a man she loved desperately.

And it changed nothing.

"Goodbye, Chance," she whispered.

His features closed up and for the first time since she'd known him, she saw him for the professional warrior he was. Hard and cold, even his amber eyes flashed out a warning. Hurt radiated from him and simmered in the anger rippling off him in waves.

He lifted one hand and gently stroked the back of Sarah's head before turning around as stiffly as if he were on a parade deck. Jennifer watched him march across the room. She watched the front door open, watched him step out and watched the door quietly close again behind him.

Then all she heard was the sound of her own tears and her daughter's tiny voice, calling for daddy.

* . * . *

Three days later, the silence in the house drove Jennifer back to the Connelly mansion. Back to work. She needed distraction. She needed to keep busy. She needed somehow to fill the empty hours that kept crawling past.

She felt as though she'd been through a wringer. Jennifer had cried until there were just no more tears inside her. And it hadn't helped. There was still an aching, open wound inside her heart and she knew without a doubt it would never heal. All she could hope for now was a return to normalcy. A return to what her life had been like before Chance had entered it.

Even though a world without Chance in it held absolutely no appeal.

She sighed, hitched Sarah a bit higher on her hip and told herself to be thankful for small favors. Like Emma telling her to bring Sarah to work with her, so she wouldn't worry. "We'll be fine, sweetie. You'll see."

"Chanz here?" Sarah turned her head back and forth, looking all over the empty hallway of the Connelly mansion.

Jennifer's gaze swept the place, too, even though she suspected Chance had left a few days ago. After the argument they'd had, she was sure he'd been more than eager to get the heck out of Dodge.

"No, baby." Jennifer shook her head and forced a smile she didn't feel. "Chance is gone."

Those three little words somehow sucked all the air out of the room, so Jennifer continued on, headed for Emma's office and her old, welcome routine.

Seth Connelly planted a kiss on Emma's forehead, then took a step back. He threw a quick glance and smile at Jennifer before turning back to the woman he considered his mother. "I'll call after I meet Angie."

"All right," Emma said, reaching up to put one hand on his cheek. "You be careful."

"I will," he said, adding uselessly, "don't worry."

With that, he turned and headed for the door, pausing only long enough to grin at Sarah. Then he stopped in the doorway, threw another smile at his mother and was gone.

Emma's own smile only drooped a little as she looked at Jennifer. "So," she said, "how's our Sarah?"

"Doing very well."

"Chanz gone?" Sarah asked, her mouth screwing up into a pout.

"Yes," Jennifer said.

"No," Emma corrected.

"He's not?" Stupid, stupid, she told herself as a white-hot flash of excitement streaked across her heart.

"Not yet," Emma told her, taking Sarah into her arms. "He leaves day after tomorrow."

The older woman watched her, and Jennifer wondered absently if Emma could actually see her heart break. He was still here. But he was going to leave. And he'd leave never knowing that she loved him.

A cold chill crawled up her spine and Jennifer wrapped her empty arms around her middle. Without even Sarah to hold on to, she felt completely alone. And the cold seeped into her bones where she knew instinctively it was going to stay.

"Oh, God," she whispered, and wished she knew what the right thing to do was.

"Jennifer," Emma said softly, "love is a rare and glorious thing. Trust me. I know." She smiled sadly and shook her head as she cradled Sarah close. "I've seen how Chance looks at you—and how you look at him."

"Emma—"

"Honey," the other woman interrupted her, "if you let this love that's between you get away, you will always regret it."

Regret. The word echoed inside her over and over again until it took on the rhythm of her own beating heart. She already had regrets. She regretted that she'd never told Chance that she loved him. She regretted that she'd been on the stupid birth control pills and hadn't conceived during that first magical night with him. She regretted that she'd sent him off to a dangerous job letting him think she didn't care.

And it would only get worse, she knew. Even as her breath strangled her, her mind filled with images of his face, his smile, his touch, his kiss. Each of these and more would haunt her for the rest of her life. And every time she dreamed about him, she would have to acknowledge that *she* was the one who'd ended it. That *she* was the one who hadn't had enough strength, courage, to grab what she wanted and hold on tight.

The coming years stretched out in front of her and all she could see was an empty black void. No laughter. No kisses. No shared secrets. No more babies. No arms holding her in the night.

"Oh my God," she said past the knot of emotion clogging her throat. "I'm so stupid."

"Not entirely, I'm happy to see," Emma said.

"Where is he?"

"He went to Navy Pier."

Jennifer grinned, leaned forward and smacked a kiss onto Sarah's cheek. "Watch her for me?"

"Sure," Emma called out as her secretary ran for the door. "But after you accept his proposal, you've got some calls to make about Daniel's coronation!" But Jennifer was already gone. Shaking her head, Emma looked down at the baby in her arms and said, "Would you like a cookie?"

* * *

At Navy Pier, Jennifer threw money at the cab-driver, yelled "Keep the change," and leaped from the taxi. The weekday crowds weren't too bad as she sprinted down the long boardwalk. It was still too early in the year for the legions of tourists that would soon be streaming up and down the promenade.

Her gaze constantly scanning the faces she ran past, Jennifer knew only that she had to find Chance. Had to convince him that she was sorry. That she'd been wrong. Had to tell him that she loved him.

A fierce wind raced across the surface of Lake Michigan and pushed at her, almost as if trying to slow her down. She shoved her hair out of her eyes and raked the crowd again, looking for that chiseled jaw, that short, brown hair and quick smile. Those amber eyes.

Music blasted down at her from overhead speakers and a clutch of school kids on a field trip headed toward the tours being given aboard a navy ship at the end of the pier. Kiosk salesmen hawked cotton candy, sodas and hot dogs and she ignored them all in her single-minded search.

And finally, she saw him. Stepping out of one of the shops, he turned his face up into the sunlight and Jennifer's heart soared.

"Chance!" She called his name and started running for him even before he turned, surprise etched on his features. She didn't give him time to think. She'd come this far, she wouldn't be stopped. Not when she'd finally figured it all out.

Throwing herself at him, she wrapped her arms around his neck and trusted him to hold on to her. He did. His arms snaked around her tightly and lifted her off the ground as she pressed her lips to his in a kiss designed to tell him what her fears had kept her from saying before.

Absently, Jennifer noted the smattering of applause her performance was drawing from the interested group of bystanders. But she didn't care. All that mattered was Chance. And being in his arms. Where she belonged.

At last, though, she broke the kiss and looked up into those eyes that held a promise of a future. And before he could ask the questions she knew were coming, she started talking, words jumbling over each other in her haste to be heard.

"I understand, Chance," she said, breathless, "I know what you were talking about the other day. Life. It's not worth living if you're not willing to risk everything."

"Jen—"

"No," she said quickly, shifting her grip on him so that she could cup his cheek, tenderly drawing the pad of her thumb across his skin. "No, let me say it. I *have* to say it."

He nodded.

"I love you, Chance Barnett Connelly." And once the words were out, she laughed, throwing her head back briefly and enjoying the pure pleasure sweeping through her. "I'm not afraid to say it anymore. I'm only afraid to live my life without you in it."

Around them, the crowd slowly grew as more and more people were drawn to the real-life drama playing out on Navy Pier.

"I finally get it," she said, willing him to believe, willing him to read the truth in her eyes. "Love. That's all that really matters. And if you're lucky enough to find it, you shouldn't be dumb enough to turn your back on it."

His arms tightened, but that was the only sign that he'd heard her. Seconds ticked past and Jennifer worried that she'd waited too long. That she'd missed the opportunity life had handed her because she'd been too afraid to grab it and hang on.

An ache settled in the pit of her stomach as Chance gingerly set her down onto her feet. When he let her go, she felt cold. And empty. But then he smiled and reached into his pants' pocket, pulling out a small emerald-green velvet box.

Jennifer's breath caught as she looked into his eyes and saw love shining back at her.

Chance felt as though someone had just lifted a three-ton weight off his back. "These last few days without you have been about the worst I can ever remember,'' he said and watched as a sheen of tears glistened in her eyes. He'd never been so glad to see anyone in his life. Hearing her call his name had sounded like the answer to a lonely man's prayer. "I'm not used to needing…well, *anyone,*" he said and paused before adding, "but I need you, Jen. You and Sarah. And you should know that I was leaving here to go hunt you down."

"You were?" she asked and swiped away a single tear that rolled along her cheek.

"Damn right," he grumbled, remembering his plan for a siege of her heart. If he'd had to, he would have requested extra leave time, just so he could stay in Chicago long enough to convince her that she loved him. "I wasn't about to let you or *our* daughter get away from me."

She smiled and his heartbeat staggered. God, how had he ever lived this long without her?

"I want to be a part of your lives," he went on quickly, saying all the words he'd been rehearsing most of the morning. "I want to belong somewhere and I need that place to be with you."

"Oh, Chance, we do belong together. I was just too scared to admit that before." She lifted her chin and gave him a watery smile. "Well, I'm still scared. But I'd rather be scared *with* you, than *without* you."

He inhaled sharply, deeply and nodded. "Good.

Good. Jen, I can't promise to live forever—no one can—but I do promise I will *love* you forever."

"I'll hold you to it," she warned.

"You do that."

"Oh, and there's one more thing," she said, oblivious to the now substantial group of people watching them.

"What's that?" he asked warily.

"More babies," she said. "I want more babies."

"Me, too, honey," he told her and gave her a quick, hard kiss that was powerful enough to curl her toes. "The more the merrier." Hell, he got hard just thinking about her belly round with his child. But first things first. Opening the small green box, he said, "There's just one more thing."

Jennifer stared down at the huge solitaire diamond winking at her and gasped. Taking advantage of her surprise, he dropped to one knee, took her left hand in his and said in a loud, proud voice, "Jennifer Anderson, I love you more than I ever thought it possible to love anyone. And if you'll marry me, I'll spend the rest of my life proving it to you."

"And I," Jennifer said, pulling him to his feet, "will spend the rest of my life thanking my lucky stars for sending you to me."

"So that's a yes?" he asked, one corner of his mouth twitching into a grin.

"Oh, you bet it's a yes," she said.

Chance slipped the ring on to her finger before she could change her mind and sealed its place with a kiss. Then he grabbed her tightly around the waist and swung her high into the air.

She grinned down at him, the cheers of the crowd ringing in her ears, and for the first time in far too long, Jennifer felt truly, magically, alive.

*   *   *   *   *

DYNASTIES: THE CONNELLYS
continues…

*Turn the page for a look
at what's in store in the
next Connellys book—*

Plain Jane & Doctor Dad
by Kate Little…

*Also included in this
two-in-one*
DYNASTIES: THE CONNELLYS
volume is

And the Winner gets…Married!
by Metsy Hingle.

*On sale in June 2003
only from Silhouette Desire*

Plain Jane & Doctor Dad

by

Kate Little

As Maura Chambers left Scott Walker's office, she knew she'd never see him again. But he didn't say "Good luck" or even "Goodbye." He merely shuffled papers on his desk, ignoring her, as if she had already vanished from his sight.

She stepped into the busy hospital corridor, resisting the urge to give his door one last, resounding slam. What good would that do her now? It would only give the major-league gossips on staff more to talk about. Hadn't they already gotten enough mileage out of her failed romance? In a matter of days Scott would be gone for good, starting a new job and a new life hundreds of miles away. And she'd be free of him. Almost…

As much as she'd dreaded facing Scott again, she'd been obligated to disclose her secret. After all, he bore his fair share of responsibility. But it only took a moment for Maura to realize Scott didn't see the matter that way. His reaction had been more than disappointing. More than cold or unsympathetic. It had made her sick to her stomach.

Well, what did you *really* expect? She should've known, after the night Scott had announced he was leaving Chicago.

Looking back, it made her angry all over again to see his calculated tactics so clearly. How he had chosen a fancy restaurant for their talk, a place so formal he could almost be assured she wouldn't make a scene. As the maitre d' had led them to their secluded, candle-lit table, Maura had even thought Scott might be planning to propose.

He had a little speech planned for her—but it wasn't about marriage.

Getting to know her the past six months had been great, he'd said. But the problem was, he'd found a great job in Minnesota. Just what he'd been hoping for. She wouldn't want to hold him back, would she? Besides, they both knew this was a casual relationship.

Then he'd patted her hand. Long-distance things never seemed to work out, he'd added, so it was best for them both to end it now. To make a clean break. In a few weeks she'd thank him for making it so easy.

At that moment she finally saw Scott's true nature. How had she been so blind?

Maura felt her eyes tear at the memory. It seemed impossible that she had any tears left after the way she'd cried that night. She leaned against the wall and reached into her pocket for a tissue.

"Maura?" She felt a touch on her shoulder and turned to see Doug Connelly's tall, commanding form beside her. "Are you all right?" he asked kindly.

"Uh, sure. I've just got something in my eye," Maura mumbled.

"Here, let me see."

Before she could resist, he took her chin in his gentle grasp and turned her face up to the light.

His questioning gaze considered her troubled expression and she was sure he could see now that she'd lied to him.

"It looks as if it might be gone," he said quietly. His hand dropped away, but he continued to gaze down at her, his warm, amber eyes filled with concern.

"Why don't we get some fresh air? You look like you could use it." Doug took her arm without waiting for her reply.

Before Maura knew it, they were outside, walking down a tree-lined path. She glanced at Doug's rugged profile and tall, lean form. He walked with his hands dug into his lab coat, his ever-present stethoscope slung around his neck.

She had first come to know Doug as a colleague, then as a friend. While they weren't close, they'd always been able to talk to each other. Which was quite unusual for Maura. She had always been shy with men. Especially men this good-looking.

"Sit a minute," Doug said as they came to an empty bench. When they were settled, he asked, "What is it, Maura? I know you were crying back there. Is this about Scott?"

"No...not at all." She shook her head.

That's what everyone must think, she realized. That she was still pining for a man who had treated her so badly.

"He didn't deserve you." Doug's tone was firm and deep.

That struck her as odd, since Doug and Scott had once been close friends.

"That's nice of you to say," Maura replied quietly.

"I wasn't saying it to be nice. It's the truth." He paused, as if uncertain whether to continue. Then he said, "I know it feels awful right now. But give it time. Before you know it, you'll forget all about him."

She turned and glanced at Doug. The look in his eye, his expression of sheer kindness and consideration, was her undoing. She burst into tears.

Then all of a sudden, she felt Doug's strong arm

circle her shoulders and pull her closer, his grip strong and warm around her, his chest firm under her cheek.

"It's okay," she heard him murmur against her hair.

No, it's not okay, she wanted to say. It's anything but.

"Oh, Doug, I'm sorry...I just don't know what to do..." Her voice trailed off in another wave of tears.

She felt Doug's strong hand stroking her hair. She felt the warmth of his body and breathed in the scent of his skin. With her eyes closed, her cheek nestled in the crook of his shoulder, she felt so safe and protected. For the briefest moment, Maura allowed herself the lovely fantasy that she could stay this way forever. How much easier everything would seem, she thought wistfully.

But that was impossible. There was no one to help her out of this mess. Doug might offer his strong shoulder to cry on, but he didn't have a white charger standing by for a quick getaway.

She took a deep breath and forced herself to move away from his embrace.

"I'm sorry. I didn't mean to make you upset by talking about Scott," Doug apologized.

"It wasn't that." She wiped her eyes and took a shaky breath. She felt him watching her, waiting for her to speak.

Finally, she said, ''It's just that I have this problem…'' She paused and, staring straight ahead, added, ''I'm pregnant.''

She wasn't sure why she'd told him. The words spoken aloud sounded so final. So overwhelming.

Doug looked shocked for an instant, and was suddenly silent. His comforting, sympathetic expression grew harsher. Angrier.

''With Scott's child,'' he said. It was a statement, not a question.

Maura nodded reluctantly. But not before she noted that Doug's warm, amber eyes had mysteriously turned into cold, hard stone.

****

Don't forget
Plain Jane & Doctor Dad *by Kate Little and*
And the Winner gets…Married!
by Metsy Hingle—both
DYNASTIES: THE CONNELLYS
stories—will be on sale in June 2003.

DYNASTIES: THE CONNELLYS

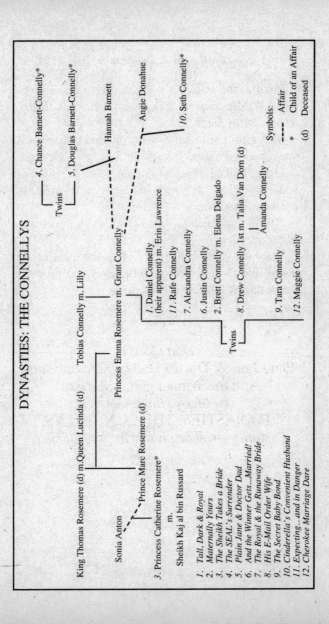

King Thomas Rosemere (d) m. Queen Lucinda (d)

Prince Marc Rosemere (d)

Sonia Anton

Tobias Connelly m. Lilly

Princess Emma Rosemere m. Grant Connelly

4. Chance Barnett-Connelly*

5. Douglas Barnett-Connelly*

Twins

Hannah Barnett

Angie Donahue

10. Seth Connelly*

1. Daniel Connelly (heir apparent) m. Erin Lawrence

11. Rafe Connelly

7. Alexandra Connelly

6. Justin Connelly

2. Brett Connelly m. Elena Delgado

8. Drew Connelly 1st m. Talia Van Dorn (d)

Amanda Connelly

9. Tara Connelly

12. Maggie Connelly

Twins

3. Princess Catherine Rosemere*

m.

Sheikh Kaj al bin Russard

1. Tall, Dark & Royal
2. Maternally Yours
3. The Sheikh Takes a Bride
4. The SEAL's Surrender
5. Plain Jane & Doctor Dad
6. And the Winner Gets...Married!
7. The Royal & the Runaway Bride
8. His E-Mail Order Wife
9. The Secret Baby Bond
10. Cinderella's Convenient Husband
11. Expecting...and in Danger
12. Cherokee Marriage Dare

Symbols:

- - - - Affair

* Child of an Affair

(d) Deceased

0403/51a

SILHOUETTE®
DESIRE™ 2-IN-1
AVAILABLE FROM 18TH APRIL 2003

A MAN OF MEANS Diana Palmer

Long Tall Texans

One intoxicating kiss from innocent Meredith Johns was enough to cast a spell on powerfully seductive rancher Rey Hart. But could their tenuous union survive *his* stubborn pride—and *her* perilous past?

THE MILLIONAIRE'S PREGNANT BRIDE
Dixie Browning

The Millionaire's Club

Businessman William Bradford's protective instincts were aroused by pregnant Diana Foster. But the passion they shared soon had him wanting their temporary arrangement to last a lifetime…

COWBOY'S SPECIAL WOMAN Sara Orwig

Single mum Maggie Langford couldn't resist the burning temptation of rugged Jake Reiner's kisses. But could she warm his frozen heart and convince her temporary housemate to stay…forever?

FOR THIS WEEK I THEE WED Cheryl St. John

Francie Karr-Taylor's marriage to single father Ryan MacNair was only supposed to last a week—but with his possessive touch and hot kisses, how could she help wanting her fake family to become real?

OF ROYAL BLOOD Carolyn Zane

Royally Wed: The Missing Heir

Aristocratic Sebastian LeMarc seemed too worldly for innocent Princess Marie-Claire—but something was brewing between them. Was it strong enough to withstand the rumours of his secret ties to the royal family?

IN PURSUIT OF A PRINCESS Donna Clayton

Royally Wed: The Missing Heir

When Princess Ariane and irresistible Prince Etienne become inseparable the prince wonders if he's finally found his bride. But if so, what will happen when he learns she's been stripped of her royal title?

AVAILABLE FROM 18TH APRIL 2003

 **SILHOUETTE**®

Sensation™

Passionate, dramatic, thrilling romances

IN GRAYWOLF'S HANDS Marie Ferrarella
VIRGIN SEDUCTION Kathleen Creighton
SHADOWING SHAHNA Laurey Bright
TEXAS HERO Merline Lovelace
OUT OF EXILE Carla Cassidy
TWICE UPON A TIME Jennifer Wagner

Special Edition™

Vivid, satisfying romances full of family, life and love

THE TRUTH ABOUT TATE Marilyn Pappano
THE PRINCE & THE PREGNANT PRINCESS Susan Mallery
HER MONTANA MAN Laurie Paige
THE PRINCESS AND THE DUKE Allison Leigh
HIS LITTLE GIRL'S LAUGHTER Karen Rose Smith
INVITATION TO A WEDDING Peggy Webb

Superromance™

*Enjoy the drama, explore the emotions,
experience the relationship*

ALL SUMMER LONG Arnold, Jensen, Hutchinson
A CONVENIENT PROPOSAL CJ Carmichael
THE BABY GIFT Bethany Campbell
HIS PARTNER'S WIFE Janice Kay Johnson

Intrigue™

Danger, deception and suspense

UNCONDITIONAL SURRENDER Joanna Wayne
PHYSICAL EVIDENCE Debra Webb
NOT ON HIS WATCH Cassie Miles
OPERATION: REUNITED Linda O Johnston

0403/51b

NORA ROBERTS

Time & Again

Two enchanting and intriguing tales about passion so powerful that it transcends time itself

Available from 18th April 2003

Available at most branches of WH Smith, Tesco, Martins, Borders, Eason, Sainsbury's and most good paperback bookshops.

0503/121/SH53

New every month

◆ SILHOUETTE®
DESIRE™

joyfully presents

ROYALLY WED:
The Missing Heir

Who can succeed the throne of St. Michel?
An heir—a son—may exist!
Now a desperate search is underway for…
the missing heir.

May 2003
OF ROYAL BLOOD
by Carolyn Zane

and

IN PURSUIT OF A PRINCESS
by Donna Clayton

June 2003
A PRINCESS IN WAITING
by Carol Grace

and

A PRINCE AT LAST!
by Cathie Linz

Silhouette Books
is delighted to present

from award-winning author
MARIE FERRARELLA

The Bachelors of Blair Memorial

Meet—

Lukas Graywolf: lover, healer and hero
In Graywolf's Hands
Sensation – May 2003

Reese Bendenetti: loner, doctor and protector
MD Most Wanted
Sensation – July 2003

Harrison MacKenzie: MD, bad boy and charmer
Mac's Bedside Manner
Special Edition – September 2003

Terrance McCall: secret agent and doctor in disguise
Undercover MD
Sensation – November 2003

0503/SH/LC59

SILHOUETTE® INTRIGUE™

*proudly presents its new Confidential series
with three sexy, rugged agents in*

Chicago
Confidential

Men bound by love, loyalty and the law—
these specialised government operatives
have vowed to keep their missions and
identities confidential…

NOT ON HIS WATCH

Cassie Miles
May 2003

LAYING DOWN THE LAW

Ann Voss Peterson
June 2003

PRINCE UNDER COVER

Adrianne Lee
July 2003

0503/SH/LC62

SILHOUETTE®
SUPERROMANCE™

is proud to present

THREE GOOD COPS

by

Janice Kay Johnson

The McLean brothers are all good,
strong, honest, men. Men a woman
can trust…with her heart!

HIS PARTNER'S WIFE
May 2003

THE WORD OF A CHILD
July 2003

MATERNAL INSTINCT
September 2003

0503/SH/LC64

SILHOUETTE® DESIRE™

proudly presents

A BRAND NEW TRILOGY FROM
BESTSELLING AUTHOR

LEANNE BANKS

The Royal Dumonts

*Each member of this royal family finds the love
they deserve in the most unlikely of places...*

ROYAL DAD
April 2003

HIS MAJESTY, MD
August 2003

PRINCESS IN HIS BED
December 2003

0403/SH/LC58

SILHOUETTE DESIRE™

invites you to enter the exclusive world of

The Millionaire's Club

where five seriously powerful and wealthy bachelors set out to find a traitor in their midst…and maybe encounter true love along the way.

May 2003
THE MILLIONAIRE'S PREGNANT BRIDE
by Dixie Browning
(in a two-in-one volume with A Man of Means *by Diana Palmer)*

June 2003
HER LONE STAR PROTECTOR
by Peggy Moreland
and
TALL, DARK…AND FRAMED?
by Cathleen Galitz

July 2003
THE PLAYBOY MEETS HIS MATCH
by Sara Orwig
and
THE BACHELOR TAKES A WIFE
by Jackie Merritt

0503/SH/LC60

♥ SILHOUETTE® SUPERROMANCE™

He's tough... He's honest...
He's sexy! He's a man who'll stand
up for what he believes in.
You can always...

COUNT ON A COP

*Watch for these four exciting novels
from favourite Superromance authors*

Are You My Mummy? by Kay David
January 2003

A Ranger's Wife by Lyn Ellis
February 2003

**My Private Detective
by Rebecca Winters**
March 2003

The Baby Cop by Roz Denny Fox
April 2003

SILHOUETTE®
SPECIAL EDITION™

proudly presents

a brand-new trilogy from

SUSAN MALLERY

DESERT
ROGUES

Hidden in the desert is a place where
passions flare, seduction rules and
romantic fantasies come alive…

March 2003
THE SHEIKH AND THE RUNAWAY PRINCESS

April 2003
THE SHEIKH & THE VIRGIN PRINCESS

May 2003
THE PRINCE & THE PREGNANT PRINCESS

0203/SH/LC55

SILHOUETTE®
SPECIAL EDITION™

proudly presents

CROWN AND GLORY

*Where royalty and romance
go hand in hand...*

April 2003 - Silhouette Special Edition
The Princess Is Pregnant! by Laurie Paige

May 2003 - Silhouette Special Edition
The Princess and the Duke by Allison Leigh

June 2003 - Silhouette Special Edition
Royal Protocol by Christine Flynn

July 2003 - Silhouette Desire 2-in-1
Her Royal Husband by Cara Colter
The Princess Has Amnesia! by Patricia Thayer

September 2003 - Silhouette Desire 2-in-1
Searching for Her Prince by Karen Rose Smith
The Royal Treatment by Maureen Child

November 2003 - Silhouette Desire 2-in-1
Taming the Prince by Elizabeth Bevarly
Royally Pregnant by Barbara McCauley

SILHOUETTE® SPECIAL EDITION™

*presents three more passionate and
adventurous stories from*

MONTANA

*Welcome to Montana — a place of
passion and adventure, where there
is a charming little town with
some big secrets...*

Her Montana Man by Laurie Paige

May 2003

Big Sky Cowboy by Jennifer Mikels

June 2003

Montana Lawman by Allison Leigh

July 2003

1 FREE

book and a surprise gift!

We would like to take this opportunity to thank you for reading this Silhouette® book by offering you the chance to take ANOTHER specially selected title from the Desire™ series absolutely FREE! We're also making this offer to introduce you to the benefits of the Reader Service™—

★ FREE home delivery
★ FREE gifts and competitions
★ FREE monthly Newsletter
★ Exclusive Reader Service discount
★ Books available before they're in the shops

Accepting this FREE book and gift places you under no obligation to buy, you may cancel at any time, even after receiving your free shipment. Simply complete your details below and return the entire page to the address below. *You don't even need a stamp!*

YES! Please send me 1 free Desire book and a surprise gift. I understand that unless you hear from me, I will receive 2 superb new titles every month for just £4.99 each, postage and packing free. I am under no obligation to purchase any books and may cancel my subscription at any time. The free book and gift will be mine to keep in any case.

D3ZEA

Ms/Mrs/Miss/Mr ....Initials................................
BLOCK CAPITALS PLEASE

Surname ....

Address ....

....

....Postcode................................

Send this whole page to:

.... Croydon, CR9 3WZ
.... ty Kildare (stamp required)